WINDOW
of the
Heart

The Stained-Glass Legacy ⛪ Book Three

Amy R. Anguish

Scrivenings
PRESS
Quench your thirst for story.
www.ScriveningsPress.com

Published by Scrivenings Press LLC
15 Lucky Lane
Morrilton, Arkansas 72110
https://ScriveningsPress.com

Printed in the United States of America

Paperback ISBN 978-1-64917-313-3

eBook ISBN 978-1-64917-314-0

Editors: Elena Hill and Linda Fulkerson

Cover by Linda Fulkerson, bookmarketinggraphics.com

To Kathy Cretsinger.
If not for her starting Ken Ten Writers' Retreat and Mantle Rock
Publishing, I never would've met the other authors in this series, and
we never would have come up with such a concept. I treasure her
friendship and the years she helped mentor me.

Chapter One

"You've got to be kidding me." Lennox Malone pointed to the front of the chapel. "Sara Beth, there's a toilet on the stage!"

Sara Beth waved her hand through the air. "That's an easy fix, Len. Don't you see the bigger picture?"

"The bigger picture?" Lennox took in the vaulted ceiling, the cracked window, the dark spots of what must be mold growing where carpet might once have been. "Sara Beth, why this chapel? Of all the venues you could choose to marry in, why this one?"

"It's so quaint."

"Quaint?" Lennox rubbed her throbbing temple. "That doesn't fit any of the words that came to mind when we walked in here. Filthy, run-down, dilapidated, yes. Those are apropos—but quaint?"

"Lennox, I know somewhere deep down in your amazing mind you can open your eyes and see the potential of this place. The sunlight filtering through that stained glass. The coziness of such a small venue. And the gorgeous trees outside that will be orange and red by the time my wedding gets here."

"Six months." Lennox motioned around them and accidentally knocked against the edge of one of the pews. The

"

decorative endpiece flew off and skittered across the floor. "That's all we have. I'm not sure this can happen in six years, much less six months."

"Brian's cousin should be here any minute, and he'll confirm it can be ready." Sara Beth crossed her arms and pouted her lips. "Besides, I should be able to get married anywhere I want to. I'm the bride."

"I think part of your brain fell out when Brian slipped that ring on your finger." Lennox shook her head as she scanned the room. Potential? The only potential she could see was the potential for this structure to be condemned.

Scurrying and scratching came from the front of the building, and Lennox stepped a bit closer to the back door, just in case some creature popped out that was bigger than she was. Sara Beth didn't seem to notice.

What must it be like to see everything through love-colored glasses? Not that Lennox truly believed in such things. After all, she hadn't seen much proof of love in her life before now. But Sara Beth had been her best friend for ten years now, and Brian came across as a good guy. So maybe things would work out for one couple in the world.

"When is Brian's cousin supposed to be here?"

"Around two." Sara Beth smiled as she typed on her phone. Must be texting her fiancé.

"It's almost two-thirty now." Lennox tapped her smartwatch.

"He'll be here. Brian promised." Sara Beth pointed to the stage. "Can't you just picture flowers along the windowsill? And candles in glass pillars. The stone in here will look great with the orange color I picked for your dress. And we might even incorporate some pumpkins and gourds. Would that be too much?"

Lennox sighed. "We can figure it out when we get closer. I'll watch for sales at the craft stores. Don't they put fall decorations out early in the summer?"

"Maybe." Sara Beth tapped her fingertip against her chin. "Gourds might be overkill."

"Are you sure you want me in orange?" Lennox fingered her pixie-cut hair. "I've been told in the past it's not a good color for my complexion."

"Wait until you see it. It's not scary orange. More like what you'd see in a fading sunset." Sara Beth's voice grew dreamy. "And with us carrying fall bouquets of mums or sunflowers or something, maybe even with some leaves mixed in—it'll be perfect."

And as maid of honor, it was Lennox's job to make sure it truly did turn out as perfect as Sara Beth dreamed. Which is why this location worried her. And Brian's cousin still not arriving wasn't a sign that things would improve anytime soon. Lennox wandered outside and took a deep breath of the early spring air. March teased them with mild temperatures and lots of sunshine this year, but that didn't mean another cold snap couldn't sneak up between now and Easter next month.

Today had turned out lovely, though not warm enough for the convertible pulling up to have its roof down. A lanky man got out, pushed his sunglasses back into his windblown, too-long hair, and flashed her a grin. Hands in his pockets, his gait said he was in no rush. Surely this wasn't the cousin.

"Hi." He stopped right in front of Lennox as if expecting her to act excited to see him.

"Ty?" Sara Beth rushed through the door of the chapel and gave him a quick squeeze. "Isn't this going to be great? It's so perfect. Just like Brian described."

Brian had described the mold and misplaced toilet to Sara Beth? Or was she talking general appearances? Either way, Lennox sometimes wished she could be as optimistic and bubbly as her friend.

"You know I love this place. I'm thrilled you want to get married here. It's been a while since we've been able to do a wedding at the chapel." Ty's gaze roved up to the roof and back down again.

"It's going to be magical." Sara Beth turned and blinked at Lennox. "Oh. Did you meet my friend Lennox? She's my maid of honor, so she's here to help figure out what all needs to be done. She thinks it's her job to make sure everything is perfect."

"I'm Ty." He held out his hand.

She took it and let go again as quickly as possible. "You were supposed to be here forty-five minutes ago."

"Yeah. Sorry about that." He shot Sara Beth a grin. Did he think women found him charming? "I couldn't resist stopping on the way out here. I saw a little fruit stand selling flowers and a few early crops, like broccoli and strawberries, from their greenhouse. I picked up a few for my mom. She's always going on about how she misses fresh fruit during the winter. Since it was so pretty out, I took the long way, not thinking about flooding from last week's rain. One of the roads was still closed, so I had to turn around to find another cut-through that would work."

"It's fine. We've just been looking around." Sara Beth looped her arm through his as if his excuse made perfect sense. "Lennox is worried we won't have enough time to get everything repaired, but I told her it wasn't that bad. What do you think?"

"I think you're right." Ty stepped into the chapel and paused as if taking in sacred ground. "There's a bit of damage there." He pointed to a spot where a tree branch had broken through the roof. "And we'll obviously need to work on the pipes so we can get the toilet back where it goes. But most of this is aesthetic more than structural. Just cleaning."

"Do we just ignore the mold? And the pews that are falling apart? And the broken glass? And the vermin?" Lennox pointed toward the front of the room.

"Vermin?" Ty and Sara Beth both shot her a glance.

"There was rustling." She shrugged, refusing to admit to being overly dramatic.

"I'll check into it." Ty failed to turn his head in time to completely hide his smirk.

Lennox folded her arms across her chest. "What about outside?"

"Outside?"

"Yes. Outside. The flower beds are a mess. And the parking lot needs work. Otherwise, how will Sara Beth's guests get their cars in and out?"

"Why do you need me?" Ty lifted an eyebrow. "Obviously, you're a general contractor or something to be able to spy all the problems."

Heat burned her cheeks. Her stupid pale skin was surely turning a bright shade somewhere between cherry and tomato right now. She squared her jaw and shoulders and lifted her chin. "I'm not a contractor. But I *am* concerned at how lightly you're treating this. I mean, if you're going to show up almost an hour late every time you have an appointment, I can't imagine your work efficiency being any better. We have a schedule."

"Being the best man, I'm well aware." Ty picked up the piece of the pew that had fallen off earlier and set it back in its place.

The best man? Of course, he was. Why would her counterpart be someone she could get along with? Someone she would *want* to walk down the aisle beside. Not that she ever truly wanted to walk down the aisle with or to anyone. Not her dream.

Ty pulled a phone out and snapped some pictures of the roof damage, the mold, and the cracked window. At least he was doing something besides grinning and agreeing to everything the crazy bride said. Where was Sara Beth anyway?

There, near the back, her eyes focused on the front and yet far away, obviously dreaming of what would happen in six months.

Sara Beth's phone rang, pulling her from her reverie. She glanced at the screen, and her face lit up. "Ty, help Lennox understand. Tell her about Evangeline. I'm going to take this call."

Before either of them could protest, Sara Beth was outside. Awkward silence ensued.

"Okay, then." Ty slid his hands back into his pockets and leaned back against the end of the front pew. It shifted behind him, and he quickly straightened, laughing. "Guess we'll add that to the list, huh?"

"You think all this is funny?" Lennox motioned around them.

"On the contrary." Ty cocked his head at her as if trying to figure out what made her tick. Instead, his expression made her want to squirm. "I take this much more seriously than you think. My great-great-grandfather and his uncle originally built the structure. It's been in the family ever since. My father never loved it as much as Gramps and Great-Great-Grandpa Brendan did, though, so he didn't check on it as often. And that's led us to this.

"I'd say that tree fell during the ice storm, which means the hole has only been there a few months. The scratching is probably mice or squirrels. The flower beds can easily be cleaned out and replanted. I don't know why you've decided to be so negative, but it's going to be okay."

Breathe in through the mouth and out through the nose. And again. How many times had she coached other ladies on breathing out their stress while teaching barre or PiYO? Lennox needed to get control of her emotions. He was right. She had been nothing but negative since they got here.

"And the toilet?" She couldn't help herself.

"Unfortunately, when indoor plumbing was installed back in the eighties, no one factored in tree roots growing several feet in either direction. The roots grew through the pipes, so we need a plumber before we can put the toilet back. But I promise, you won't have to worry about it being on stage during the ceremony. I wouldn't want it to take attention away from your beautiful dress."

"No one's going to be looking at my dress when they can stare at someone as gorgeous as Sara Beth." Lennox ran her fingers through her hair as she surveyed the room again. "But thanks for the assurance. How can I help?"

"Stay out of the way." Ty shrugged. "Seriously. Much of this even I can't do. But I have all the contacts we need through my dad's contracting company, and I'll get people scheduled to get in here and work as I can."

"As you can."

"Yes. We have until September. It'll be okay if they don't get here right away. Except maybe the roof guy. That's a priority." He turned to face her fully. "Sara Beth mentioned Evangeline—the story of the first wedding that happened here."

"It's okay. I'm not romantic. And she'll never know if you tell me or not." Lennox leaned back, trying to see her friend through the open front door, but there was no sign of her.

"It's sweet. Some people say it's what's blessed all the marriages that have started in this chapel since then." Ty grinned and tossed his head back, knocking a loose strand of hair out of his eyes. "If you believe things like that."

"I don't."

A glimmer of something flashed across Ty's face at her blunt statement but disappeared just as quickly. "Well, if you change your mind, I'll be happy to tell you."

"Right. I guess I better give you my number so you can keep me updated on how things are going." Lennox pulled her phone from her pocket.

"I'll make sure Brian knows how things are going or if we run into any problems." Ty gave her a side glance. "Unless you simply wanted an excuse to give me your number."

"What?" Lennox took a step back. "No!"

"I'm not that repulsive." Ty chuckled and once again moved the hair out of his face.

"You just need a haircut," Lennox muttered as she turned toward the door.

"Hey." Sara Beth peered up from where she sat on a rough-hewn bench a few feet from the chapel. "Everything squared away?"

"I guess." Lennox shrugged.

"Great." She glanced behind Lennox and gave Ty a huge smile. "Thanks again for meeting us. I know you helped Lennox understand that everything really will be perfect."

"As perfect as a shaggy-haired sloth can make things." Ty's reply brought that flush of heat back to Lennox's cheeks.

"Okay." Sara Beth waved. "I'm sure we'll be seeing you a lot over the next few months. Thanks for all your help."

Lennox slid into the passenger seat of Sara Beth's car and buckled in without another word. So much for her remark not being heard as she left the building. A glance in the vehicle's mirror showed Ty watching her. What was he thinking? Did he dread being best man to her maid of honor as much as she dreaded being paired up with him? A little niggle told her the issue was something altogether different. And she wasn't at all sure she wanted to know.

Chapter Two

"How did Sara Beth end up with a best friend like that?" Ty glanced over at Brian as they filled their plates at the monthly family Sunday lunch.

"Like what? Lennox?" Brian added a chicken wing, then another. "She's okay. Nothing like Sara Beth. But she's pretty cool."

"Uptight seems more like it." Ty added a spoonful of the next dish to his plate before he realized it was Jell-O salad. He wrinkled his nose but moved on rather than trying to find a discreet way to scrape it off.

"Really?" Brian grabbed several rolls. "What makes you say so?"

Ty flopped down on the brick hearth in Aunt Mary's den. "Maybe because she practically had a conniption when I didn't show up right at two the other day. Then she acted like I needed to keep her informed of when everything would be done. Doesn't she know you and Sara Beth are in charge of the wedding? And she wouldn't let me tell her the story of Brendan and Evangeline. Claims she's not romantic."

"Not everyone is like you. Some people actually believe in punctuality. Or don't believe in the magic of getting married in some old chapel." Brian stuffed a bite of corn casserole in his mouth.

"But you *are* getting married in that old chapel."

"That's because I'm marrying someone who *is* romantic." Brian wiped his mouth and took a swig of sweet tea. "Lennox and Sara Beth are polar opposites. But they've been friends forever. Like, since the first day of high school. Something about being forced to be partners in science class or something. I don't know. I don't have to understand. Lennox is part of the Sara Beth package, so I roll with it and go on."

Ty sat silent for a moment, contemplating all Brian had said.

"She does lead a mean kickboxing class, though." Brian playfully nudged Ty's arm. "I'll give her that."

"Kickboxing?"

"She's one of the owners of that little workout place on the square. Sara Beth likes to go take her barre classes."

Ty spluttered the drink he was taking. "Bar?"

"Barre with an *E*. Like what ballerinas do." Brian motioned with his hand to show where the barre would be hooked on the wall. "She also does PiYO and a couple of other things."

"PiYO? What kind of language is this?" Ty pushed the Jell-O salad over to the side of his plate so its artificial cherry-ness wouldn't ruin any of the good stuff.

"Workout language. I think PiYO is a combination of yoga and something else." Brian snapped his fingers a few times as he thought. "Oh, yeah. Pilates. I don't go for those classes. Just the kickboxing. Sara Beth said she loves the way I look. Gotta keep her happy. Besides, by taking these classes, we're also supporting her friend."

"Right. Rub it in some more, why don't ya?" Ty set his mostly empty plate aside.

"What?" Brian flexed his arms. "That my body is better than yours?"

"No." Ty scoffed. His lean frame might not look like much, but most of it was muscle he kept toned using his home gym several times a week. "That the younger cousin is getting married before the older."

Brian guffawed, causing several heads to turn toward them. He waited until the attention was gone before lowering his voice and replying. "So what? If you think about it, this is only the second generation where something like that could happen. Before our parents, there were no siblings."

"Apparently, it makes me look like a slacker. Because I have no marriage prospects at the ripe old age of twenty-seven, I'm obviously hopeless." Ty pursed his lips and scowled at his cousin, sending him into another round of laughter.

Brian shook his head. "Seriously, man. This is ridiculous. Are they really riffing you over my getting married first?"

"Today, I've already been asked four times if I'll ever find a girl and settle down. Don't I know I'll be twenty-eight next year?"

"I can't believe it. Who asked you such things?"

"Your mother, for one. And Aunt Tunene. And Uncle Ford." Ty ticked each name off on his fingers. "And don't forget my mother. Everyone's asking if I'm going to be as late to marriage as I am to everything else in life."

"Well, we obviously need to hook you up with Lennox so you can get married right away. Maybe even a double ceremony. Then, you can live up to the family's unreasonable expectations." Brian leaned over, his elbows on his knees. "Because obviously marrying someone just to make sure you're not still single at twenty-eight is a completely sane and realistic reason to do something so permanent and life-changing."

"Or not." Ty mock-punched Brian's shoulder. "Something tells me Lennox and I wouldn't even get along long enough to make it all the way up the aisle."

"Well, you better find a way. You have to walk that aisle together this fall." Brian stood and motioned toward the kitchen. "Let's go find some dessert."

"Right. She's the maid of honor. I guess that's why she's acting like a bridezilla?"

The edge of Brian's lip quirked up. "No. I think she's just more detail-oriented than Sara Beth. Lennox takes her responsibilities seriously. You know, in the olden days, people used bridesmaids sort of like decoys so the evil spirits couldn't tell which one was the bride and descend on her."

"What?" Ty almost dropped his spoonful of banana pudding —a near travesty.

"Yeah. One of those magazines the girls were poring over had an article about it. People believed all that stuff way back when, so to trick the spirits and keep the bride safe, all the girls wore similar dresses. Crazy, right? I don't think bridesmaids are supposed to do that much anymore, but the checklist for the maid of honor is never-ending."

"What's the list for best man look like?" Ty followed his cousin onto the back porch.

"I don't know." Brian shrugged. "I sort of tuned out after that. You need to make sure you get to your fitting on time for your tux. And plan the bachelor party. Hand me her ring during the ceremony. And ..."

"And?"

"No. I better not tell you that one." Brian tapped the end of his spoon against his chin. "I don't think Sara Beth would like me to remind anyone of that particular tradition."

"Oh, come on, man. You can't leave me hanging."

"Decorations." Brian's dad, Uncle Matt walked up with a grin. "The best man is in charge of decorating the getaway car."

"Dad!" Brian's frown morphed into a grin.

"Just want to make sure you get the full experience, son." Uncle Matt chuckled, then turned serious as he faced Ty. "But more importantly, Ty, your duty as best man is getting that chapel ready. My future daughter-in-law has her heart set on that place. Are you up for it?"

"It's one of my greatest desires to see that place brought back to its former glory." Ty pressed his right palm to his heart. "I love that chapel. I want to make sure it's repaired more for myself than for this guy over here."

"Well, thanks a lot," Brian scoffed. "Glad you're doing this for me. I figured you were doing it because you were tired of having an eyesore across the yard from your house."

"Eyesore? No way. Even a little rough around the edges, that chapel is gorgeous. It just needs a little TLC." Ty smirked. "Besides, some of those pews are probably in such rough shape because of our shenanigans growing up."

"Shenanigans!" Brian shook his head. "We were perfect angels."

Uncle Matt guffawed. "Not sure that's the term I'd use. Or have you forgotten that summer when Gran wanted you to come over and help with the dogs? Except you two took them for a walk by the creek. And ran into a skunk."

Ty chuckled. "I bet if the old cabin hadn't been torn down a few years ago, it would *still* stink. Seeing as we were told we had to sleep there until the stench wore off."

"Gran didn't mess around." Brian ran a hand through his hair. "But the trick was on her. Because we had more fun camping in that old cabin than we would have staying at the big house."

"Something tells me she knew." Ty sighed. "There's a lot of good memories on that piece of property."

"Agreed." Brian nodded. "Good thing Gran left the house to someone who cares enough to do something with the chapel."

"I'm doing it for all of us. It's been in the family since the 1920s, and we've neglected our duties. If I can't live up to one family expectation, maybe I can at least do this."

If only he could achieve both, but with no prospects in sight … He would settle for salvaging a piece of their family heritage.

"Sounds good to me." Uncle Matt clapped him on the shoulder. "Did Brian tell you about our wedding invitation get-together?"

Ty raised an eyebrow at his cousin.

Brian shrugged. "Evidently, we're not supposed to send invitations out until like two months before, but Sara Beth figures if we go ahead and address them, we'll be ready when that time comes. She said we might as well address them at the same time we're doing the *Save the Date* cards, whatever those are. She also wants to do a cake testing, so she figured it would be fun to turn it into sort of a party. Eat cake, address envelopes, and talk about tuxes, evidently."

"Ooh, fun." Ty's voice dripped with sarcasm. "I'm sure it will give Lennox another opportunity to tell me to get a haircut."

"Did she really?" Brian laughed.

"Your hair is a bit shaggy." Uncle Matt tugged on a strand.

"You should have seen how pink her face got when she realized I heard her." Ty grinned. If Lennox wasn't so uptight, she'd be rather cute. He'd never paid attention to girls with super short hair before—hair shorter than his—but it flattered her round face and petite form. The color intrigued him as it changed shades of red under the light coming through the chapel's stained-glass windows.

"Oh man, this is going to be so much fun." Brian's smile stretched from ear to ear. "I think you both may have met your match."

"You forget. She's not romantic. And thinks I'm unreliable. And, did I mention, my hair is too long?"

"We'll see." Brian pulled his phone out. "I'll text you the information for the invitation thing so you'll have it."

"Great." Ty opened the message and saved it to the calendar app on his phone. "Maybe I'll show up early just to throw Lennox off."

"There you are." Ty's mom walked up. "Discussing wedding plans?"

"Is there any other topic right now?" Uncle Matt squeezed his sister-in-law around the shoulders.

"Maybe Brian will rub off on Ty and remind him the clock is ticking, and the water is fine." Mom emphasized the last three words with a jab to Ty's chest.

Ty rubbed the sore spot. "Mom, that's not the way things work, and you know it. Things are different now. People wait longer to marry. Just because you married young doesn't mean it should happen forever."

Brian rubbed the back of his neck and ducked his head. "Maybe Ty's right. Maybe you guys are focusing too much on age. What if Sara Beth and I hadn't found each other so early? Would you disown me or something?"

"We're mostly teasing." Uncle Matt patted his son's shoulder. "You know we'll love you both no matter what road your lives take."

"I would like time to get to know my grandchildren, though." Mom shot Ty a look that said she might not completely agree with Uncle Matt.

"Well, in the meantime, maybe I can at least get the chapel back to proper order." Ty pushed away from the porch railing and held his phone up in the air. "I'll see you later, Brian."

Mom's words and actions proved he was destined to be the black sheep in the family, and nothing he did would make that better. But he'd try anyway. He truly loved the chapel. He would start there. Then …

Ty shook his head as if he could shake away the niggling thoughts Brian planted. Lennox couldn't possibly be a girl for him. They were polar opposites, and despite the popular belief that opposites attract, he couldn't imagine it working out between two people so completely different.

No. His focus would be the chapel. Tomorrow he'd locate workers for the repairs. Just a matter of eking out the time to make the calls. How hard could it be, with all Dad's contacts?

Chapter Three

Lennox pinched the bridge of her nose, but the tension remained behind her eyes. The pain had settled in around the time she met Brian's cousin—Ty. The strain worsened the longer she went without hearing any progress. It had only been a week and a half, but still ... shouldn't he at least have scheduled someone to look at the roof?

The music from Presley's class thrummed through the walls into Lennox's office. Sounded like aerobics tonight, too fast-paced to be yoga. The bassline pulsed in synch with the twitch of Lennox's eye.

Why couldn't Sara Beth want to get married in a normal place like any other bride? She had to pick a place that needed tons of work and an overseer who couldn't even bother to be punctual.

"Mama Said" interrupted Presley's upbeat song. Mom's ringtone. Lennox's fingers hovered over the screen a moment before answering. After all, she'd already avoided three earlier calls from her mom by using her classes as an excuse.

"Lennox? I was beginning to wonder if your phone was working." Mom's gravelly voice reverberated in Lennox's already tender head.

"No. Just a busy day. I taught three classes."

"Well, I'm glad you're free now. You're still free on Thursday evenings, right?" Rustling sounds came through the phone. What was her mother doing?

"I am, but I'm already busy this Thursday."

"But I want you to meet George." Mom's whine made Lennox grimace.

"George?"

"My boyfriend. You're going to like this one, Len. He's an accountant."

"I thought you were dating someone named Roy." Lennox gave up on the bridge of her nose and moved to pressing her temples. "Last week."

"Well, he never showed up for our last date, but ... George was across the bar, so I struck up a conversation, because, you know, I thought maybe he'd pay for my drink." Her mom giggled. "And he did."

Now the important facts were coming out. George must be well-off. Lennox rolled her eyes. "And you never tried to call Roy again, did you?"

"Why should I? He stood me up." Her mother snorted, and a loud bang caused Lennox to hold the phone at a distance. "Besides, George is different from the others."

"All, what? Twenty of them?" Lennox flopped on her couch and leaned her head back, banging it softly against the leather.

"Lennox, don't use that tone of voice with me. It's not easy to find a soul mate."

"Soul mate. I don't even think that's a real thing."

"Well, if you come to dinner on Thursday, I'll show you. I really think George is it, Len."

"Sorry. I said, I already have plans." For the first time since Sara Beth informed her of the cake-testing, envelope-addressing party, Lennox was glad to be part of it.

"Like a date?"

"Hardly." Why did an image of that slob Ty run through her head? "I'm helping Sara Beth with wedding plans."

"Don't you waste all your time planning *her* wedding so you won't have time to find someone and plan your own now." Her mom tutted. Another clang rang out.

"What are you doing?" Lennox finally gave in to her curiosity.

"I'm looking for the wok."

"Wok?" Lennox frowned. "Do we have a wok?"

"I thought we did. I seem to remember your dad getting me one when we were on a stir-fry kick once." More bangs and thumps. "But I can't remember where it might have gone."

"Maybe he took it twelve years ago." Lennox didn't even try to keep the scorn out of her voice.

"Why would he take a wok? He didn't take anything else. Not even his wedding ring."

There was no hope for this headache. No massaging or pressure points would take care of it at this point. Lennox refused to answer.

"Are you sure you can't get out of that thing with Sara Beth? I mean, her wedding isn't for a while yet, is it? Your sister's coming." Lennox's mom's voice held that whiny tone once more. "It's not every day you get to meet your mom's boyfriend, you know."

Now it was Lennox's turn to snort. "Just every few months, huh?"

"Lennox Paige! You show some respect. I'm doing the best I can, okay?" Now came the pouty voice. Their conversations followed the same pattern. "When your dad walked out and left me to raise you two girls by myself, I had to give up everything. My health, my time, my youth. Now that you're both grown up and moved out, I can try to claim a bit of happiness for myself. Are you so unfeeling that you'd deny your mama a chance at love?"

"I don't believe in love, Mama." Lennox kept her voice even, her tone cool. "But I won't stop you from chasing the pipe dream. Just leave me out of it. I'll stop by next week, okay?"

"Great. I'll check with George and see what his schedule's like.

He's really busy with tax season, but maybe he can squeeze something in." Her mom sounded more reasonable. "Maybe Sara Beth will rub off on you and remind you that love is real."

"She'll try." Lennox smirked. The old adage about people in love was true—they thought everyone else should be too. "You have fun and tell Macy I said hi."

"Sure." Her mom sighed. "Sometime you two are going to have to sit down and find a way to get along."

"I love my sister." Lennox stood and paced again. "I just can't stand to see her throw her potential away."

"You mean because she's turning out like me?"

Lennox chewed her lower lip. She couldn't deny some truth to the statement. Instead, she needed to end the conversation before it took an even worse turn. "Take care, Mama. We'll see each other soon. Have fun on Thursday."

"Love you." Her mom's closing words echoed through her head.

Love.

It was a beautiful concept, if misconstrued. Lennox flopped back on the couch, her legs aching from the two PiYO sessions earlier in the afternoon. She was surrounded by people who believed in the fantasy of happily ever after, but she didn't see much of it coming true in real life. No. When life got rough, somebody usually ended up leaving.

No need to become attached to someone and learn to lean on him only to have to relearn to live by herself later on. Or worse yet, to have to raise children by herself, like her mother had done. Lennox refused to end up bitter and whiny down the road.

"You still here?" Presley stuck her head through the door, wiping her brow with a towel.

Lennox hadn't noticed the silence. "Yeah. I was finishing up a bit of paperwork and got interrupted by a mom call."

"Oh, man." Presley made a face. "New boyfriend?"

"She's rather predictable, isn't she?"

"It's usually either that or wanting something." Presley tilted her head. "You okay?"

"Just tired. A little stressed about this wedding. Didn't need mama drama too." Lennox waved her hand. "I'll be okay."

"Maybe this will cheer you up. Someone came by earlier asking about your kickboxing class." Presley tapped her fingers against her chin. "Taller than me. Wavy hair. Chocolate eyes."

It couldn't be. "What did you tell him?"

"I told him to come by on Saturday. He was a little scrawny to be wanting to work out, but who am I to judge? I mean, every new member helps pay the bills, right?"

"Right." Lennox sat up and scooped up her bag. "You good to lock up?"

"Consider it done." Presley play-punched her arm on the way out. "And quit stressing about your friend's wedding. That's her job. Exercise is supposed to increase endorphins. You're walking around like you haven't coached three classes today."

"A good night's sleep will have me back to myself in the morning." Lennox waved over her shoulder as she slipped out the back door.

Would she be able to sleep? Not knowing she'd have to see Ty at least once this week, if not twice. He couldn't really be interested in her kickboxing class. Most of the classes offered at Twisted Barre were women only. How had he found out about one of the two that allowed men?

Sara Beth or Brian. The traitors. If they tried to set her up, so help her …

Chapter Four

Late again.

Ty ran a hand through his hair and let out a deep breath as he stood on Sara Beth's porch. All his good intentions of showing up early had come to naught. And this time, it wasn't even his fault—not that Lennox would believe him.

Why was he thinking about Lennox? He was here to support Brian and Sara Beth. Lennox was simply the other friend helping out. It didn't matter what she thought of him, so long as she walked down the aisle on his arm at Brian's wedding.

Brian swung the door wide. "Hey! You're just in time for dinner."

"I meant to be here earlier. Dad needs a new electrician. The guy showed up half an hour after his appointment time. And then, the interview ran long." Ty followed his cousin to the kitchen.

"No worries, man. We were just talking until the lasagna finished anyway. Sara Beth wants us to eat neatly because we don't need sauce on the envelopes." Brian slid his arm around his fiancée and gave her a squeeze.

"How would you feel if you went to open something with a red smear on it?" Sara Beth poked Brian in the chest.

Lennox wrinkled her nose. "Ew."

"See?" Sara Beth waved at her friend.

"So, it's time to eat?" Ty rubbed his hands together.

"Yes. We just got everything on the table." Sara Beth pulled out of Brian's arms and led them to the dining room where her parents stood. Aunt Trish and Uncle Matt were there too.

Sara Beth's dad led them in prayer, although Ty noticed Lennox didn't bow her head. Was she being extra quiet tonight? Or maybe the tirade she'd displayed the one time he'd met her was misleading. There he went thinking about her again.

Ty scooped out a huge helping of pasta. "So, Sara Beth, we're addressing invitations tonight?"

"And *Save the Date* cards. I figured it would be easier to do them at the same time." Sara Beth passed the breadbasket to her mom. "And we need to come up with our hashtag."

"Hashtag?" Lennox cut a glance at her friend. "What does that mean?"

"Like on social media." Sara Beth grinned. "All the brides and grooms are using cute hashtags now so people can post wedding wishes and pictures. They'll all appear together when someone searches for that phrase. But I don't know what we can do. I mean, Brian's last name is Dunne. And we're not done—we're just getting started."

Sara Beth's mom shook her head, "I'm not sure I get what you mean, honey. Why not just #dunnewedding?"

"That's not cute or original. And it might even be taken. We have to make sure we don't use someone else's. All our posts would mix in with theirs and be totally confusing." Sara Beth forked a bite of lettuce.

"So, you're wanting a play on words using our last name?" Ty ripped off a bite of bread.

Sara Beth gave a little bounce. "Exactly."

"There's *oneandDunne*. Like, you're never going to love another." Brian winked.

Lennox held up a finger, then quickly typed something into her phone before shaking her head. "It's taken."

"Really?" Brian blinked a few times. "And I thought it was original."

"What about *dundundunDunne*? Like the wedding march music?" Uncle Matt chuckled.

"But without music, they could change the tune." Sara Beth frowned.

Ty snickered. "Yeah. They could turn it into one of those dark Beethoven pieces." He hummed the deep notes.

"Okay. No music." Sara Beth's mom agreed.

"Maybe something simple like *MrandMrsDunne*." Sara Beth tapped her chin while Lennox typed that one into a social media site.

"Nope. That's been done too. No pun intended."

"This is harder than I expected." Sara Beth sopped up the last of her sauce with her bread. "Let's move on to addresses and keep thinking about it. Everyone have clean fingers?"

Brian held up his hands for her to examine. "What? No dessert?"

"Not until you've addressed at least twenty envelopes."

"Um, you know what my handwriting looks like. Are you sure you want me to be one of the ones writing on them?" Brian pulled out Sara Beth's chair.

What would it be like to be in a relationship like that? Before he could help Lennox in a similar fashion, her scowl had him returning his attention to the happy couple.

Lennox perched on the edge of the couch and picked up a *Save the Date* card. "How many are we doing?"

"We figure we can't fit more than a hundred and fifty max in that chapel." Sara Beth handed out pens. "But not everyone will be able to come, either. So, we're inviting about two hundred."

"Two hundred envelopes?" Ty missed the sofa and landed on

the floor. Maybe if he stayed where he was, no one would notice the mishap. Besides, down here he was closer to the coffee table. Yeah. That would be his excuse.

"No, silly." Sara Beth laughed before continuing. "We're inviting that many people, but a lot of them have more than one person in the family. It's less than two hundred envelopes. And if we each do a few, it won't be much at all."

Ty picked up a *Save the Date* card. "We fell for each other, a dream come true, and want you here this autumn for our *I dos*." The words were printed over a picture of Sara Beth and Brian playing in leaves.

"Man—this poem." Ty shook his head.

"I wrote it." Sara Beth straightened. "Isn't it perfect? Sort of a play on the word *fall*—you know, the season we're getting married."

"And the season we had our first date. And our first kiss." Brian beamed over at her.

"It's ... sweet." Ty hoped his words came across more authentic than they were. He didn't want to hurt Sara Beth's feelings. Was Lennox smirking?

"Well, there's your hashtag." Sara Beth's dad pointed to his daughter. "*FallingforDunne*."

"Oh!" Sara Beth gave another bounce. "It's so cute."

Brian crossed his arms. "I don't know. You already fell for me. It's not something you're still doing."

"I plan to fall in love with you a little more each year for the rest of our lives." Sara Beth tapped him on the nose.

Aunt Trish rolled her eyes. "Okay, you lovebirds. Let's get busy."

Each person was given part of the list and a stack of two different envelopes to address. Ty laid his first set aside and glanced Lennox's way. Her hand gracefully curved out a letter *S* prettier than he'd ever seen. He leaned over to watch more closely.

"Something wrong?" Lennox didn't even look up, focusing instead on her calligraphy.

"Nothing. You just caught me off-guard."

She finished the envelope and set it aside. "Why?"

"You didn't strike me as that kind of a girl."

"What kind of girl would that be?" Lennox raised an eyebrow.

"One who puts extra swirls and flourishes on her letters." He refused to look away from her disdain.

"Because I teach kickboxing?" She poked her pen in his direction, although she didn't actually touch him. "Or something else?"

He leaned back and cocked his head to the side as he studied her. "This doesn't fit the impression you gave me the other day. And the fact you teach kickboxing definitely doesn't change that original idea."

She pursed her lips. Would she give him a piece of her mind? No, she straightened her shoulders and pulled two more envelopes her way. "You better get busy. Unless you plan to be late for dessert too."

"I didn't mean to be late for dinner." He followed suit and returned to addressing envelopes, although he snuck more glances at her from the corner of his eye.

She huffed and peered over at him. "What?"

"What, what?" He focused on making his *G* neat.

"You keep *looking* at me. Do you want me to ask you why you were late earlier? I assumed it was because you're always late."

"And you can make such an assumption after only meeting me twice?" He pushed his envelopes aside.

"Why not? You can make assumptions about me, it seems."

"*Touché.*" He held out his hand. "Truce?"

She hesitated before sliding her fingers around his. "Try to get along well enough to help our friends get married in a few months and then never have to see each other again?"

"If that's the way you want it." He clasped her smaller hand in his, wondering at the rightness of it being there. "But you might like me if you gave yourself a chance."

"Don't hold your breath." She tugged her fingers free.

"Are you two done trying to outdo one another?" Sara Beth pulled Ty's attention back to the others in the room. "We're ahead of you by five envelopes."

"Right." Ty tapped his pen to his forehead in a mock salute. "At your service."

"Did you finish reading your chapters for this week yet?" Sara Beth poked Brian.

"Um, some of them." Brian's tongue peeked out of the corner of his mouth as he wrote another name. "But we're not meeting with Brother Phillips until Saturday."

"Right. The day after tomorrow." Sara Beth poked his shoulder.

"What are you two reading?" Ty set another envelope aside, secretly comparing the height of his stack to Lennox's—still shorter.

"It's a book for our counseling sessions. The book is supposed to help us come up with some questions for each other." Sara Beth chattered a mile-a-minute as she wrote, and Ty wondered if her envelopes would be any neater than the ones he had finished.

"Why do you need counseling? Aren't you two getting along?" Lennox set two more in the *completed* stack.

"It's pre-marital counseling." Brian studied his list as he continued. "A few sessions to help us make sure we get our marriage started off right. Helps us have a better idea of what we're getting into and some tips to make our life together work better. After all, nothing half-done is done right."

"That's it." Sara Beth's dad snapped.

"What, Daddy?"

"*Marriagedunneright.*" Sara Beth's dad pointed at Lennox's phone. "For your hashtag."

"Ooh. Maybe. Do you think it's already taken?" Sara Beth leaned forward as Lennox typed the words.

"It's available."

"Sweet!" Sara Beth and Brian sealed the idea with a kiss.

Lennox rolled her eyes and went back to her calligraphy. She was a conundrum. She wore her hair almost as short as a guy's and taught workout sessions, but then wrote in fancy scripts on her friend's envelopes. She swore she didn't believe in love, but was here helping plan a wedding, even going so far as to come up with a ridiculous hashtag. The more he learned about her, the more he wanted to know.

"If you're late to dessert, I'm going to eat your helping." Lennox didn't even look up, but somehow sensed he'd been staring at her again.

"Not if I can help it." Surely, he could write faster than she could make all her swirls and curlicues.

But could he get this growing desire to know more about her out of his head when she so obviously wanted nothing more to do with him than was absolutely necessary?

"Have you found someone to start working on the chapel?" Lennox asked, pulling him back to reality.

"I've been calling around to get the best price." He tried to keep the defensiveness out of his reply.

"You know it's supposed to rain quite a bit this weekend." Her stare bore into him.

"It has a tarp over it for now. Believe it or not, I have *some* idea what I'm doing." He met her blue gaze without flinching. "I'll do my part in this wedding, and you can do yours."

"Speaking of your part in the wedding, Len." Sara Beth chimed in from the other end of the coffee table. "We're dress shopping next week."

Had a look of utter disgust crossed Lennox's face before she schooled it back to its normal smoothness, or had he seen things?

Len. The nickname was more feminine, somehow. What would she do if he started calling her that? And what would she look like in a dress?

"Tux fittings too, guys." Sara Beth pulled him back to reality once more.

Now it was his chance to turn up his nose. He didn't mind getting dressed up every now and then, but a tuxedo had more parts than any outfit had a right to. The idea of someone measuring in certain areas made him cringe. But, with the right dress, a tuxedo was appropriate. Especially if he could spin that dress—and the someone in it—around the dance floor a time or two.

Hmm. The wedding talk was obviously getting to him. Focus. Address the envelopes, eat dessert, and go home ... away from all the kissing and talk of marriage. Let it be chocolate.

As if she could read his mind, Sara Beth said, "Dessert tonight is four different kinds of cake. I couldn't decide, so we're going to taste them together and pick. Classic white, of course, and peanut butter with raspberry filling, and lemon, and chocolate."

Every one of them sounded amazing to him, though chocolate was his favorite. Did Lennox like chocolate?

Focusing was harder than Ty realized.

Maybe he'd skip that kickboxing class he'd been considering. Time away from a certain redhead might be a safer option. And he needed to make sure the tarp was secure.

Chapter Five

"Need help with anything, Mom?" Lennox tapped the Formica countertop in her mother's kitchen, wishing to avoid the awkwardness of this situation.

"This isn't my first rodeo. I've made dinner for you before now." Her mom gave a head of lettuce an extra-hard chop.

"Mostly dinners out of a box or the freezer, though. Not like this." Lennox indicated the various pots and pans bubbling on the stove.

George gave Mom's shoulder a squeeze. "You should show some respect for your mother." He wasn't anything like Lennox expected. Her mother's age—maybe a year or two older—with graying temples and a mustache. Not trim. Not fat, either. His sweater vest over a striped shirt made him look rather dashing. "She's raised two girls to womanhood, mostly alone. That's not easy, you know."

Had any of her mother's other boyfriends shown such support?

"I meant no disrespect." Lennox crossed her arms over her chest as she leaned against the sink. "I simply don't remember anything this fancy."

"I'm showing off for George. I'm sure he hasn't had a home-cooked meal in a while. Not since his wife died four years ago." Her mom piled the chopped leaves in a bowl and added some cherry tomatoes and carrots.

"A few, but not nearly enough." He picked up the salad and a bottle of dressing to take to the dining table.

"Sorry, I'm late." Macy rushed through the front door as Lennox carried the last dish to the table. "I had to run an errand for Jared, and it took longer than I expected."

"No worries, dear. We're just sitting down." Her mom motioned them all to the table.

"*Whew.*" Macy flopped into the chair across from Lennox. "Jared uses this dry cleaner all the way across town, and by the time I got off work, everyone was picking up their clothes, so I had to wait at least ten minutes. Then, I couldn't find the ticket stub to give the attendant. And finally, I had to coerce them into looking it up by his name instead. I don't know, but whatever I said, they bought it and let me pick up his suits. I don't know why he has so many suits."

Lennox raised an eyebrow as she waited for her sister to finish the story. She didn't understand why her sister would want to pick up her boyfriend's laundry in the first place. Relationships weren't worth it, if that's what it took.

George cleared his throat as Lennox reached for a roll. "Would you like to pray first?"

Lennox froze—her hand in mid-air. "Oh. Um, sure."

She glanced over to her mom, who already had her head bowed. Macy was lowering hers as Lennox took her in too. When had this happened? Prayer had never been a thing in this house.

"Father God, we thank you for this time together as a family and for this delicious food. Please bless the hands who prepared it as well as the mouths that will eat it. Give us all safety back to our homes this evening, and let us be a blessing to You. In Jesus' name, Amen." George's voice rumbled through the room, and probably straight to God's ear, assuming He was up there somewhere.

Lennox had never heard a petition less rote.

"That was beautiful, George." Her mom passed a bowl of potatoes to him with a smile. "As always."

"Thanks, but it's not about how pretty it is. As long as it's heartfelt. That's what God wants." George scooped out some spuds and placed the bowl in Lennox's hands before she even realized it was coming.

The weight knocked her knuckles against the table. She quickly recovered and served her helping as she tried to understand this new man in her mom's life. A Christian? Since when did her mom pick up guys who were supportive *and* Christian?

"Busy week, Lennox?" Mom broke into her ponderings.

"The usual."

"Tell me about your gym." George forked a bite of chicken and gave her a nod that was probably supposed to be encouraging.

"I am one-third owner of the Twisted Barre downtown. We offer classes, mostly for women—barre, PiYO, yoga, spin, aerobics, and a few others. I do a kickboxing class a few times a week where men can join too. And I think some of Hattie's spin classes allow men, but mostly it's female-only. We wanted a place where women could feel safe to work out without being gawked at." Lennox picked at her asparagus. Would he make a comment about feminism?

"That's a great idea."

Lennox almost dropped her fork.

"My daughter might be interested in something like that. What'd you say the name was again?" George wiped his mouth.

"Twisted Barre." Lennox leaned back, out of her element. "We came up with *twisted* for things like yoga and PiYO and Pilates. *Barre* for barre, obviously."

"And what is barre?"

"It consists of poses and stretches, similar to what a ballerina might use." Lennox held her hand up waist-high. "With a barre across one wall, hence the name."

"But you don't have to be a ballerina to do it?" George leaned in, his focus more on her than the food in front of him.

"No. We simply use their forms and movements as a basis for the workout."

"Lennox got a degree in health and physical education and then went on to learn all these different ways to stretch and bend and move." Mom motioned toward her with a fork. "She's put a lot of work into making this gym a success."

What was going on? It was the first time Lennox could remember her mom sounding supportive of her occupation.

"Lennox is a little obsessed with being healthy." Macy forked a bite of chicken. "I'm surprised she was even able to get off work today."

"Hattie took my class tonight, and I'll cover one of hers on Thursday. It will all work out." Lennox shot her sister a dirty look. "What about you, Macy? How's your job search going?"

"*Ugh.* You'd think people would be willing to pay more for all the things they want employees to do. If I have to stock shelves and clean and help people look for things and possibly work the register or something else—that deserves more than a couple dollars above minimum wage." Macy rolled her eyes.

Lennox wanted to ask her sister if she appreciated those workers now that she realized how little they got in return for their hard work. George changed the subject again, and the conversation flowed more easily for the rest of the meal.

After Lennox helped load the dishwasher and put away leftovers, Mama stepped on the front porch with a cigarette. Lennox wrinkled her nose and headed toward the back porch door. The view wasn't great in the trailer park, but at least she wouldn't be in here when her mom came in reeking of smoke.

A moment later, George joined her at the railing looking over into Mrs. Petowski's garden of pink plastic flamingoes. "It's a lovely evening."

"It's turned out better than I expected." The weather was finally warm enough to not need a jacket after the sun dipped below the horizon. The sky was a mellow orange turning to gray and then deeper black scattered with a few early stars. The smell of hyacinths wafted over from the edge of the garden.

"I take it you weren't sure about me?" George's mustache twitched with the beginning of a grin.

Lennox leaned her back against the rail and studied the stars overhead. "I honestly never know what to expect from my mom's boyfriends. I guess you know there have been many. After my dad left us, she went a little crazy, as if she felt like there was something wrong with her, that it was her fault. And she's been trying to convince herself otherwise ever since. Hence, the cigarettes and drinking."

"She's promised to try to give up a lot of that." George nodded once. "That cigarette she's smoking now is the first for today."

Lennox's head jerked his way. "Really?"

"Really."

"That doesn't even make sense. Didn't she meet you in a bar? Why would she give up drinking and smoking for someone who does the same thing?" This night was giving Lennox a sense the whole world had turned upside down.

"I don't drink. I was at the bar that night as an accountability partner to keep a friend from going too far. Not to mention as a ride home." George fixed his eyes on Lennox with a look of pure seriousness. "When Faye came over and asked me to buy her a drink, I agreed, but only if she'd go out with me another time, one when alcohol wasn't involved."

"Why?" Lennox shook her head. "Sorry. That sounded bad, but I simply don't understand."

"Her eyes. They reflected pain like that in my own life. We've both lost someone we loved. She lost your dad when he walked out, and ... I lost my wife to cancer. There's a kindred spirit there. And I wanted to see if I could find more." He took a deep breath. "Obviously, I did. We've had several dinners now and have more in common than you might think. She has a great sense of humor."

"I guess I can't imagine." Lennox studied her mom as she re-entered the doublewide. "I've known her one way for so long, it's hard for me to believe she can live another."

"You'd be surprised what can change with the love of Jesus."

There was that Christian talk again.

"You don't believe me." George leaned back against the railing next to her. "Well, that's okay for now, but I don't promise to quit talking about it."

"I don't believe in love of any kind, George. I've seen it fail too many times to count."

"Then it wasn't love." George patted her arm as he straightened to go back in. "Love never fails."

Well, that was a bunch of malarkey. Of course, love failed. The divorce rate was proof enough of that. And wasn't this family complete evidence? Nothing had lasted here except the heartbreak that came after a supposed love.

Through the window, George gave her mom a hug and kissed her temple. Her mom smiled up at him and looked happier than Lennox had seen her in years. Was this guy for real? Or was more heartache coming their way? Lennox didn't believe George could work miracles simply because he believed in God. In her experience, God wasn't working miracles anymore.

No. Love had to be a once-in-a-lifetime thing. Like Sara Beth and Brian. They were the couple who might make it. But for someone as broken as her mom or herself? No. Love couldn't live in a broken heart.

Not even for someone as nice as George.

He'd leave, too, just like all the others, and Lennox would have to sweep the pieces up of her mother's broken heart once more.

Chapter Six

Trying on a tuxedo was not Ty's idea of a fun time. Whoever invented such a constraining contraption should be made to wear one twenty-four seven.

But this was for Brian and Sara Beth. For them, he would let someone measure him in all sorts of awkward places. If that wasn't true love, he didn't know what was.

Letting out a breath, he pulled the door handle. A bell chimed above him as he stepped into the only formal boutique in Park Haven. Yards of filmy fabric, ruffles, and lace filled the room. It was worse than the three years his cousin Lindsey had participated in pageants.

"Ty!" Sara Beth rose from a chair in the corner, a water bottle in hand. "You made it."

"Am I on time? Because if so, mark the calendar." He gave her a quick hug.

Her laugh tittered around the room. "Close enough for me. Ms. Betty is helping Lennox into her dress right now and couldn't have helped you until after she's done anyway."

"Lennox is here?" Ty rocked back on his heels, hands in pockets, probably not coming off as nonchalant as he intended. "I guess I didn't realize you'd scheduled us so close together."

"I didn't originally, but her work schedule got switched around this week so she could go to dinner at her mom's on Tuesday. So now she has a class this afternoon when we'd originally scheduled her, but Ms. Betty did some amazing juggling for me."

"Here we are, dear." Ms. Betty's voice, one he'd recognize anywhere after years of hearing it in Bible school, interrupted them as she stepped through the curtain. "She looks lovely, of course."

Ty waited, but no one followed Ms. Betty from the dressing area. Sara Beth bounced on her toes but evidently saw only the older woman as well. Ty's heart skipped a beat at the thought of seeing Lennox all fancied up.

"Len, if you don't come out here right now, I'm going to drag you by the ear." Sara Beth hollered, her Southern accent thickening as her voice raised.

"Sara Beth, are you sure about this color?" Lennox emerged, her head down as she fingered the creamy orange fabric of her satin skirt. "I don't think it's right for me at all."

She raised her gaze to Sara Beth and froze. He couldn't blame her. Ty was rather frozen, too, seeing her in that gown. The simple empire-waisted bodice hugged her form perfectly, showing off her sculpted shoulders and arms. From the waist, the skirt hung in elegant flowing lines all the way to the floor, where her toes barely peeped out in shiny sandals. And the color didn't clash with her hair—it enhanced it.

Would his heart ever beat a normal rhythm again?

"Lennox, it's perfect!" Sara Beth jumped up onto the platform with her friend and grabbed her hand to spin her around. "Just like I pictured."

"Really?" Lennox's face was full of doubt.

"You look amazing." He said it before he could stop himself.

"See?" Sara Beth winked at him. "Ty wouldn't lie about something like that. Especially since he's the one walking you down the aisle."

Lennox winced. Was it more because of him or the walking down the aisle part?

"Well, there you go. If Ty approves, that's all that matters, right?" Lennox's voice dripped with sarcasm.

"C'mon, Len. You look gorgeous. That cut is perfect, and so is the color." Sara Beth did a little cheerleader move and squealed. "Exactly how I imagined. How great is this dress going to look with the sunflower bouquets?"

When Sara Beth made Lennox spin again, a small sliver of creamy white showed between where the zipper ended below her shoulder blades and the dress buttoned at her nape. His fingers itched to run up that slip of exposed skin, but he knew better. No way on earth would she be amenable to that idea.

"It doesn't even look like it needs any alterations, Ms. Betty. Am I right?" Sara Beth stepped back and examined Lennox from tip to toe.

"I'm thinking it doesn't. As long as Lennox is okay with the length." Ms. Betty clasped her hands in front of her chest.

"These are the shoes you wanted, right?" Lennox lifted a foot, showing off more of those toes. They were painted a dark maroon, and the color suited her.

"Yes. It's all perfect." Sara Beth gushed.

Lennox frowned as she studied the strappy heels on her feet. "I'm not sure about spending hours in these things, but I'll practice between now and then."

"You'll do great." Sara Beth puffed out a disbelieving breath. "I've seen the way you move in your classes. You'll probably be more graceful than I will walking down the aisle. And I'll have my daddy's arm to hold on to."

"Okay, Ms. Sara Beth, you next." Ms. Betty motioned toward the curtain behind them. "I'll get you in your gown so you can see the two together, and then I can help you both out again. Just have a seat and make yourself comfortable, Mr. Dunne. I'll be with you after I get the girls finished."

"No worries. I've got some time." Ty gave the older lady a

grin, secretly thrilled to have a few moments with Lennox to himself.

"The chapel repairs must be going well." Lennox pulled him from his admiration.

"What?"

"I said, the chapel repairs must be going well." She tucked her hands into her hips. "You mentioned having time, so that must mean the repairs are on schedule. Otherwise, you'd be more rushed. Right?"

"Right." He absent-mindedly rubbed the back of his neck. "I've got some of the best companies in the area lined up to work on it." He wasn't about to mention they couldn't start working before late June due to having earlier commitments. What Lennox didn't know wouldn't hurt him.

"I look forward to seeing it in better shape soon." She glanced over her shoulder as if she could see the progress of Sara Beth through the curtain.

"That dress really does look stunning on you." He couldn't help himself, despite knowing she wouldn't appreciate the compliment.

"I'm doing this for Sara Beth. I'll probably never wear this dress again, but for a few hours, I can handle a color that does nothing good for my complexion and hair." Her fingers dashed through her short locks as if they had a mind of their own.

Ty shook his head. "But you're wrong."

"What?"

"You're wrong." He reached out toward the hair and then stopped himself before discovering how soft it was. "It's perfect for your hair and ivory skin. This dress has just enough of a peachy shimmer to set it all off and make the hue less orange. Besides, peaches and pinks look great on redheads."

"And how would you know that?" She lifted an eyebrow.

"My mom is a redhead. Although hers is a bit brighter than yours." He shrugged and stepped back to lessen the temptation to touch her. "Anyway, I've heard a lot of discussions on what she can and can't wear. Trust your friend's instincts. This one is spot on."

Lennox pressed her lips together and studied the feminine room around them as if she didn't want to discuss anything further. He'd leave it alone, for now. But he didn't want her to think she wasn't beautiful, because she was stunning. He could barely keep his eyes off her.

"What do you think?" Sara Beth's voice pulled both their gazes to where the curtain had parted. The bride stood, beaming in her ivory lace dress. It had simple lines and a full skirt but was elegant and screamed her Southern personality in all the intricate details.

"It's perfect for you." Lennox joined her and squeezed her hands.

"You're both absolutely lovely." Ms. Betty moved around them, fidgeting with seams and the way the fabric lay. "Yes. Those colors are a great choice, dear. And you wanted the boys' vests and ties to match the bridesmaid dress, right?"

"Yes, ma'am." Sara Beth peered passed the older lady and winked at Ty. "What do you think, Best Man? Can you rock a tie and vest in this color?"

"Can it be a bow tie?" He tilted his head and gave what he hoped was a puppy dog look. He'd never been sure if he'd perfected it or not, considering how often it didn't work.

Sara Beth giggled. "Of course. I think that will be charming."

Lennox rolled her eyes. "Can we get out of these now? I have a class this afternoon."

"Of course." Ms. Betty ushered her back behind the curtain, and Ty let out a breath of disappointment as he lost sight of her.

"Don't give up, Ty. She might be softening just a little." Sara Beth pulled his attention back to her.

"What?"

"I can see you're attracted to her." She put a finger over her mouth. "But that is my little secret. Just be warned. She's a hard shell to crack. Her past ... hasn't been easy. And it's left her jaded when it comes to love."

"Any tips?"

"If I think of anything, I'll let you know." Sara Beth shook her head. "In the meantime, I'll find every way I can to throw you two together."

"Well, in that case, let me praise you some more." He motioned for her to twirl. "Brian is going to fall over when he sees you walking down the aisle in that dress. I'm going to have to hold him up."

Her laughter filled the small space. "It's going to be fun being a member of your family. Thanks for the compliment. I guess I better go slip out of this before someone who shouldn't see it walks by."

"I made sure Brian had plans on the other side of town because a little birdie told me you were having your fitting this morning. My mom suggested it."

"Well, thank your mom. I'm sure you'll look just as dashing in your tux."

"I'll do my best."

She slipped behind the curtain, and he slid down into the chair. He couldn't imagine looking half as well as Lennox had in that gown of hers. But maybe together, they'd even each other out. Assuming she let him near her that day for longer than the ceremony.

Lennox walked by without glancing his way, back in her workout gear, a loose shirt emblazoned with *Twisted Barre* and black leggings with neon stripes down the side. Back to her strong side instead of the feminine one. The bell jangled as the door closed behind her.

He'd have to keep thinking of ways to break down her walls. Or maybe find a gate. Did ramparts like that have gates? He was willing to find out.

"See you later, Ty." Sara Beth stopped in front of him. "Have fun being fitted. And please make sure Brian makes it to his appointment later. I know he doesn't care as much, but I wouldn't want him to look less handsome than his groomsmen."

"I'm at your service." Ty stood and bowed. "Whatever you need, just let me know."

"Thanks again, Sir Dunne." Sara Beth gave a perfect curtsy and was away through the door.

Ty turned to Ms. Betty, who waited expectantly in front of the curtain.

"Your turn, dear."

"Yes, ma'am. Lead the way."

In the black pants and white shirt, he stood, his arms out, so Ms. Betty could measure and tug at the fabric, making sure she had him in the right size, that the hem would be the correct length, and that the vest would fit when it came in. He didn't pay much attention, though. His mind was five months down the road, asking Lennox for a dance in that dress, and wondering if his fingers might graze that little slip of skin on her back.

Miles to go before that could happen, though, he reminded himself as he changed back into his jeans and polo. First, he had to find a way to get to the other side of that wall. What was it about her that made him want to work harder at this than he'd wanted to do anything else in his life?

Hopefully, Sara Beth would find another excuse to throw them together—and soon.

Chapter Seven

"Go ahead and find your spots, guys." Lennox jogged into the room and geared up her mind for the kickboxing class Saturday morning. While many of her classes called for high energy and focus, this one required the most. It was pretty much non-stop for forty-five minutes.

Sara Beth waved from her normal position at the end of the first row. Brian stretched his hamstrings beside her. A backpack kept anyone from taking the spot next to him, the one almost directly in front of her. Lennox narrowed her eyes. Surely, he wasn't saving a place for his cousin. He wouldn't still have that on his mind, would he?

Well, Ty wasn't here yet, and it was time to start. Maybe if she played the music and got people moving, he'd be too embarrassed to walk in front of everyone after showing up late. It was worth a shot.

"Everyone ready?" She held her finger over the button on her music player.

"Wait." Sara Beth shot her a guilty look. "I forgot my water bottle in the changing room. Mind if I grab it really fast?"

If anyone else had made that request, Lennox would've started anyway and let them miss the first minute. But she gave her friend a begrudging nod and set her player back down.

Brian glanced behind him, but not in the direction his fiancée went. He looked toward the front door of the studio. Evidently, her hunch was right. Tension crept into the space between her shoulders and settled in like a cat right before a nap. She rolled her neck and let out a breath of relief when Sara Beth came back in before anyone else could.

"Okay, guys. It's been a rough week. Let's blow off some steam, shall we?" She started the upbeat music and jogged in place at the same time. "You know the drill. Time to warm up."

"You know, don't you?" Brian's voice was just loud enough to carry to her at the front. No one else glanced their way. The other dozen participants were used to the random conversations.

Lennox simply lifted an eyebrow at him but gave no certain answer.

"He's not as bad as you seem to think. You're not even giving him a chance." Brian followed her into shoulder rolls.

"A chance for what?" Lennox shot as the music picked up a bit more speed. She raised her voice so the rest of the class could hear. "Okay, guys, let's do this thing."

The right-hand punches came first. Lennox jabbed hard, picturing people who currently annoyed her.

"How about a chance for friendship?" Brian bounced along with her, thrusting his fist in front of him. "He's a great guy."

"He can't even be on time—ever." She shifted and motioned for the rest of her class to switch to their left hand.

"That's not true," Sara Beth chimed in. "He was on time at the fitting the other day."

"The fitting that *just happened* to be the same time as mine?" Lennox sent her friend a dirtier look than she usually would. "None of our accidental meetings are on purpose, right?"

"Lennox, your schedule changed." Sara Beth grabbed a breath. "They weren't originally back-to-back." Breath. "And you know it." Sara Beth pouted a bit but continued to follow as Lennox shifted once more and added low kicks.

"And today?" Lennox kicked a bit harder than she meant to and almost lost her balance. Obviously, having a conversation while teaching was a bad idea.

"He was interested in the class." Sara Beth huffed. "Brian bragged about the workout."

"It's probably a good thing he didn't show up." Lennox shook her head. "He doesn't look like he could keep up."

As she turned to lead them in lunge kicks, she caught sight of Ty standing in the open back doorway. She missed a step but quickly added a half-beat to catch back up. How long had he been there?

He leaned against the frame, his arms crossed over his chest. His face was unreadable, but his eyes never left her. Had he overheard their conversation? Surely not. And it wasn't like she'd said anything that would offend. He was late all the time—he even acted proud of it.

She fixed him with a glare as she added high kicks to the routine. Well, if he wanted to waste his money and simply watch the class instead of participating, she wouldn't stop him, despite the awkwardness. She'd rather have him back there than right in front of her, where she might be tempted to close the gap and kick more than air.

He studied her another minute, then lifted his fingers to his forehead in a mock salute before turning and walking away. Her heart tripped, though she wasn't sure why. No time to analyze now. She needed to keep focused on the next movements and steps for the routine.

Speaking of which, time to add some more punches. Oh, for something more solid to hit than air, which seemed thinner every second of this class. Sara Beth frowned. She must have seen Ty there ... and leaving.

Just because Sara Beth and Brian were happy together didn't mean the whole world needed the same kind of relationship to be happy too. Lennox punched with extra force and then took a deep breath through her nose to try and calm down a bit. Only twenty more minutes of the routine, and then she could hole up in her office with her punching bag.

She cringed as she punched too hard once again, a twinge of pain running through her bicep. Who was Ty Dunne to come in here and mess up her adrenaline rush by making her mad? It wasn't her fault he was too late to join the class without making a fool of himself. It wasn't her fault he knew about it at all. She hadn't mentioned it in any of their *chance* meetings over the last few weeks.

Just because Sara Beth and Brian were together didn't mean she and Ty should be too. They were maid of honor and best man, not a second bride and groom, for crying out loud. Thankfully, it was time for the kick-punch-swerve section of the routine. It required more attention. And she needed something else to focus on besides the exasperating man who walked out of here as if he understood something she didn't.

By the time the workout was over, Lennox's heartrate was higher than normal, even after such a straining session. Ty Dunne was bad for her blood pressure. That's all there was to it.

Sara Beth came over, mopping her face and neck with a towel. "Well, you sure weren't kidding when you said you wanted to push it today, huh?"

"It's the same class as always." Lennox turned her back to her friend.

"No. It was definitely more intense." Sara Beth placed a hand on Lennox's shoulder. "Listen, I'm sorry if I had anything to do with it. We weren't trying to upset you. I thought you'd appreciate another member in the class. You know, more students, more money coming in each month."

"There's more to life than money, Sara Beth." Lennox unplugged her music player from the speakers and wrapped up the cords. "I'm doing okay without another person signing up for my class."

"Lennox, seriously." Sara Beth caught her arm before Lennox could walk away. "What's up with you lately? I know you've never been one for gushing or being overly emotional, but you're acting more prickly than normal. Is it because of our wedding or something else? I don't want the stress of *my* wedding to cause *you* stress. Being the maid of honor was supposed to be something fun. Not another job."

"I'm fine. I'm just dealing with a lot right now. My mom's dating a new guy. And I'm trying to make sure I hold up my end of the load with classes and income. And, yes, your wedding has added a few extra ounces of stress, but not enough to worry about. I promise."

"So, it's just Ty, then?" Sara Beth gave her a saucy grin.

"Don't push your luck."

"Okay, okay." Sara Beth raised her hands in defeat.

Brian walked up with both their bags. "Got your gear loaded up, too, sweetheart."

"Thanks." Sara Beth accepted her duffel and a quick kiss. "See you later?"

"Wouldn't miss it." Brian nodded at Lennox. "Great workout today. See ya later."

"Bye, Brian."

"He's such a cutie." Sara Beth fanned her face with her hands. "How did I get so blessed?"

Lennox shook her head. "You're hopeless."

"Hopeful, you mean." Sara Beth play-punched Lennox's arm. "How can I not be with a whole lifetime of love ahead of me?"

Lennox bit down her snarky remark about how she wasn't sure a lifetime of love was achievable. Even George hadn't been able to pull it off, with his wife dying early from cancer. Nothing was certain. Not even that word people kept throwing around —*LOVE.*

"Oh, I noticed the craft store has their silk flowers on sale next week. Want to go look with me and see if we can grab enough to make bouquets later?" Sara Beth rocked on her heels, excitement all over her cute little pixie face.

Lennox let out a breath and nodded. "Okay. I'm in. Thursday night? I don't want to switch my schedule around too terribly often."

"I guess I can wait until then." Sara Beth's voice dripped with enough sarcasm to let Lennox know she wasn't as disappointed as her words sounded. "I mean, surely not many people are shopping for sunflowers in April."

"I wouldn't think so." Lennox shook her head.

"We can grab a bite to eat after. There's a new café in town."

A girls' night did sound fun. It had been a while since she and Sara Beth had been able to do much without Brian tagging along. And it would only get worse after they married in September. Might as well take advantage of it while she could.

"Okay. We'll go get a bite to eat too. Do you have ideas about what you want, or are we going in with an open mind and seeing what's available?" Lennox walked her friend to the back of the now-empty room and flipped off the lights.

"Oh, man. I have ideas, but I don't know if I can describe them or not." Sara Beth wrapped the end of her blonde ponytail around her finger. "I'll look up some pictures online and send them your way."

"Sure." Lennox wondered if Sara Beth would remember later that she'd promised to do that. The bride had been rather absent-minded lately.

"See you later." Sara Beth paused in the hallway. "And, please, don't be too hard on Ty. He's a really sweet guy who could probably use a friend right about now."

"Why?" Lennox's curiosity took control before she could stop the question.

"His family's being sort of hard on him. Something about Brian getting married before him. They all got married in their early twenties, but here he is, twenty-seven, with no girlfriend or any prospects. His aunts and mom are really pushing him about letting the family down. Gran Nancy joked about him being even later to get married than he was to everything else.”

“You’re serious? Because he’s not the first to marry?” Lennox grimaced as she ran a hand through her sweaty hair.

“Yeah. It’s weird.” Sara Beth shook her head. “I think that’s why the chapel means so much to him. Like it’s something else important to the family that he can restore to make up for not living up to their other expectations.”

“But he doesn’t act like he cares about the chapel.”

“Seriously? Couldn’t you hear it in his voice when he told you the story of Evangeline and Brendan? The way he tells those stories, it’s hard to miss.”

“Oh, yeah. I guess …” No way was she about to admit she hadn’t let Ty tell her his love stories. Better to keep Sara Beth in the dark. What was in those stories that was so important?

Sara Beth waved and walked out into the sunny morning. Lennox wandered past Hattie’s spin class toward her office. She should get some paperwork done before her class later today.

Problem was, though she stared at her computer screen with all her might, her mind kept wandering back to the man who walked away from her class rather than joining in. Had she truly hurt his feelings by talking about how he was always late? If Sara Beth was right, his lateness might be a sore spot lately.

Even though she didn’t want to, her curiosity had been piqued. The chapel became more interesting to her every time the topic was brought up. But was it enough to make her want to spend time with Ty Dunne? Maybe long enough to have him tell her that story?

Chapter Eight

Ty stepped through the sliding doors and took a deep breath. Nothing in the world smelled like a craft retailer. A combination of paint, candles, paper, and fabric permeated the air and drew him further in. Other men might prefer the aromas of a hardware store, but this place was like Christmas to him.

It had been a while since he'd had time to wander through this store, but the floral section was still to the right of the entrance, full of cheerful blooms and sprays. About halfway back, a blonde and red-head could just be seen over the colorful aisles. He headed that way, bracing himself. Sara Beth would give him a warm welcome, but he had a feeling her maid of honor wouldn't be so kind.

"Sara Beth." Loathe as he was to interrupt the lovely picture of the two girls with their arms laden with blooms, he was on a mission and couldn't let the groom down.

"Ty! What are you doing here?" Sara Beth spun around, the expression on her face almost as bright as the blossoms in her hands.

"Well, unfortunately, I've come as a messenger." He tapped

his watch. "Brian wasn't sure if you remembered that you're supposed to be seeing Gran tonight."

"Oh." Sara Beth's hands both went to her cheeks, the summery sprigs falling to the floor. "Tonight? No. That was supposed to be ..."

"Thursday?" Ty finished her thought.

"Yes. Oh, man. Lennox, I'm so sorry." Sara Beth grabbed her friend's hands. "What are we going to do? The sale ends Saturday, and I know you won't have time to come back. This isn't nearly enough for all the bouquets and corsages and boutonnieres. I've made such a mess."

"Relax, Sara Beth." Lennox started picking up the dropped stems. "I'll buy these and maybe a few others. It'll give us a start. We can pick up anything else we need later and just use a coupon if it's not on sale. We're months ahead of schedule."

"But ... but dinner." Sara Beth twisted her purse strap in her hands.

"I'm a grown woman. If I can't find food for myself by now, I deserve to starve." Lennox gave Sara Beth a gentle push. "Go. Brian is probably waiting for you in the parking lot."

"But you rode with me."

"I can give her a ride." The words probably wouldn't be welcome, but Ty wasn't about to leave a woman stranded at the craft store with countless bundles of flowers.

"Oh, I forgot you were here. That's perfect." Sara Beth snapped. "Ty, you're probably even a better option for helping Lennox find the flowers we need anyway. And it takes a load off my mind that she won't be left here alone. Thank you so much."

Before he or Lennox could protest, Sara Beth dashed toward the door. He released a breath and then knelt to help Lennox grab the last few sunflowers. As they straightened, he fixed her with a stare.

"I know. I know. You don't want me here any more than you wanted me at the gym on Saturday." He held his hands up in surrender. "But we're here now, and the store closes in two hours.

We can have a stare down and waste time, or we can gather up as much as we can for Sara Beth and get out of here so I can drop you off wherever you need to be."

Lennox released a slow stream of air through her lips. There was an obvious desire to argue written all over her beautiful face, but she was fighting it. Her teeth tugged on the edge of her bottom lip.

"About Saturday—"

"Let's not bring up anything that might cause an argument." He set his flowers in the cart and glanced through what had been gathered, trying to get an idea of their plan.

She pursued the subject anyway, her arms crossed over her chest. "I never said I didn't want you there."

"Your body language spoke very clearly." He raised an eyebrow. "If I'd been in the spot Brian saved for me, your punches and kicks would have had me black and blue."

Her mouth hung open, eyes wide. Was she shocked he'd said it, or shocked he had known? Either way, he was ready to move on.

"So, tell me Sara Beth's plan, because I'm not figuring it out by looking through this." He motioned to the greenery and florals between them.

She opened her mouth, but then pursed her lips and narrowed her eyes. A battle raged across her face for another second, but then she squared her shoulders, straightened her chin, and gave a short nod. "Sunflowers with a few little accent pieces for the bouquets. Smaller for the three bridesmaids and larger for Sara Beth, obviously."

"Does she want the kind of bouquet that trails down or the kind that's all round on top?"

His question seemed to flummox Lennox. "What?"

"Here." He pulled out his phone and did a quick search for bridal bouquet pictures. "See how this one is a cascade, and it sort of waterfalls down from the main cluster? That's what my mom had. But this one is round. Or there's the trend right now of bridesmaids carrying only one large flower instead of a bunch."

"Why are there so many options?" Lennox ran a hand through her hair, leaving a few strands sticking up in the front. His fingers twitched with the desire to reach up and smooth them down, but he resisted. No use aggravating the girl who was actually acting friendly right now.

"So, any idea?"

"I think she's leaning more towards the round kind for all of us. Does that help?"

"Yes. Let's see what you've got." He rummaged through the mixture in the cart, pulling out several sizes of sunflowers, a few garlands of greenery, and some daisies. "Good start. I'm thinking we need a bit of red and maybe orange to incorporate everything else. Your dress is somewhere between a dark coral and a pumpkin-y shade of rust, right?"

She blinked. "Yes?"

"You don't remember that gorgeous gown you tried on the other day? Do you have a picture of it?"

She pressed her lips together but then pulled out her phone and swiped several times across the screen before handing it to him. In the photo, she stared off to the side, her expression something of a combination of wistfulness and aggravation. He stifled a chuckle before it could escape. She would think he laughed at her instead of how much of her personality was captured in this one shot. At least it confirmed his memory of the color.

"Perfect." He spun around, searching for the colors he wanted. Everything nearby was yellow and green. "Let's find the red and orange section."

She followed him as he wandered back a few feet to a row of roses and tulips and lilies. His eyes scanned up and down the blooms, hoping the right shape would appear amid the more elegant blossoms. There. He pulled out a couple of small chrysanthemums bushes in deep fall colors. Comparing the orange to her dress confirmed his hunch. This would work wonders.

"Are the men going to have much in their boutonnieres? Or plain and simple?" He grinned a bit. "I prefer simple, but it's not my wedding."

Lennox ran her finger up and down the side of the buggy, refusing to meet his gaze. "It sounded like Sara Beth trusted your judgment."

He plopped the fake flowers into the cart. "Brian probably told her I have a degree in design."

Her eyes jerked to his. "Really?"

"Really." He steered them over and grabbed a couple stems of fake Queen Anne's lace. "I double-majored in design and business, much to my father's disappointment."

"You're just disappointing your family all over the place, huh?" She clasped a hand to her mouth, eyes wide. What did she regret more? Her brazen question or letting him know how much she knew?

"I take it Sara Beth gave you some of my backstory?" He swallowed the lump of regret that she held more knowledge of him than he did about her. And she still didn't want him around. Was he truly so heinous? "My family holds high expectations. It goes all the way back to the 1920s when some of our family chose a rather ... well, let's just say they considered themselves above the law. Since then, *this* side of the family, with few exceptions, has made sure to be above-board and perfect in everything so as to not be mistaken as associating with *them*."

"Goodness. Were they liquor runners or something?"

"Mobsters." Ty couldn't resist laughing at the expression on her face.

Pure shock. She hurried to catch up to him as he turned down an aisle of greenery. "You're not serious."

"I am. But that was a hundred years ago. It doesn't mean as much to me as to some members of our family." Ty shook his head. "I'm sure Gran wanted to meet with Brian and Sara Beth tonight to reiterate that they only get their inheritance if they remain good girls and boys." His voice had turned a bit mocking by the end, but he couldn't help himself.

Gran Nancy had become more serious about her matriarchal duties over the last few years, losing some of her lighthearted fun, and becoming ... well ... crotchety, of late. Maybe when the cancer stole Gramps five years ago, it took some of her heart with him.

"Wow." Lennox shook her head and then smiled as he handed her a package of red leaves.

"What do you think about putting those with a small sunflower for the boutonnieres?" He tilted his head as he tried to picture the combo in his mind.

"Sounds cute to me, but like you said earlier—it's not my wedding."

"True." He took the pack back and held it up with a flower. "If Sara Beth doesn't like it, she can return it and get something else."

Lennox opened her mouth to say something, but her phone started singing from her pocket. Was that a song from the fifties? She held up a finger and wrinkled her nose as she glanced at the screen. Even though she obviously didn't want to answer, she held the device to her ear and said, "Hello."

He tried not to listen in, but it was next to impossible with them right there on the same aisle, only the quiet elevator-style music playing in the background breaking up the quiet on this side of the store.

"George said she was giving that up." Lennox's voice rose a little, a bit of hysteria on the edge of the words.

Ty added some off-white lace and burlap ribbon to the cart, thinking it might be a great way to wrap the bouquet stems together. In went some floral wire and tape too.

"Where is she this time?" Lennox's fingers massaged her forehead. "No. I'm not sure how quickly I can get there. I'm not home right now. I was helping Sara Beth get flowers for the wedding."

Ty searched the section one more time to see if anything else caught his eye that might work in the decorations. But his attention was more on the woman pacing at the end of the aisle, distress obvious in her every move.

"Okay. I know. I know it's my turn. I'll be there as quickly as I can."

"What's wrong?" Ty steered the cart back toward the front of the store as she rejoined him.

"Don't worry about it." Lennox jabbed her phone back into her back pocket, her chin locked in a position that had to be to keep it from trembling. "I just need to get home now."

"Sure. Let's check this out, and I'll take you wherever you need to go."

She nodded but didn't say anything else.

He stashed the bags in the trunk of his car, almost wishing he drove something bigger. By the time he closed the hatch, she had already climbed in the passenger seat without waiting for him to open the door. Sliding in, he paused a moment with his hand on the key. A niggle, be it divine or curiosity, urged him to offer more help, but he wasn't completely sure of the situation.

"Anything wrong?" She glanced down at the ignition.

"Yes, but you won't tell me." He turned the car on. "So, where am I taking you? Because it sounds like you're only going home to leave again. Why not let me drive you instead so you don't have to backtrack?"

She opened her mouth, closed it, and opened it again. He wondered if she'd give him any kind of an answer when she finally spoke. "Okay. You asked for it. My mom is drunk at the bar on the edge of town—Goldie's. My sister called me because, evidently, it's my turn to play designated driver. I guess Mom's boyfriend is working tonight or something, so he can't do it. And my sister is ... well, if we started that discussion, it would take all night."

She shared much more than he'd expected, so he wouldn't push for more. "Okay, let's go get your mom."

"Just like that?"

"Just like what?"

"You're not going to question the sanity of my family? Or wonder what you got yourself into when you offered me a ride? You're not going to worry about my mom throwing up in the tiny backseat of your fancy car?" Her voice raised with each question.

"No." Though he inwardly cringed at the last question, he could honestly say it didn't stop him from wanting to help. "Help me find this place, because I've not paid much attention to the bars at the edge of town, and I want to make sure I get the right one."

She turned her head toward her window. Was she crying? Nothing he could do about it now. But he wasn't taking her directly home after dropping off her mom, either. Because she needed a listening ear whether she wanted one or not.

Chapter Nine

"There." Lennox pointed out her window to her mother's favorite watering hole. Exactly as she remembered from the last time she'd played designated driver. The cinderblock walls were a dull gray under the neon lights blazing from the windows. Music blared so loud it could be discerned word for word without stepping foot inside.

Ty stopped her with a hand on her shoulder. "Want me to go in with you?"

She was tempted for half a second. After all, it would be nice not to have to walk in there alone, trying to find her mother and then coax her into leaving. But then the thought of him seeing more than he already had ... and would, when her mom came out—no.

She squared her shoulders and shook her head. "Thanks, but I can handle it."

He caught her hand once more before she could get all the way out. "Let me give you my cell number at least, so you can call if you change your mind."

She pulled her bottom lip between her teeth and hesitated. With a long breath, she handed him her phone and waited while he punched in his digits. Now she'd have it for when she needed to call him about the chapel repairs. That was the excuse she gave herself in her head, at least.

"I'll be back as quickly as I can." She shut the door behind her before he could stop her again.

She walked into the dim interior, scanning the various people occupying the bar stools. No luck there. On to the tables. She waded through the room, checking the patrons as she went. Her mother had chosen the table in the very back corner—that wasn't like her. Normally, she would've been at the bar where she could be seen more to pick up men.

"Mama." Lennox placed her hand on her mother's slumped shoulder. Was she asleep? "Mama."

Her mother twitched and then lifted her head a few inches. "Whatchoo want?"

"Mama, it's me. It's Lennox."

"Lennox? No. Lennox is too good for this place. She doesn't go in bars." Her mother's head moved back to the table. "Quit trying to trick me, and let me be miserable in peace."

"Mama, look at me." Lennox shook her arm.

"Len?" Her mom's eyes blinked a few times as if she were having trouble focusing ... and considering the number of glasses on the table, she might be.

"Hey, Mama. Let's get you home, okay?"

"I don't wanna." Her mom jerked her arm away from Lennox's grasp. "Besides, I have one more before Billy cuts me off for the night."

"Naw, Faye. Go on now and let your girl take you home." The man behind the bar flapped his apron at her. "We'll settle up next time you're in."

"How much does she owe?" Lennox pitched her question at Billy with the hope her mom wouldn't pay attention. She had her head back down on the cool wooden surface, so there was minimal risk, but Lennox still didn't want her mother's ire raised.

"I'll tally it up for you." Billy waved her over to a register at the corner. "Thanks for coming. When Macy answered earlier, she sounded like she was in the middle of something, but said she'd take care of it. Guess it'd been a while since you'd been in here, and it slipped my mind Faye had two girls."

"That's fine, Billy. Thanks for looking after her." Lennox accepted her credit card back, dismayed she wouldn't get it paid off this next month after all. Her mom probably wouldn't even wonder why she didn't have a tab at Goldie's next time she came in, so there was no hope of getting the money back from her.

Now, back to the task at hand. The steady rise and fall of her mom's form confirmed she was completely passed out this time. Lennox let a huge breath escape through her lips. She really didn't want to have to call Ty for more help than he was already offering. She squared her shoulders and marched back to the corner table.

"Mama." Lennox gave her mother's shoulders a firm shake. "Time to go home."

Her mom moaned but didn't give any other response.

"Mama, come on. I've got a sweet ride to take you home in. A convertible." And considering the smell emanating from her mother, they might want to lower the roof despite the risk of rain moving in.

"You don't own a convertible." Her mother's words slurred at the end. "You're too … uptight for something so fun."

Lennox bit back the hurt, reminding herself that her mother wasn't herself right now. "Well, it's one that belongs to …" How did she even describe Ty? Acquaintance? No. Her mother would never believe she'd hopped into the fancy car of someone she barely knew. But *friend* sounded wrong. *Ugh*. Why did this have to be so complicated?

"Did you finally pick up a guy?" Her mother's head raised at last and fixed her with enough of a stare to make Lennox squirm.

"No. He's Brian's cousin, and we were helping pick up a few things for the wedding. Sara Beth had to leave, so he offered me a ride."

"A wedding? Lennox, you're getting married?" Her mom grabbed her hand and flipped it over, obviously looking for a ring.

"Mama! Focus. *Sara Beth* is getting married. Remember?" Lennox jerked her hand back. "Now, can we get out of here?"

Her mother's eyes narrowed. "Why should I?"

"Because if you don't, you'd be denying me the privilege of escorting you home." Ty's voice came from right behind Lennox, and her mom's eyes widened.

Chills ran down Lennox's body. He was supposed to stay outside.

"Well, Len. Good job. This one's even cuter than the one your sister's caught." Her mom rose on shaky legs and braced herself against Lennox's upper arm. "What's his name?"

"Ty Dunne, at your service." Ty slipped his hand under her mom's other arm, and the pressure eased up on Lennox's.

If he expected gratitude, he had another thing coming.

"Tydon?" Her mom frowned. "That's a strange name. But if Lennox likes you, I will too."

Ty's lips twitched as he helped steer her mom through the tables and toward the door.

"I told you I didn't need any help." Lennox hissed in his direction.

He kept his focus on the door. "I waited fifteen minutes."

"I'm sorry it took longer than you thought it should." She clenched her teeth.

At his car, they stopped while he opened the passenger door and leaned the seat forward for her mom to slip in the back.

"Are you sure you want her back there?" Lennox wrinkled her nose. "What if—?" There was no easy way to put this. "You know. What if she needs to—" Lennox motioned with her arms and mouth as if vomiting.

"Then, I'll have to have it serviced tomorrow." Ty shrugged. "It will be okay. But back there, she can lean over and rest if she wants."

He drove a car like this and didn't mind if it was thrown up in? She gave herself a mental shake to pull away from the conflicting things she was learning about him. With a jolt, she realized he was waiting for her to climb in. She slipped into the front passenger seat and buckled while he walked around to the driver's side.

"Okay, Navigator, lead the way." The engine purred to life, and he backed out of the parking lot.

On automatic, she directed him where to turn to get back to her mom's trailer park. He pulled into the gravel drive, then glanced in the back, where her mom snored softly. Lennox rubbed her forehead and swallowed the humiliation of this situation. Nothing she could do about it now.

Ty broke the silence. "Do you think I need to carry her?"

"No." For one thing, Lennox wasn't sure Ty *could* carry her mom. "Let's try to rouse her again, and I'll get her inside."

"You're the boss."

It took a few minutes, but they finally managed to wake her mom enough to help her out of the vehicle and up the steps. Lennox didn't even bother with lights as they wound through the double-wide. She'd done this enough times that she could avoid the obstacles and get them back to her mom's bedroom without much trouble.

"That man, Len. You hang on to him." Her mom tried to shake a finger at her while Lennox slipped a nightgown over her head.

"He's just a friend, Mama." The word came easily this time. Not that she had a clue what to think about it, but it was truer than anything else at this moment. "Not every woman needs a man to make her happy."

"But even if you don't need one, they're nice to have around." Her mom leaned back on the bed and closed her eyes.

"Where's George tonight, Mama?" Lennox couldn't keep the question inside.

"George." Her mom's eyes flew open again as she spit his name out. "George is busy with tax season. Don't I understand that? Well! George doesn't understand that sometimes a woman just needs a man to listen to her for a few minutes because she had a bad day."

Lennox tossed the dirty clothes into the hamper in the corner. "Accountants are really busy for a few more weeks, though. It's a legitimate reason. And without that job, he wouldn't have all that money you're so fond of."

"You think I like George for his money?" Her mom propped up on one elbow. "That's ridiculous. Obviously, you don't know him very well. We just had a misunderstanding tonight. I'll probably forgive him tomorrow."

"Mm." Lennox kept her opinion to herself. She'd seen her mother's fluctuating moods for too long to believe half of what she said, especially after having so many drinks. "Well, sleep well, and call me in the morning if you need a ride to pick up your car."

"As if I'd go back to work at that stupid diner after the way they treated me this afternoon." Her mother simpered on her pillow. "It's disgraceful."

"What happened this time?"

"Three teenagers, that's what happened. No one teaches them respect anymore."

While Lennox partially agreed, she didn't know that disrespectful teenagers were enough to cause her mom to go on such a bender. "What did they do?"

"They all ordered huge meals, ate every last bite, and then slipped out without paying their bill. That's what." Her mom hit the mattress with her fist. "So, of course, it had to come out of my paycheck, which is hardly enough to pay bills as it is."

Lennox bit her tongue to hold in the rebuke that if her mom would quit spending money on beer and cigarettes, she'd have more for all those bills she couldn't afford. "Well, you're home now. Get some rest, and things will probably look better in the morning."

"I'm sorry I interrupted your date." Her mom's eyelids were dropping again, so Lennox decided it was a waste of breath to argue once more about her and Ty's relationship. If it came up again in the future, she'd explain it again then.

She shut the bedroom door behind her as she came out into the living area. Ty stood in front of a bookshelf, a picture frame in his hand. She peeked over his shoulder at a photo of her and Macy around the ages of twelve and nine. Her haircut should have been declared child abuse. She ripped the frame from his hand and put it back in its spot. Maybe it was too dark in the room for him to truly make out the full awfulness.

"Sorry. I guess curiosity got the best of me." Ty glanced over his shoulder. "Is she settled okay?"

"Yeah. She'll have a headache, but she's used to it."

He followed her back out of the house and down to his car. He didn't wait for her directions as they left the park but turned left onto the highway out of town. She frowned and straightened.

"Where are we going?" She pointed with her thumb behind them. "I live that way."

"I thought you might need a little time to decompress." He never even glanced her way. "I know this evening turned out nothing like you originally planned."

"Ever since I met you, nothing has." She leaned back and crossed her arms.

"Oh, come on. It hasn't been all bad, has it?" His lips did that thing where only one corner turned up. Sort of halfway between a smirk and a grin.

"I'm amazed your ego fits in this little car."

"Well, it's a tight squeeze." He gave a nod of concession. "But worth it."

"Where are you taking me?" She squinted down the road as if she could make out their destination. "I could consider this kidnapping, you know."

"There's something I want you to see."

The only thing she really wanted to see right now was her

apartment building, but that wasn't an option as it was behind them. Maybe if she complied, he would turn this fancy car around so she could go home and go to bed. Something told her that wouldn't be the way things went down.

Chapter Ten

This might not be the best plan he'd ever come up with, but it was all Ty could think of on such short notice. He walked slightly ahead of Lennox as they entered the dark chapel and wondered the best place to sit. His favorite place might not be something she'd consider clean enough. Not that anything in here was actually clean.

"Okay." He stopped just in front of the first row of pews, in line with the window. "On a night like this, it should be perfect."

"What should be perfect?" Lennox's voice was full of skepticism.

"The light."

She scanned the room. "Does this building even have electricity?"

"Normally, yes. It was wired for it in the eighties. But I have it cut off right now until I can get the electrician back out here." He let her pompous attitude toward this beloved structure roll off his shoulders. But he also wasn't about to suggest she sit on the bare stone floor without something underneath her. He started to unbutton his overshirt.

"Wait a minute!" She scurried back. "Hold it right there,

mister. I don't know what you thought I was agreeing to in coming out here, but it definitely didn't involve you removing your clothes."

"Lennox, chill your bones. I'm taking off my *outer* shirt so you can have something to sit on. I have a T-shirt on underneath." He slid the cotton over his shoulders and placed it on the floor in front of him with a flourish. "Besides, I'm not that kind of a guy."

"Just don't take off anything else." She motioned toward his body with a single finger and edged around him, as far away as the narrow aisle would allow, before gracefully lowering herself to the makeshift spot he'd just prepared.

"I wouldn't dream of it." He sat next to her with much less poise, then gazed up at the window.

"So, what are we looking at?"

"That." He leaned toward her a bit and pointed up to the various colored panes that sparkled every so often from the starlight behind them. The clouds from earlier had broken up.

She didn't say anything, so he peeked over to see what she was doing. Her eyes were fixed on the glimmering spectacle above them, and he could almost see some of the stress ease from her shoulders. A weight he hadn't known was there lifted off his own. He honestly hadn't been sure this would work, but suddenly his plan was perfect.

"Most people only think to look through a stained-glass window during the daytime, when the sun is brightest. But I grew up coming out here. This chapel was part of our playground growing up. We spent many a night playing cemetery or sardines. One evening, I happened to stop long enough to pay attention to the window ... and it mesmerized me." He leaned back on his hands. "Now, whenever I need to decompress or think or pray, I come in here and watch God's nightlights through my great-great-great-uncle's window. There might be another great in there, somewhere. I lose track."

"God's nightlights?" Lennox shook her head. "Now you sound like George."

"Who is George? You mentioned his name on the phone." Ty's curiosity would probably get him in trouble one day—possibly this one. But there was something else besides curiosity. Something he wasn't ready to name. Lennox tensed a bit beside him.

"Mom's boyfriend of the week."

"Wait." He jerked his head her way. "Week?"

"Let's just say that ever since my dad left, my mom's gone a little crazy in trying to find the ever-elusive *love*." She rolled her eyes as she dragged out the last word.

"That sounds rough."

"I won't lie and say it was easy." She folded her legs up so her chin could rest on her knees.

He stayed quiet to see if she'd say anything else.

"Dad left when I was twelve. Mom was doing okay, but decided she'd have better opportunities in a slightly bigger town, so she moved us here when I was in ninth grade. That's when I met Sara Beth."

"That explains why I don't remember you. You were a few years behind me in school." Ty started to lean on the pew next to him, but when it shifted under his weight, he straightened again. Maybe Lennox hadn't noticed. A quick glance showed her focus still on the window.

"I guess. We were the year behind Brian, evidently." Even her shrug was graceful.

"And he was two behind me. So, you would have been a freshman my senior year."

"And then you were off to college to get your double major."

"It wasn't my original plan, but it's what happened, yes."

She sat quietly. Where were her thoughts? She didn't seem anxious to leave, but he wasn't one to be able to not say anything for very long, either. He nibbled on the inside of his cheek, trying to control the urge to break the silence.

"She's not always like tonight, you know." Lennox's words

were quiet, but still full of anger. She shook her head. "At least not for the last little bit."

"Maybe she had a rough day."

"That's her story. Something about some punk kids walking out without paying their bill. The owner of the diner she works at takes it out of her check." Lennox pressed her palms to her eyes, weaving her fingers through the short hairs at the top of her head. "I guess maybe I let myself believe George the other day."

"What did he say?"

"That my mom was trying to give up smoking and drinking." She lowered her hands and leaned her head back. "I should have known better. People don't change that quickly. Nor do they change for other people. I guess I pushed aside my normal self-preservation and let myself believe in miracles for a few days. Stupid, huh?"

"Not stupid." Ty tentatively put a hand on her shoulder, and when she didn't flinch away, he gave it a gentle squeeze. "But you're right."

"I'm right, or I'm not right. You can't tell me I'm both." Lennox leaned away, and he removed his hand.

"What I mean is, you're right about people needing to change for something other than another person. Change often starts because of someone they care about, but they need to do it for themselves ... and even for a higher purpose."

"A higher purpose? You mean God?" Lennox scoffed.

"There's no higher reason to do things in the world." He lifted a shoulder. "But I won't try to convince you of that tonight. I'll just have to hope my actions speak loud enough each and every time we're together that you can see Him in me."

Lennox dropped her head to her knees again. "I'm surrounded by idiots."

"I guess so. Even the Bible says the gospel is foolishness."

"It does?" She cast him a wary glance. "Then why follow it?"

"Because it says it's foolishness to them who don't believe." He shifted to face her a bit more. "I do believe, and I've seen past the parts that don't seem reasonable. I know it's worth it, even if the world deems me a fool."

She was quiet for a moment. Had he made a breakthrough? His words didn't seem like enough, but different things reached different people.

"You said you weren't going to try to convince me tonight." She stood and stretched one way then another.

"And I won't. But I will say one more thing." He clambered up beside her, and then stooped to pick up his shirt again. "Change takes time. And sometimes there are setbacks. Be lenient with your mom. It could still happen."

"Maybe." She started back down the dark aisle. He studied her silhouette for a moment before following. "You're actually having work done here, right? You didn't leave the lights off just so I couldn't see that nothing had changed?"

And ... the hopeful mood was broken, just like that.

"The roofer is coming in next week, for your information." He beat her to the car and opened the door for her.

She gave him a skeptical look before sliding in.

The ride back to town was silent except for the few directions she gave him to her apartment complex. It was easier to give her the time to process everything. He'd planted a few seeds. That George guy could water them.

"I guess I'll see you at the next wedding-planning event, huh?" He killed the engine in front of her building.

"Yeah." She motioned over her shoulder. "We should probably get those flowers out of your trunk so I can take them in."

"Aw. You're going to take away my reason to see you again so soon?" He winked but hit the button to open the back.

"I'm sure you'll find another excuse to show up in the near future." She hefted two bags over her arms and then frowned at the five remaining.

"I got these." He slipped the last bags into his own arms.

"Thanks." She led the way up the stairs. "I figure you'll probably try kickboxing again, right?"

"Only if you want me to."

She glanced up from where she'd been inserting the key into the deadbolt. "Really? You'd give up so easily?"

Was that a tease? A flirt? He couldn't begin to tell.

"You bringing those in?" Her voice from the other side of the door pulled him out of his ponderings to realize she'd left him on the stoop. "Just drop them on the couch. I hardly ever use it anyway."

He set them down on the red microfiber sofa. The colors suited what little he'd put together of her character. His eyes roamed the rest of the room, taking in the small television, polka dot chair, and the bright painting of a sunset on the wall. No knickknacks or personal pictures. Instead, one corner housed a collection of various workout equipment.

"Well, Mr. Designer. Will it do?" She shot him a grin through the window cut in the wall between the living area and kitchen. "I know it's not much, but for just me, I don't need more."

"I love the reds. The bright tones fit you."

"Thanks. Not bad for bargain finds, huh?" She held up a kettle. "Want any coffee or tea or something?"

Was she going to let him stay longer? This night was full of surprises. "I'm not much of a tea drinker." He walked over to lean against the kitchen doorframe. "What kind do you like?"

"Green. Tonight, I thought I'd do the peach flavor. But I also have ginger, blueberry, and mint."

"Very healthy."

"I try." She straightened her back but ducked her head. "Listen. I know I haven't shown it, but I really do appreciate all the help you gave me tonight."

"I would have done it for any of my friends." He meant it, but if it came right down to it, he'd do just about anything for this girl —a scary thought considering how little he knew about her, even after all these interactions.

"So, we're friends now?" She fiddled with a mug as the water heated behind her.

"We did declare a truce at the invitation party, remember?"

"A truce doesn't necessarily mean friendship, though." And her hackles were back.

He shook his head. "Lennox, relax. Friendship is a good thing."

The kettle whistled and made them both jump. She jerked around to make her tea, and just like that, it was time to go. Not that he wanted to, but he wouldn't press her any farther tonight.

"I better get home. Work in the morning." He knocked on the door frame.

"Right." She nodded, bouncing her tea bag in the hot water. "I guess I'll see you Saturday, then. At kickboxing."

It took all his willpower to not ask her if she were sure. "Sounds great. I'll try to make sure I don't schedule anything beforehand this time."

"We'll see."

"You sure you're going to be okay?" Just one more minute with her wouldn't hurt.

"Fine. Remember? I've been dealing with my mom like this since high school."

He cringed and quickly schooled his face, hoping she hadn't noticed. "Saturday, then."

"Ten o'clock. Earlier, if you can."

"Okay." He glanced over his shoulder at the top of the stairs. She stood in the doorway, the light from behind casting a warm glow around her. He tripped down the first two steps before recovering.

"You sure you want to try kickboxing?" Her teasing question followed him the rest of the way down, and he laughed.

Something had changed between them tonight. Oh, they might not be anywhere close to best friends or even barely more than acquaintances, but still. Much better than the previous times they'd met. Now, to make sure they didn't go backward.

Hopefully, he'd be able to reach that electrician tomorrow. Assuming he found a few minutes to make a call that wasn't work-related. Dad ran a tight schedule and had a strict no-nonsense policy. If only he could get that chapel repaired, he could stay on Lennox's good side. A side he found he liked a lot more than he thought he would.

Chapter Eleven

"There's a man here to see you." Hattie's ponytail swished as she poked her head in Lennox's office Saturday morning.

"Already?" Lennox swallowed a gulp of green tea, wincing as the hot liquid scalded the back of her throat. "He wasn't supposed to be here until my ten o'clock class."

A glance at the clock showed ten minutes before nine. Ty was over an hour early? She hadn't even been sure he'd show up. Not after the other night. She still couldn't believe she'd invited him in for a cup of tea.

"You were expecting this guy?"

"Honestly?" Lennox raised a shoulder. "Maybe, but not until a few minutes after ten."

Hattie laughed. "This guy doesn't look like the kind who waits until after something starts. I'll send him back."

Lennox frowned. Had Ty gotten a haircut? In her mind, he definitely fit the profile of someone who was perpetually late. Though he'd surprised her with other details of his life the other night. Like having a degree in design. She hadn't expected that. She clicked a few more things on her computer so she'd at least look busy when he walked in.

A sharp rap on her doorframe pulled her attention that way once more. She blinked. Not Ty. George. *What on earth?*

"Hi, Lennox. Is this a bad time?" George tapped his fingers on his upper arm.

"Oh. No." She jumped up and moved a stack of papers and towels off the couch in front of her desk. "I just wasn't expecting you."

"Your friend said you were, which rather surprised me." He lowered himself onto the sofa, and she plopped back down in her own chair, probably the most ungraceful movement she'd made in the last five years.

"Miscommunication." Lennox cut her hand through the air. "I thought you might have been someone who said he wanted to try my class this morning."

"Is it starting now?" George glanced back at the clock.

"At ten. We've got a few minutes." Lennox picked up a pencil and twirled it around her fingers, unsure why he was here. Uncertain she wanted him here. Wondering why she was so fidgety while he sat there so calmly.

"Speaking of miscommunication." George dusted off an invisible piece of lint from his plaid shirt.

"You're here about Mama, aren't you?" Lennox should've known. "Did she send you?"

"No. No. She doesn't know I had any idea of coming this way." He shook his head. "But I wanted to apologize."

"Apologize? To me?" Lennox leaned back against her chair. "What for?"

"I had no idea she'd take the couple of missed calls and a quick response that I was busy with a client as ... well ... as a rebuff, so to say. She took it much more personally than I thought she would."

"My father left us when I was twelve. Just walked out our door." Lennox leaned forward, resting her palms on her paper-covered desk. "So, yeah, she has issues with neglect and rejection."

"I'm aware of her history. But I didn't realize it would look like I was rejecting her simply because I was working. I've never spent much time with someone who has a past like hers. It's going to take me time to learn how to navigate this path."

Lennox rubbed her temple. "So, are you apologizing for ignoring my mother or something else? Because I'm confused."

"I'm apologizing that you had to clean up the mess." He pressed her hand still on the desk before sitting back again and letting out a deep breath.

"I guess she called you the next morning for a ride?" Lennox released a sigh of her own. "She never called me, and I know her car was still at Goldie's."

"No." George ran a hand through his graying hair. "I ran by the diner Friday morning to see if I could talk with her on break, but she wasn't there. Manager said she hadn't shown up and would lose her job if she wasn't careful after the day before. Needless to say, I ran over to her place and banged on the door. One look and I knew she'd had a rough evening, so I made coffee and listened while she told me what happened."

"What happens now?" Lennox fought against the stream of anger burning her up on the inside. "She's supposed to just go back to the way it was before, as if none of this happened? Until the next time you can't answer your phone, and we start all over again?"

"No." George pounded his fist on his leg. "No. That's not what I want. I was serious when I told you she wanted to give up on that lifestyle. I was just arrogant enough to believe I would be enough to help her change her ways. It was stupid of me. I let her flattery go to my head."

Lennox leaned back again, wrapping her arms around her middle. "A ... friend ... told me the other night that someone can't change her lifestyle for another person. It wouldn't work."

"Same friend you are expecting this morning?" George's lips twitched up on one side. "Your mom mentioned there was a guy with you when you came to her rescue. Sounds like a good one."

Lennox lowered her head and schooled her features. "She *would* remember that part of the night."

"Don't worry." He winked. "All she could tell me was he has a red car."

Lennox shook her head. "I can just see her studying all the red cars in town, trying to figure out who her daughter is dating."

George raised an eyebrow. "*Dating?*"

"Don't go there. We're not." Lennox pinned George with a stare and waggled her finger at him. "But Mama made that jump in logic, and she probably won't remember the several times I tried to correct her."

"Well, whatever he is to you, *his* logic is sound." George tapped his fingers on his knees. "Here's what I'm planning. I'm going to see if she'll start attending the support group for people trying to quit certain lifestyles that meets at church. I know several people it's helped. And I'll even go with her."

"Isn't this your busiest season?" Lennox narrowed her eyes. "I thought that's how we ended up in this mess, to begin with."

"Just a few more days until April fifteenth, and things will slow down a bit." He held up a finger. "But something I've learned through the years. Even when work is busy, it doesn't always have to come first. *People* are more important. And over the last few weeks, your mother has become important to me."

"Actions speak louder than words, George." Lennox couldn't resist the barb.

"And I'm sorrier about that than you'll probably ever know." George rubbed his hands over his face. "But I promise it won't happen again. And I promise to do all I can to find her more help too. More than just me."

"If she's only changing for you, it's not going to work even with more help. You agreed with that statement only a few minutes ago."

"I know. That's why I want to try the program the church offers. It gives a better reason for changing than another person. It shows them there's more to life than the here and now. That God gave us a purpose and a plan."

"You're going to shove your Christian propaganda down her

throat?" Lennox shook her head. "That won't work any better. She's dealt with Christians before. They've only offered judgment and hypocrisy."

"Then it's time she met some who are different." George stood.

"I know you came to apologize, but I'm not ready to accept yet. Not until I see that my mom really won't end up like she was Thursday evening again. I've seen her go through this cycle more times than you can count, and it's not easy for either of us." Lennox crossed her arms over her chest.

"I accept that. But I will do my best to show you there's more to the church and God than you think. And that things don't always have to be like they have been." He fixed her with a serious stare. "And I'll do my best to earn that forgiveness—and your trust."

He glanced over his shoulder again. "I better get out of your way so you can prepare for your class."

She didn't know how to respond. None of her mom's other boyfriends had ever cared what she or her sister thought. Half of them hadn't even cared what her mom thought. George was at least different in that area ... so far. But would he be able to live up to his plans and promises?

No one had before now.

Not her dad.

Not her mom.

Not her sister.

And none of the other men who had been in and out of her life all these years.

If anyone had lived up to the trust and friendship she had for her, it was Sara Beth. Brian had slowly eased his way into being tolerable. But anyone else? Lennox's trust didn't stretch far. It couldn't. It was too easy for hurt to creep in when she let her guard down.

She stared at the empty doorway for several minutes after George walked through it. He hadn't told her whether he'd helped Mom save her job or not. If not, that would probably mean more bills on top of her own for a month or so until Mom got her feet back under her. Her sister wouldn't be any help. She could barely pay her own bills.

Lennox pulled her thoughts back under control. Fifteen minutes until class started. Time to focus her brain on leading others in the series of kicks and punches that would help accelerate their heart rates and sweat off some calories. Honestly, nothing sounded better than kicking and punching right now.

In the empty studio, she made sure her music was pulled up and then started in on a few stretches to ease her muscles into the exercise they would endure for the next hour. A few early students trickled in and started their own stretches. Sara Beth gave a little wave and smile before taking her usual spot at the end of the row. Five minutes until start time, Brian sauntered in, beaming at his fiancée.

And Ty was right behind him.

Her heart skipped a beat as Ty took the section right in front of her. He came, after all. Had he read more into her actions Thursday evening than she meant for him to? She'd been so confused and emotionally wound up by the time they got back to her apartment. When she realized he had to help her carry the bags, she hadn't known what to do. Inviting him for a cup of tea simply slipped out.

At least, that's what she told herself.

He raised an eyebrow at her and motioned to his watch.

Oh!

It was a minute after time to start. She quickly hit play and greeted the class, carefully looking anywhere but right in front of her. With any luck, she'd get all the way through without forgetting what move came next. Surely three months of teaching the same routine would help, wouldn't it?

Even with someone shooting her a cocky grin every time her gaze connected with his?

Chapter Twelve

Something was bothering her. Lennox might think she hid it through her expression and actions, but Ty could tell. And it wasn't only in the way she avoided meeting his eyes. She looked everywhere but at him, as she led the class through the various repetitions of her kickboxing routine.

Sure, she had to tense her core to pull off some of the punches and kicks, but this tension through her shoulders was practically viable. It radiated from her. He was almost afraid to stand so close.

After the other night, he thought they'd eased past some of the distance between them, but now he wondered if something had happened to knock him right back to square one. He couldn't think of anything he'd done or rather, not done, that would've changed her mind. Nothing she should be able to know about, anyway.

She wouldn't like that he was still working to line up people to work on the chapel. The wedding was five months away. He had time, whether she'd admit it or not. He just had to get through the next few weeks until his brother came home, and then Ty could give the chapel repairs more of his focus.

Ty thought about the job he was basically stuck in, one he'd never asked for but had always been expected to take, adding a bit more thrust behind his punches. It wasn't that he despised the family business. Nothing like that. After all, it was Great-Grandpa Connor's legacy. Ty just preferred to use his other degree more than his business one. Though his dad would never understand his desire to work in design.

"Okay, just a few more minutes, and then we'll go into our cool down." Lennox motioned with her hand to three different spots in front of her. "We're going to do our three-point kick now. Remember to do high, medium, then low, moving across. Ready? Let's do ten on each leg. One! Two! Three!"

Ty gritted his teeth as he worked to follow her graceful motions. He wasn't great at balancing on a good day, and when he was more distracted than not, he was even less. His goal this morning was to not fall on his bottom and embarrass himself in front of the whole class ... and especially Lennox. She already thought him enough of a slacker.

Her eyes met his for a second, and he could tell the moment she realized where she was looking and moved her gaze somewhere over his left shoulder. So much for the hope, he'd left her apartment with the other night. Was the awkwardness this morning because of that, or was it residual from before? She'd said they were almost finished with this class. He had to hang in there a few more minutes, and then maybe he could catch her before she disappeared again.

"Great job today, guys. Let's start cooling down now. Finish up with ten jumping jacks, and then we're going to walk in place for a few minutes." She was graceful even when bouncing.

Maybe he should be grateful she hadn't been watching him this whole time. He didn't want to think about how jerky and rough his motions had been. He avoided glancing in the mirror behind her for a reason.

"That's it. Roll your shoulders. Big arm circles moving forward." Did she lift weights? Her biceps were well-toned and covered in freckles. Very distracting.

Not that his arms were bad. Since installing a weight table last year, he'd been able to keep up with the regimen adopted in college. His baggy T-shirts simply covered the muscle underneath. Would she be more impressed if she knew?

He gave himself a mental shake as he realized the rest of the class had moved to lunges, and he was still walking in place. Perhaps he should listen to what she was saying *now* instead of trying to figure out what to say after class. He quickly leaned into his bent right leg and relished the stretch in his left muscles. Except for jogging a few days a week, his legs were more neglected than the rest of his body, and today's workout had been tougher than he expected. Brian was right. Lennox taught a fierce class.

A few more stretches, and the music stopped.

"Great workout, everybody. Thanks for joining me this morning. I'll see you next week." Lennox gave a wave and then turned her back on the class to fiddle with the speakers behind her.

Ty picked up a towel and wiped his face, his heart pounding in his chest. Was the rate still up from the routine, or was it because he was about to wade back into *enemy* territory? Or both?

"Glad you could make it today, man." Brian clapped him on the shoulder.

"Yeah. Thanks for the recommendation." Ty ripped his sight away from Lennox only for a second to greet his cousin. "I think I better go tell the teacher what a good job she did."

"You do that." Brian gave him a smirk and then turned toward his fiancée.

Ty took a deep breath. He could do this. After all, he'd spent several hours with her the other night and had even been invited in for tea. A simple conversation now should be no big deal. He walked over to her right as she was turning around.

"Oh!" Lennox's hands pushed against his chest as soon as she bumped into him.

"Sorry about that." His hands grabbed her elbows, mostly to keep her from stumbling again.

She pulled her arms back. "I see you made it today."

"Early, and everything." He looped the towel around his neck. "It was a great class, Lennox. Thanks for not chasing me out today."

"Yeah, well, someone told me last week it was bad business to chase away new students." Her gaze shot over to where Sara Beth stood. She rubbed a hand up and down one arm while shifting her weight every few seconds.

"What's wrong?" Ty caught her hand under his to still the nervous movements.

Lennox pulled her fingers away and scanned the area, though there was nothing else to pick up. "Who said anything was wrong?"

"Your body language." Ty motioned to her. "Even during class, your punches could have busted through brick. I was glad I wasn't a few feet closer. And now, you're fidgeting and rocking on your heels and avoiding eye contact."

"Oh." She stared at the ground, but her fingers continued to wrap and unwrap the cord she'd removed from her phone.

"Lennox, seriously. I thought we agreed to be friends. Are you that upset about me being here?" Ty took half a step back, swallowing the fear she might say "yes."

"No." She let out a breath, glanced up. "No. It's just ... George was here before class."

"Your mom's boyfriend?" Ty almost slumped, he was so relieved it had nothing to do with him.

She nodded.

"Hey, Lennox. Did you remember to bring those flowers for me this morning?" Sara Beth stepped between them, a smile on her pixie face.

"Oh. Yeah. Um, they're in my car. You know where I keep my keys?" Lennox pointed toward the back of the building. "Feel free to grab them. Just don't leave without bringing my keys back."

Ty waited until Sara Beth left with Brian before resuming the conversation. It helped that everyone else from the class had left as well. He didn't feel as much need to keep his voice low.

"So, George, huh?"

"Yeah." Lennox wrapped her arms around her middle. "He said he wanted to apologize for Thursday night. As if it were his fault."

"He apologized for your mom's drinking?"

"For not realizing she would consider his not answering the phone as rejection." Lennox shook her head, a look of utter disbelief on her face. "I mean, she was abandoned by my dad. What did he think she'd consider something like that?"

"If he's never dealt with someone who's been left before, it probably didn't even cross his mind. I don't think it would have occurred to me." Ty had to force himself to not reach out and wrap his arm around her shoulders. She appeared so lost, wrapped in on herself like that.

"Well, now you know. Rejection doesn't just go away. People wear that hurt for the rest of their lives." The pain in her expression cut him straight to the heart. She wasn't only talking about her mom—she was talking about herself too.

"So, what did George say besides being sorry your mom thought he'd rejected her?"

"He talked about some meeting at his church. Said it was for people struggling with things like alcohol. Said he was stupid to think he'd be enough incentive for her to change. And he promised I wouldn't have to deal with that again." She lifted a shoulder.

"Sounds like he really wants to help her."

"I don't know. I guess I don't see what's in it for him." Lennox stared off toward the other side of the room. "I mean, why bother to go through all of this for someone who's obviously so messed up?"

"Why not?" Ty gripped the edge of his towel—anything to keep his hands from reaching out to hold her.

"Because who does that, Ty?" Lennox's arms came free, slicing through the air as she stomped a foot. "It's not ... not real. It's not normal. Mom comes with more baggage than anyone would want to claim. No one has ever apologized to me for not being there when my mother had one of her breakdowns. And he didn't even seem worried when I told him I wasn't ready to accept his apology, either. He just said he would earn it. Who does that?"

"The kind of person who acts in love instead of self-interest." Ty's heart broke a little that she'd never been around enough people like that to realize they existed. "And yes. They do exist."

"Not in real life." She started walking away.

He grabbed her hand and jerked her back around a little harder than he meant to. "Yes, in real life. *This* is real life. George is real. Just like Sara Beth. And Brian. And me. And I could introduce you to so many more."

She yanked away from his grip. "Don't ever grab me like that again." She shook out her fingers. "You weave a great theory. But I can't accept it right now. I'm supposed to believe you don't act in self-interest when you can't even show up to an appointment without being late most of the time?"

He let out a long breath as she marched out of the studio. Obviously, he needed to work more on teaching the truth in love. Hopefully, George would have a better chance at reaching her, because Ty was better at bringing out her ire. He gathered his water bottle and headed out.

So much for talking her into going to lunch with him after class. So much for all the dreams that had started seeming possible after their evening together Thursday.

He wanted to take all her pain onto himself so she wouldn't have to deal with it anymore, but that was impossible. Only One could do that for her, and she wasn't anywhere near ready to accept Him.

Ty sent up a silent prayer as he left the Twisted Barre that God would shine His light through George and himself, and somehow find the cracks in her heart so the light could penetrate the darkness. He ended with a personal plea that he could show her love was real and worth it.

"Please, God. She needs to be loved whether she knows it or not."

And Ty had someone in mind who would gladly volunteer for such a job.

Chapter Thirteen

T he chapel appeared different from the last couple of times Lennox visited it. Of course, the first time had been over a month ago, when the trees were barely turning green. And the last time had been in the dark. But she wouldn't think about that time, or any of that night, or what had come after.

No.

She was here for one reason and one reason only. She needed to see for herself if any work had been done yet. Despite Ty's insistence he had it under control, she had a sneaky suspicion the chapel's interior would look much the same as it had the first time. Possibly worse, considering how much rain had fallen between then and now.

Lennox sighed as she took in the scraggly gardens around the exterior. She couldn't judge the whole thing on that, though. Landscaping came last, right?

Was anyone even here? Would it be unlocked? She hadn't considered that when she drove out here on the spur of the moment. Sara Beth had said Ty was supposed to be working out here this morning. Pounding sounded as Lennox neared. Was she about to be impressed?

She pushed against the wooden front door, and it creaked slowly open, allowing her entry. With the trees shading the area, the stone walls, and the time of day, the temperature was at least ten degrees cooler inside than out. April had decided to act more like summer than spring the last few days, and the coolness was a relief.

The interior's musty smell had her wrinkling her nose. Mold and disuse and something else did not make a happy aroma. They'd have to air out the building before Sara Beth's wedding. The small foyer was dim. Sara Beth said the little hallway to the right had two tiny classrooms they could use as dressing rooms. The bathrooms were to the left, but she could see through the open doors into the main auditorium that the toilet remained where she'd found it originally. Lennox rolled her eyes and took a step farther into the sanctuary.

The light sparkled through the window this afternoon ten times brighter than the starlight had that night. No. She wouldn't think about the last time she'd been here. She glanced around.

The glass still had a crack in it. The stains remained. She avoided looking down at the floor as she made her way up the aisle, afraid to see any more filth. She might have sat on his shirt that night she wouldn't think about, but she didn't want to know what his shirt covered up, either.

Lennox flopped onto the front pew, completely unimpressed by all that had been done—or rather, hadn't been done yet. A creaking sound warned her only a second before the bench leaned to the right, and then crashed to the ground. She sat, stunned for a few seconds, waiting for her body to let her know if anything was hurt more than her bottom.

"Are you okay?" Ty rushed in through the back door and skidded to a stop next to her. "What happened?"

"I sat on this pew you said you were going to fix." Reluctantly, she accepted his hand and borrowed some of his strength to pull herself off the floor. "What if this had been the wedding day, and it was Sara Beth's mom sitting there? It would've ruined the whole thing. What happened to your list? What happened to you taking care of things?"

"I told you I would do things as I could get guys scheduled. The pew wasn't a priority." Ty knelt down and studied the damage. "Looks like we need to replace the braces that attached the seat to the ends."

"If you'd taken my number when I offered it back when all this started, you could've kept me apprised of what had and hadn't been done, and then I wouldn't have sat on a broken pew." Lennox pointed with her whole arm at the mess on the floor.

"How was I supposed to know to warn you it hadn't been fixed yet? I didn't even know you were coming out here today. Besides, you could have called me—you *have* my number." He caught her hand before she could hit him as she waved it around the room. "Are you hurt?"

"No. By some miracle, I'm fine." She barely kept herself from rubbing the spot that ached. That wouldn't do at all. "Just a little sore. Unpadded pews don't offer much cushion."

"I'm glad you're fine. But why are you here? Not that I'm complaining about seeing you. It's just unexpected."

"Sara Beth said you were working out here today. It's been a month, and I wanted to know what's been done. I'm supposed to be helping, and I can't help if I'm not informed." She poked him in the chest. "I thought you were going to keep us informed."

He caught her hand before she could jab it in him again. "I've told Brian everything."

"And what is everything? Because all I see is the branch being gone from the roof. The mold is still here. The window is still cracked. The pew is still broken. And there sits the toilet." She fisted her hands to her side, frustration oozing out of her. "Have you done anything at all?"

"I was fixing the roof when I heard the crash. We can't work on the interior stuff until the exterior is done, and it took a while to get the roofer lined up for a project like this. A chapel doesn't take priority over all the houses in town with wind damage from the storms last month." He pressed a hand to his forehead, and she almost felt guilty for letting him have it. *Almost.*

"I didn't see your car. If not for the pounding, I would've wondered why the door was unlocked."

"I parked at home. The roofer's truck is over on this side of the building, so he'd have his tools handy." He thumbed over his shoulder. "And again, you have my number. You know phones work both ways, right? You could have called and asked what had been done."

"And have you give me some half answer again?" She huffed in frustration. "No, thank you."

"Your choice." He shrugged. "But I don't promise to help you up next time you break a pew."

"Next time I—" She couldn't believe his audacity. Was he serious? "You've got to be kidding me! I could have broken a bone or something. I had no warning. One second I was sitting, and the next, I was on the floor. I mean, you're practically asking for a lawsuit here."

He closed the foot and a half distance between them, grabbed her face with both hands, and pressed his lips to hers. She froze, completely caught off track. Then, her senses kicked into high gear, taking in the caress of his mouth moving so softly against hers, his chest much firmer under her fingers than she'd first guessed from his thin build, his hands weaving their way through her short hair, and sparks flying up and down her middle, building into a flame she had no desire to ignite. She quickly shoved him back and took another step for good measure.

Touching her lips with her fingertips, she took only a second to catch her breath. "Why did you do that?"

"Why?" He dashed a hand through his messy hair, accidentally knocking his sunglasses to the floor. "Because I wanted to get your attention and make you stop talking for a minute."

"You kissed me to shut me up?" His audacity had reached new levels.

"And because …" He took a step toward her and back again, his hands raised as if he were trying to grab his thoughts from thin air. "I think I'm falling in love with you."

"Love." She spluttered. "Love? Kissing has nothing to do with love."

"Of course, it does." He started to move toward her again, but she held up her palm, and he stopped.

"No. Kissing is about lust. About someone wanting something from someone else. And then, when you're tired of it, you just move on. There's no such thing as love." She grabbed her bag off the floor where it fell during the crash and turned to go.

"Kissing is an outward expression of an inward feeling." He caught her elbow. "It's not only about lust."

"Feelings can't be trusted. They change quicker than the Tennessee weather."

"Okay, I'll concede at least part of your point. Feelings shouldn't be the whole foundation of a relationship. But they're great for getting things started. And I think we're starting down the road toward love."

"You can't love me. There's no way." She shook her head. "We haven't even known each other that long. We're barely even friends."

"Well, every relationship has to start somewhere. Why can't this be the start of something more?" He waved toward the back of the building. "I could show you several records of marriages that started right here, and the couples hadn't known each other very long."

"You might think you love me today, but you don't really. Maybe you're attracted to me for some unknown reason. Or maybe you're caught up in your little romantic bubble that seems to exist in this chapel. But you'll realize you don't even know me. If you did, you'd know I'm unlovable." She jerked her arm away from his grip and marched toward the door.

"Someday, I'm going to kiss you, and you're going to know

love is real." His voice was low, but she could still hear it halfway to the back of the chapel.

She paused a second, the desire for his words to be true raging with the reality of her experiences. She'd never let him know that when he kissed her a few moments before, she hadn't sensed any lust in the embrace. If anything, she'd felt cherished.

But it didn't matter.

She walked on, hoping he didn't notice her hesitation. Because she was cut from damaged cloth, and there was no way she'd let someone else weave their own with hers. It would only lead to more tears and rips and frayed edges.

No. She'd stick to what she knew. And she knew love wouldn't come her way.

Not ever.

Chapter Fourteen

A plan.

Ty needed a plan. And he needed one better than the one he had in place now, which was … none. Well, that wasn't totally true. His plan was mostly to wait until his brother Eric got back from school in a few weeks, and then they would tackle everything. Assuming his brother actually deigned to put in some hours at the family business this summer.

He had to. That's all there was to it. Eric had to agree to work in the office enough so Ty could find the time to work on the chapel too. Not only for Brian and Sara Beth's wedding. But because he needed to prove to Lennox that not everyone went back on their word. That he really was a guy she could rely on and trust.

And it wasn't only because he was intrigued by and attracted to her. Though he was. No. This went further and deeper than any of that. He needed to show her Christ through his actions and words and life. Not an easy task, if she refused to spend any time with him.

What had he been thinking? He leaned back in his office chair and ran a hand through his hair. Maybe it *was* a bit longer than he normally let it grow. The strands wrapped around his fingers all the way down the top of his collar. Hmm. He had two choices—cut it or let it grow long enough for a ponytail. Wouldn't Lennox just love that?

He shook his head and leaned forward. She was in his thoughts most of the day, no matter how much he tried to focus on what was in front of him. Like the stack of bills he needed to double-check before mailing. They should've gone out yesterday, but he'd set them aside to help a new customer needing advice on what tile to use in her kitchen remodel. And the designer in him hadn't been able to resist the chance to come out and be useful.

Sure, he could design a kitchen. Or arrange flowers for a wedding. Aesthetically pleasing jobs were where his heart lay. But for some reason, his dad had insisted the office job was where Ty should be. Not acting as one of his contractors, working with him in the field. Maybe Eric would be the son who could live up to everyone's expectations. Ty managed to fail in every aspect of his life.

"I see you're working hard this afternoon."

Speak of the devil. Eric leaned against the doorframe and gave a cocky grin, his arms crossed over his chest. Though he was five years younger, he stood a couple inches taller than Ty, and had broader shoulders. Lennox would also say he had the better haircut, but Ty brushed that thought aside.

"I was pondering a problem." Ty leaned back once more. "What are you doing home?"

"Mom insisted she needed me for Easter this year. I'm not sure why."

"Easter?"

"You know. The holiday with bunnies and eggs. Girls usually wear something froufrou, and boys wear polos and khakis. Mom makes Gran's ham with pineapple and brown sugar, and Aunt Tunene cooks asparagus and potatoes."

"I know what Easter is." Ty shot his brother a dirty look.

"Really? Because I could have added jellybeans. And those yucky marshmallow chicks. And—"

Ty threw a paper clip at his brother, shutting him up for a moment. "Thanks. I get it. I guess I just missed that it was this weekend. I've been busy."

Eric walked over and flipped through the stack of bills that still needed to go out. "These are dated yesterday."

"I know. I got tied up with a client, and they got pushed aside until this morning. Which somehow turned into this afternoon." Ty snatched them back from his brother. "They were next on my list."

"I'm sure Dad's bank account appreciates that."

"Funny. Nice to see your sense of humor hasn't improved while you've been away at school."

"Sounds like I have more of a sense of humor than you, big brother." Eric flopped into the chair across the desk, ignoring the short stack of papers already occupying it.

"Mm. I've just been busy." Ty flipped a pen around in his fingers.

"Let me guess. Working on that stupid chapel?" Eric raised a brow.

Ty held up a finger. "One, it isn't stupid. Two, it's a part of our family heritage. Three, I *need* to be working on the chapel to get it ready for Brian's wedding this fall, but I keep having to stop working on that so I can work here instead. When do you get out for summer?"

"Why? You don't seriously expect me to be sequestered here all summer when I could be out relaxing and letting my brain rest, do you?" Eric shook his head. "Not in my plans, thank you very much. After this semester, I've earned my time off."

"We'll see what Dad says about that." Ty wasn't ready to give up so easily. After all, this was the best plan he'd come up with. The only plan, granted, but still the best.

"What Dad says about what?" Their father stuck his head in the doorway, a *Dunne Contracting* cap covering his balding head.

"Ty is begging for help in the office so he can run off and work on his precious chapel." The way Eric said it made it sound like the chapel didn't belong to him at all. Which was ridiculous, because its heritage was an integral part of their family.

Ty fixed his brother with a glare. "Are you or are you not a Dunne?"

"Oh, I'm a Dunne, all right." Eric motioned to his face as though he were a game show hostess. "Can't deny these genes. But that doesn't mean I have to latch on to your little romance story about the hundreds of marriages that started in Park Haven Chapel through the years. Not my cup of tea, if it's all the same to you."

"I'll remind you of that someday when you're begging me to let you have your wedding there." Ty shook his head.

"Is that before or after *you* finally get married?" Eric let out a loud guffaw. "Because at the rate you're going, I'm betting before."

"Boys, boys." Their dad came the rest of the way into the office and closed the door behind him. *Uh-oh.* Time for a lecture.

"Dad, he knows I was just kidding." Eric straightened, the papers crackling underneath him.

"Well, that's good, since you will be putting in at least a few hours here each week this summer. It's what your brother did when he was in college, and it's what you'll do too. It's the least you can do, considering we're paying for all your schooling."

Ty exulted watching his brother get told what's what ... until Dad fixed his gaze on him.

"And Ty is right to want to restore the chapel. It is a big part of our family history as well as local history. Brian is counting on him." Dad held up his hands to stop both boys before they could say anything. "That being said, his first job is here, and he needs to remember that. We count on him to keep things running as smoothly as possible."

Ty didn't say anything. What was there to say? Even if he

wanted to protest, he couldn't. The law had been laid down, and he had to live with it for now. Eric also remained silent, whether from feeling the same weight of disappointment or something else, Ty wasn't sure.

"Am I understood?" Dad glanced between them.

"Yes, sir."

Dad straightened his hat and opened the door once more. "A few more hours of work, and then we'll be done for the weekend. No more fighting."

Eric, his back to their dad, winked at Ty. "Yes, sir."

Ty quickly ducked his head and skimmed the bills in front of him, afraid if he made eye contact, he'd start laughing. Nothing like being reprimanded by the father you hadn't lived with in four years. Would he ever outgrow that?

Eric didn't let him work for long after their dad left. "So, what's this I hear about you learning kickboxing because of a girl?"

Ty jerked his head back up. "What?"

"Apparently, Brian talks to his sister more than you talk to me. And Lindsey said you were trying to impress Brian's maid of honor. And that she has no interest in you." Eric smirked. "Must be a hard pill to swallow for a flirt like you."

"Younger siblings talk too much—mine and evidently Brian's. Lindsey doesn't know the whole story. And I'm not a flirt." Ty folded one of the two bills he'd taken care of and stuffed it in an envelope.

"But you don't deny the rest?" Eric leaned forward. "I need to meet this girl. I can't imagine someone not falling all over herself under your charms."

"Because you're no playboy, either." Ty sealed off a second envelope. "Please. How many girls did you leave pining for you at school?"

"Not one. I've decided to stay single until my senior year."

"How very unlike you. Someone break your heart?"

"You wish." Eric crossed his arms.

"I would never wish that on anyone." Ty thought back to the hurt written in every inch of Lennox as she stormed away from him the other day. She wore her pain like a shield, thinking it protected her from future suffering. And the person who had hurt her was one of the ones who ought to protect and cherish her most. She wasn't abandoned by a lover—she was left by her father.

"Been through it yourself?" Eric frowned, evidently noting the seriousness in Ty's voice.

"Not really. But I'm friends with someone who has." Ty focused back on the stack in front of him, working to finish this task so he could move on to the last few of the week.

Eric remained quiet for a few minutes and then tapped the desk in front of him. "Look, man. You know I was mostly kidding earlier. I know this isn't your dream job."

Ty peered up, a protest on his lips, but Eric's stare cut him off. His brother was right. As long as his dad wasn't as aware of that as his brother evidently was, maybe Ty could keep from offending anyone else in the family.

"Anyway, I'm here now. What can I do before the end of the day to help with the chapel?"

Ty's mouth hung open. His brother was willing to help with the project he had just been making fun of? It didn't even make sense. But he wouldn't look a gift horse in the mouth, either. He pushed the stack of bills over to his brother to finish and pulled his personal to-do list out.

"Here you go. And thanks."

"You're welcome, I think. But you might owe me an extra roll on Sunday. Or your chocolate bunny or something." Eric's lips turned up on one side in the grin that almost mimicked Ty's own.

"Hmm. I don't know. I mean, Mom only gives us one bunny each now. And a guy doesn't want to miss out on his one opportunity a year to eat the ears first."

"Oh, please." Eric waved at the paper in front of Ty. "Just work on your project, and let me get this done already."

"How long are you in town for?" Ty thought ahead, wondering if he could get a few more things done on Monday too.

"I'll go back after lunch on Sunday. I really don't know why Mom thought she needed me here for such a short time, but she was insistent enough that I decided to come."

"Strange. She hasn't said anything to me."

"Well, you're already here." Eric lifted a shoulder and then stuffed an envelope.

Ty didn't respond. He skimmed through a list of workers on the computer, debating which one would be the best to repair the ceiling now that the roof was fixed. With the wood paneling covering the whole thing, it would take someone expert in matching the grains and keeping it as close as possible to the original.

Then they needed a plumber to see what could be done about those stupid tree roots. And the whole place needed a deep clean so he could get in there and spray down the mold and mildew. And air the place out. Maybe an exterminator? Lennox had mentioned scurrying. This list was long. Maybe she'd been right about how little time they had to accomplish tasks.

But he'd never tell her.

Because if she discovered she was right about one thing, she might think she was right about the rest.

And she wasn't.

Love *was* real. And it was worth it. And he planned to prove it to her, one way or another. First, with the chapel. Then ... well, he hadn't gotten that far yet.

The reason Eric had been called home was revealed the next day. Gran Nancy wanted to see all the grandkids, one at a time.

Growing up, Ty would've jumped at the chance for some time with his grandmother. After all, helping take care of all the dogs, roaming the old family farm, and exploring the old cabin was more fun than anything at home.

Gran and Gramps were special people. Ty could hardly believe it when Gramps told him the old house was going to be his one day. Nor had he expected to be able to move in so soon. But when Gramps passed away several years back, Gran decided the big old house was too much for just her. After raising four children in it, being there alone must have been very quiet.

Now, she resided in her fancy recliner at Park Haven Assisted Living. Eric shrugged as they passed in the hallway Saturday afternoon. Ty rapped lightly on Gran's door and entered with a smile on his face, though he had no idea what to expect. Gran had been ... crotchety lately.

"Hi, Gran."

"Mikey." She reached out a wrinkled hand. "My boy."

He swallowed a lump as he wrapped her fragile fingers in his. Did he look that much like his dad?

"You've always been my boy, haven't you? Even before you were mine. It's like God knew exactly what I needed."

Before he was hers? What was Gran talking about? Ty's dad was the oldest of Gran's four children. When wasn't he hers?

"It's Ty, Gran."

"Ty." She blinked. "Of course, it's Ty. I've known you your whole life."

"Yes, you have." He slid down onto his knees beside her.

"I was the first one to hold you after your parents, you know. You look so much like your dad." She moved a strand of white hair over her shoulder. Only in recent years had it been chopped off to just below her shoulders. Before that, Gramps had called it her crowning glory.

"I know, Gran." He swallowed a lump. "Mom said you wanted to see me."

She stared at him as if she didn't recognize him again. "I did?"

"It doesn't matter. Any excuse to come spend time with you is always a good one."

"You're a sweetheart, Ty." She patted his cheek. "But something's wrong."

What was she talking about? "It is?"

"Things are falling apart. Are you taking care of my house?"

"Your house looks great, Gran. And soon, the chapel will too."

A slight smile spread her lips. "The chapel? I got married there, you know."

"I know." Ty squeezed her fingers. "Brian is getting married there this fall. So, I'm spiffing up the place."

"Brian is getting married? What about you?"

"I haven't found the right person yet." The explanation came out easily, though his heart argued with it. *Had* he found the right person?

"It surprised me when MC came back to town. I just knew he was going to steal the clinic from me. Turns out, he stole my heart instead." Tears glistened in the corners of her eyes. "But when someone steals your heart, what can you do?" She chuckled. "You help him make a family and share the veterinary business, that's what."

Ty laughed with her. There was the spunky Gran he knew and loved. "Well, if I ever find someone wanting to steal my heart or share the construction business, I'll make sure to not let her get away."

"You do that. Otherwise, I might take my house back." Gran wagged a finger under his nose. "I still can't believe you're letting Brian tie the knot before you."

"It's not that bad." Ty took a deep breath. "Brian's closer to me than my own brother. How can I not be happy for him?"

"You're a good boy." She patted his cheek again. "You're taking good care of the dogs, right? Rusty doing okay?"

Rusty had been gone long before Ty was born. But Gran's memory slipped more and more, it seemed.

"Rusty's doing great, Gran."

Ty's heart, on the other hand, was suffering. To go from good moments to bad in the blink of an eye couldn't be a good sign. And it seemed to happen more and more lately. What would their family do without Gran Nancy? And what might she say in the future if she was already acting like this now?

Chapter Fifteen

"I don't know what he sees in her." Lennox leaned against the deck railing in George's backyard Easter Sunday. The weather had been a roller coaster lately, reaching up into the eighties and then back down to the upper fifties on other days. Between giant thunderstorms and an occasional frost still, Lennox hadn't been sure how the day would turn out, but the sunshine beating on her head made the slight breeze more pleasant than not.

"Don't worry. He really does care for your mom." Jane, George's younger daughter, came to stand by Lennox. They watched her son Benjamin pick up plastic Easter eggs scattered below. The toddler's short legs moved fast, and his grandfather had his work cut out for him to keep up.

"I don't know that I'm worried so much as I simply don't understand." Lennox scanned George's place, shaking her head at how different it was here compared to the trailer park she'd come from. His two-story brick house was immaculate, with a big open floor plan on the first story that most of her mom's double-wide could fit inside. His shaded yard was perfectly landscaped and even included a small swing set for his grandchild.

"Well, she's nothing like our mother, that's for sure." Jane cringed. "That came out wrong. Sorry. I just meant that when my sister and I found out he was dating again, we wondered if she'd be a lot like Mom. Their interests differ, yet there's something there that just fits with Dad. I can't quite put my finger on it, but I can sense it."

"He wants to save her." Lennox huffed. "That's all."

"No." Jane shook her head. "Don't me wrong. He's the type who is always looking to help others. But that's not all that draws him to her. I don't know. I think maybe it's their sense of humor. But I need to see them together more before I'm sure."

"How can you be so certain it's not only because he wants to play the hero with her?" Lennox turned her back on the sweet scene of her mom and George helping Benjamin count his eggs. "Since I met him, it seems to be the main focus of our conversations."

"Have you seen the way he hovers, as if looking for ways to be of service? Or the way he opens her door and helps her in and out of a car? Or the way he reaches over to squeeze her hand or give her a hug?" Jane waved her hand toward their parents. "It's more than just a savior complex. My dad has dated maybe once or twice since Mom passed, and I've never seen him take to someone the way he has Faye. I think she's just as good for him as he is for her."

Mom was good for someone? The thought jiggled around in Lennox's head but couldn't find a spot to land. Wasn't her mom just as broken as she was? Wasn't she someone who only stayed with another person long enough to get what she could out of them and then moved on? What was Lennox missing? Sure, she hadn't spent a ton of time with her mother since moving out several years ago, but her mother couldn't have changed that much, could she?

"Lennox, you made it." Her mom flashed a smile. "Have you had something to eat? We have leftovers."

Lennox had been invited to join them for worship services that morning, too, but she'd passed, claiming she was too worn out from teaching her classes the day before. It had been a crazy week, teaching with a bruised bottom, thanks to the collapsing pew.

Not to mention her thoughts being muddled by the confrontation with Ty afterward. He hadn't shown up to the kickboxing session yesterday, and she was relieved. Mostly. She'd just keep telling the disappointed part of her to shut up.

"I had a late breakfast, so I'm good." It wasn't a lie. She had stuffed herself on mini quiches she'd found on sale the week before. It was a holiday, after all.

"Well, you're just in time for cake." George grabbed one hand of his grandson, and her mom clasped the other. Together, they lifted the boy up each step to get back up on the deck. "It's coconut cake—a family tradition. Shaped like a bunny, of course."

"Did you find all the eggs, Benjamin?" Jane took her son from their parents. "Oh, there's so many! Tell you what. How about you go lie down for a nap, and then I'll let you have some candy from one, okay?"

"I want candy now. No nap. I not sweepy." He rubbed his eyes and laid his head on his mommy's shoulder as she walked him back inside.

Lennox's mom gave her shoulder a squeeze. "Did you see your sister?"

"Yes. Macy and Jared are in the living room talking to Jane's husband. I can't remember his name."

"Spencer," George offered.

"Right. We said *hello* after Jane let me in, but she wanted to see Benjamin hunting eggs, so we walked on through." Lennox gestured around. "Your house is beautiful."

"Thank you. It's taken me a while to get things the way I wanted, but I've come to love it. And I love having enough room for the kids to come back and visit." He placed a hand on her back as well as her mom's. "Now, I think I hear that cake calling my name. Jane made it this year, and I think she might even have figured out how to make it better than her mom used to."

Lennox had to admit the confection was beautiful. A layer of white coconut flakes covered the entire thing to look like rabbit fur. A big blue bow tie was at the bottom, and the eyes were a glossy brown, almost the same shade as Ty's. Not that he was the only person in the world with that color irises. Just the first one to come to mind now, for some reason she didn't wish to explore.

George passed a stack of plates to her mother and pointed to a drawer in front of Lennox where a knife should be. Lennox handed a square of dessert to her mom as the others wandered in, including Jane with a baby monitor in hand.

"Why didn't you bring that young man of yours today, Len?" Her mom passed the slice to someone else.

Lennox focused on her task of cutting even pieces, not wanting to ruin a perfectly nice afternoon with a biting comment.

"You have a boyfriend?" Macy leaned against the counter, her top dipping much too low at the neckline for Lennox's taste.

"No." Lennox carefully passed a piece of cake to her sister, though she would much rather shove it in her face. "Mama, you know he's not *my young man*. Just a friend."

"Friends don't do what he did for you that night." Her mom shook her head. "I'm betting you just don't want to admit there's more yet."

Lennox set the knife down, grateful to be done with the task of serving. If she held that utensil much longer, it might become a weapon. How did her mother remember anything about that evening? She hadn't even been able to keep her head up. There's no way she could have seen or heard much of what happened between Ty and Lennox. And there was no way she knew about Lennox's crazy tea invitation afterward.

"Believe what you want, but he's a friend. Nothing more." Lennox took her cake into another room, leaving her mama to give some description to Macy of how cute Ty was. The only correct depiction was that he had long wavy brown hair. The rest could have been anyone.

"Don't take it too hard." Jane sat down beside Lennox at the table. "My dad used to give me fits when I'd bring a guy home. It's how I recognized Spencer was the one."

Lennox frowned. "What?"

"Every boy I brought over for any reason, be it a youth event for church or a date or whatever, afterward my dad would joke about how long a relationship with that particular guy would last … or not. He might give any of them a few months." Jane licked some icing off the back of her fork with a grin. "But the first time I brought Spencer by, Dad didn't say anything at all. Several months into our relationship, I finally asked him about it. He told me he couldn't see that far into the future."

"You're telling me you married Spencer because your dad didn't think you'd break up?" It made more sense than falling in love, but still …

"Nope. I'm telling you, he was right about every single boy I ever brought home. And Spencer was the only one he could see me actually working things out with." She reached over and gave Lennox's fingers a squeeze. "Maybe you should have Dad meet this guy. If he thinks nothing will come of it, you can tell your mom to back off."

There was one major problem with that theory. Lennox savored the last bite of her cake as she mulled the story over in her mind. Assuming George did meet Ty, what if he thought they had a chance together as more than friends? That would only encourage her mother, which was the exact opposite of what Lennox needed to happen. Because despite the kiss that had left her heart racing and her insides on fire, she was sticking to her original statement. She didn't believe in love. She couldn't.

"Dad told me you work at Twisted Barre." Jane brought up a new subject Lennox was much happier to talk about.

"I do."

"Ever since I had Benjamin, I've wanted to do something to get rid of the last few pounds that won't go away. Any recommendations on which classes might be best for me?" She motioned toward her empty plate with a laugh. "Not that I'm eating like I want to lose pounds."

Lennox smiled back. "It really depends on exactly what you're wanting. We offer a variety. Some are geared more toward strengthening and stretching like yoga and Pilates. Others are more for burning calories like kickboxing or spin. And then, there's barre, which does a bit of all of it."

"Do you offer childcare? I'm not sure about it, schedule-wise, either. I'm a stay-at-home mommy, and Spencer works crazy hours some weeks at the clinic."

"No childcare yet, although I might suggest it to my partners, as you're not the first to ask about it." Lennox pulled her wallet out and removed a business card. "Here's the website so you can check out what we offer. Each class has the level of difficulty and what to expect. And you're welcome to contact me with any questions."

"This sounds great, Lennox. Thanks."

"The service this morning was wonderful." Mom squeezed George's arm as they joined Lennox and Jane at the table. "Thank you again for inviting me. The preacher said some things I'd never thought of before."

"Oh, yeah?" George sat, a second piece of cake on his plate, if Lennox was right. The wink he shot at her said she probably was. "What did he say that was new to you?"

"About Jesus being a sacrifice for us. And that every time someone commits a sin, we're putting Him right back up on the cross." Her mom shook her head. "I'd heard the story of Him dying, of course. But the way the preacher described it this morning was powerful. Made me look at some things in my life a bit more. And how I'm more like one of the guys who hung on either side of Jesus than I am Him."

"You really believe all that, Mama?" Lennox leaned back, her arms folded across her chest. "That God somehow loves us all so much He sent His Son to die?"

"I'm starting to." Mom picked at a cuticle on one hand. "It definitely makes more sense now."

All this Jesus talk made something bubble inside Lennox until she wanted to scream. "I can't even believe someone here on earth would love me half that much. How can you believe in a God who loves you more?"

"It's easier for me to believe the One who created us loves me more than anyone than it is to think someone on Earth could love me so much." George set his empty plate aside. "Though I also believe it's the task of all of us to show God's love to others through our own actions. I'm sorry you haven't seen enough of that in me to be able to believe it's possible from Him."

The One who created us. Lennox shook her head. "My father helped create me, and that didn't seem to make him love me at all. So, no. I don't think it would be that easy for me to believe in such a thing."

"Lennox!" Mom reached out as Lennox pushed back from the table, but Lennox dodged her.

"No, Mom. Thanks for inviting me, George, but I'd better go. The cake was great, Jane." Lennox set her plate in the kitchen, waved at her sister, and stalked out the front door.

"Lennox." George grabbed her car door right before she could slam it. "Can I have one minute?"

Lennox squared her jaw. "One."

"Your father didn't do what he should have by you. But you know what? That's on him. It isn't your fault. It isn't even fully your mom's fault. He made a choice. A bad one. You can't compare our perfect heavenly Father with an imperfect earthly one. Because God will never walk away from you."

"Time's up. Thanks again for the cake." She tugged at the handle, and after a couple of seconds, he released his grip so she could close the door and leave.

It all sounded good. But how could she believe in a love so big? In love at all? How could she believe in a God who supposedly loved her, when she'd never seen any examples of it?

Sure, George was turning out better than any of her mother's other boyfriends. He obviously had his life together, a good job, a perfect house and family, and maybe he even cared about her mother—for some strange reason, Lennox still couldn't grasp. But she also wasn't sure it would last.

Honestly, she was amazed her sister's boyfriend Jared was still around. Macy usually went through men faster than anyone, and now Jared had been in the picture for two months. Maybe because Macy was willing to do anything for him.

She didn't know Jane and Spencer well enough after such a short visit to be able to tell what kind of a relationship they had. Didn't all marriages start out well? It was after a few years, they went downhill.

Lennox shook her head and drove back to her apartment. She'd need much, much more proof of love before she'd admit it was real. Or achievable. Especially the kind that supposedly came from God. It was hard to accept something she'd never experienced.

Chapter Sixteen

"Yes, sir." Ty penciled the date onto the back of a receipt in his car. He'd put it in his phone later. "Not a problem. That still gives us plenty of time. And I appreciate you sharing your expertise. With the wedding not until September, the end of June should be fine."

He chatted just a few more minutes with the glazier and then ended the call. Out in the warm late-May air, he took his time walking from his car to the chapel. His brother returned for the summer two weeks ago, and with him helping around the office in the afternoons, Ty had accomplished a few more things on his list. Not that he could brag about it to Lennox anytime soon. He hadn't seen or heard from her since before Easter—when he'd made that stupid mistake and kissed her a month ago.

It wasn't that the kiss itself had been bad. He thought it had been going quite nicely up to the point she ended it and started yelling. That was when he realized she wasn't ready for anything of the sort. Ty released a long sigh. Lennox was dealing with a past full of hurt and neglect, so he'd have to overcome that pain to have any kind of hope for a future with her.

He needed to see her again. It was more than a want or a

desire. He longed to be able to get back to wherever their relationship had been headed before his stupidity interrupted it.

Inside the hallowed building, he tilted his head back and studied the newly repaired ceiling. The only way one could tell it wasn't original to the structure was to climb a ladder and look closely. The contractor had meticulously matched the colors and grain of the wood, so even Ty, who was familiar with every inch of this building inside and out, couldn't tell where one ended and another began. That should win some brownie points.

Maybe he could come up with some sort of excuse for Lennox to help him work on the chapel. The plumbers started tomorrow. But no one wanted that job.

The pew still needed repairs. Honestly, they needed some love. Would she be willing to help him tighten screws and polish wood? The Lennox he'd become acquainted with didn't back down from a challenge or hard work.

The new carpet wouldn't be laid until after the plumber and painters were done. No point. That only left deep cleaning the interior. And in four weeks, the crowning glory—the stained-glass window his ancestor had brought over from Ireland back in the early twentieth century—would be repaired. While he was loath to trust the project to someone else, it called for expertise.

He could research online how to fix cracks or tighten the cames that held the individual pieces of glass together, forming the Celtic Cross pattern. But if anything more serious needed to be done, an expert should handle such a fragile piece of history. Ty wouldn't be able to live with himself if that window were broken further.

Needless to say, he couldn't get Lennox out here to help with that project. And he was still iffy about the pews. Though she had complained about how filthy the place was, he couldn't ask her to help clean, either. He'd probably pay double to do that monumental task because this place really was beyond disgusting in some areas.

He stood and took in the beauty of the sunlight sparkling

through the colored panes for a few more minutes. When nothing else could calm him down or give him peace, he found it here. As if the glimmers of light shining green and red and blue and yellow were pieces of God drifting in and settling around him to help him bear whatever burdens he carried.

If only he could convince Lennox that God could do the same for her. Was there a way to convince someone whose heart was so bruised that she *could* be loved, really and truly? She said she didn't believe in such an emotion, but love was more than feelings. It was an action, a choice, and so much more.

He'd never persuade her of anything if he never saw her again.

He hit his fist against the back of a pew and immediately regretted it, as it swayed from the beating. He caught the seat and stilled its movement, but also made a note to bring some screwdrivers so he could stabilize these old benches. And maybe some Murphy's Oil Soap.

Once he was sure the structure wouldn't collapse when he removed his hand, he gave one more glance around the area and then turned to go. Standing here wasn't bringing any new revelations or ideas, so he might as well head back out.

As he locked the old wooden doors, the overgrown flower beds bordering the whole building caught his eye. Yes. That was something he could use some help with. And while a dirty task, maybe not so grotesque as cleaning the structure's nasty interior.

But how to convince Lennox it would be a good idea? Sure. She was probably curious about how things were going, but she was too stubborn and angry to risk contacting him to find out. In some ways, it was a relief, but in others, he missed being able to rile her each time she asked.

Another problem—while she had his phone number, he'd never been able to talk her out of hers. He had no way to contact her except for cornering her outside her job. And he didn't think that would work. Nothing to stop her from using some of those kickboxing skills she had and getting in her car to drive off. It's not like he could keep her from driving off wherever he might see her. Not without her keys.

Keys.

Something niggled in the back of his mind to do with those jingly pieces of metal, but what? What was he trying to remember? Something about one of the last times he'd seen her. She'd mentioned her keys for some reason. What was it?

Ty paced in front of the old chapel, willing his brain to go back through what Lennox might have said. Not at the craft store. She hadn't driven that night. When had he seen her next?

At the workout session. With Brian and Sara Beth. Ty snapped. That was it.

He pulled his phone from his pocket and quickly dialed his cousin.

"Ty? What's up?"

"Is Sara Beth with you?"

His cousin let out a loud guffaw. "We're not even married yet, and you're already calling my phone to talk to her?"

"I don't have her number." Ty rolled his eyes despite the fact Brian couldn't see him. "But I assumed since you're off work that you're probably together."

Brian mumbled something Ty couldn't make out and then said more legibly, "Yes, she's here."

"Well, can I talk to her, please?" Ty yanked on the ends of his hair.

"Yeah, yeah. But no funny busin—" Brian's joking warning cut off before he could finish. Ty could only assume Sara Beth had jerked the device from his hands.

"Hey, Ty. What's wrong?" Sara Beth's voice came over the line.

"I don't know that anything's wrong, but I need a favor." Ty leaned back against his car and considered the enormous job he was about to try and get Sara Beth to help him with. "Lennox has Thursday afternoons and evenings off, right?"

Ty presented his longshot idea to Sara Beth and waited for her response.

After a pause that felt like hours, she finally said, "Ty, it's practically kidnapping."

He smirked. "I'm getting pretty good at kidnapping, evidently. This will be my second time."

"What?"

"Never mind." He started pacing again. "I just need to know if you're willing to help me."

Sara Beth paused for so long, he was sure she would refuse. Instead, she finally said the words he hoped for. "Okay. Let's make sure we have all the details straight so this will work. And don't you dare mention my name as being an accomplice. I'd rather not lose my best friend, if it's all the same to you."

"My lips are sealed. Promise." He bounced on the heels of his feet. It was all coming together in his head.

Sure, Lennox would be mad, but at least it opened the door to some time with her. Maybe if she'd listen long enough for him to explain the project to further the chapel renovations, then he could lure her into spending enough time to really talk again. And that might give him enough leeway to aim them closer to where he wanted them to be.

The plan was foolproof.

Right?

Chapter Seventeen

A creepy sensation washed over Lennox's head and shoulders the moment she walked through the studio doors. Someone was watching her. Slowly, she peeked up from checking her phone messages and met his smirk across the parking lot. Her heart tripped a few beats. How long had it been since she'd seen him? A month? More? She'd begun to believe she'd finally convinced him she didn't want him around. But here was Ty Dunne in the flesh.

No problem. She didn't have to speak to him as he sat there on the hood of that ridiculous convertible of his. She'd just get in her—

"Where's my car?" Her hand shook as she pulled her keys from her bag.

"At your apartment." His words made sense, but didn't. Because she'd parked in her usual spot this morning. The one right next to where he was now.

"No. No, no, no." She flipped her keychain over, looking for the fob that remote unlocked her vehicle. Not there. "How? How did you do this?"

He didn't answer.

"What do you want?"

He still didn't answer.

"Obviously, you want *something,* or you wouldn't have gone to such trouble to steal my keys and move my car. Why can't you just leave me alone?" Lennox stomped and then cringed at the childishness of the action.

"All I wanted was an opportunity to get your help."

"My help?" She hoped her mouth wasn't hanging open as much as it felt like. "What on earth could I possibly help you with?"

"I thought you wanted to be more involved with fixing up the chapel." He slid off the hood and gave her one of those cheeky grins of his, one side of his mouth slightly higher than the other.

She pressed the achy spot in the middle of her forehead. "Please tell me you're not just now starting to work on the chapel."

"Nope." He walked around to the passenger side and held the door open as if he expected her to come over there with no more argument.

"Then what exactly am I supposed to be doing? I know how to teach exercise classes, not fix roofs or pipes or dispose of rodents." She kept her feet planted firmly where they were. There was no way she would go easily.

"Well, you mentioned how awful the flower beds were. I thought maybe you could help me pick out some plants and start cleaning up that disaster." He motioned with his hand for her to get in. "The roof and pipes are fixed. And an exterminator is scheduled."

They were? She schooled her expression, unwilling to show him how much those facts impressed her. Plus, she needed to stand her ground at least a few more minutes, lest he consider himself victorious. That wouldn't do at all. He needed to know kidnapping wasn't acceptable.

She crossed her arms. "I can't believe you'd involve my best friend in your stupid schemes today."

"And what's that supposed to mean?" He cocked his head.

"You know what it means. Only Sara Beth or my coworkers know where I keep my keys during the day. Sara Beth is the only one you know personally *and* the only one who would easily give in to your suggestion to steal my car." Lennox shook her finger at him. "Not nice, Mr. Dunne. Not nice at all, corrupting a sweet girl like her."

"I didn't coerce her into doing anything she didn't want to." Ty left the car and walked over to stand in front of her.

That was basically an admission, and while satisfaction came with knowing she was right, it didn't ease her anger. "You mean like you're trying to do to me?"

"I won't *make* you go with me. Not any farther than your apartment, anyway. I feel obligated to make sure you get home today, since it's my fault you're in this situation." He reached over and tugged her hand. "But I really do hope you'll come with me. Because I would love the help and the company. And I'd love to show you the improvements."

She pulled her fingers out of his grasp, but not angrily. It was a beautiful afternoon. And it wasn't like she had any other plans. She sighed. "Fine."

"Yeah?" He stepped backward a few times. "Really?"

She stalked over to the open door. "Let's just go before I change my mind."

"Yes." He waited for her to climb in and then eased into the driver's side, sliding his sunglasses into place. "Let's go."

She crossed her arms over her seatbelt. "I'm still not going completely happily."

"Of course not." He gave a half-serious shake of his head. "I would expect no less."

She pursed her lips and chose not to say anything else. Better to maintain silence than give him more fodder for his mockery. He was one of the most exasperating men she'd ever met. But she was rather excited about seeing what had been done. Though she tempered her expectations, lest they grow too high and be dashed by what still needed to be accomplished.

"We're going to the nursery first. It's on our way, and we can grab a couple new things that will complement the bushes and other salvageable plants already out there." He maneuvered his car through town, the air ruffling his still-too-long hair, though it did appear shorter than the last time she'd seen it.

"Fine." There. One word. He couldn't make anything out of that, though his lips twitched as if amused.

The tires crunched over the gravel in the parking lot of the biggest nursery in town. Flowers of all colors covered the grounds and continued into the greenhouses, interspersed by various shrubs, bushes, trees, and vegetable plants and herbs. A few sections included statuary, wind chimes, and bird baths. She allowed him to help her out of the car and followed him into the lush vegetation, unwilling to admit to how much she loved wandering through places like this. Living in a double-wide growing up and now an apartment hadn't allowed her to nurture a green thumb, but she'd always loved the idea of gardening. Maybe someday ...

"I looked for my mom's old work gloves for you to wear, but couldn't find them anywhere, so let's get another pair, huh?" Ty plopped a floral pair of gloves into her hands. She blinked and grabbed them before they could slip to the ground. "Should we look at shrubs and bushes first?"

"I guess?" He was asking the wrong person if he wanted gardening expertise.

"I mean, I'd love to get some bulbs in there for next spring, but it's a bit late for them to bloom this year so I'll wait until the fall for that. And when it starts cooling off, we can add some mums to the beds to give us lots of fall colors in the time for the wedding. So, mostly what we're looking for today is structure. Hearty plants that can provide a bit of greenery and maybe some color around the outside, but not need much maintenance in the long run." He meandered through the various tables toward a big display near the back of the property with larger pots and bigger plants.

She followed at a more sedate pace, running her fingers over various leaves or reading the names of flowers that caught her eye. Maybe she could come back another time and fix up a few pots for her tiny balcony. She couldn't even think what had stopped her from doing such a thing in the past. Why hadn't it crossed her mind? Sure, it wouldn't be the great big garden she might like to have, but it would be better than nothing, right?

As she neared him, about fifteen different shades and shapes of roses had her pausing again. She leaned over to breathe in their rich fragrance, closing her eyes. If only she could grow one of these on a balcony.

"Lennox?" Ty's voice pulled her eyes open again. "Hey, there you are. *Ooh*. Nice. I've always loved that shade of rose. Gran planted one in the backyard."

"Did she?" Lennox fingered the soft petal one more time. "It's very pretty."

He lifted the tag and flipped it around. "This says they can handle being in shade too. What if we do roses on either side of the front door?"

"Oh." Was he changing his plans just for her? "I mean, sure. If that's what you want."

"I want you to have some say in this too. That's why I invited you along." He indicated the various plants. "Which colors are your favorites? We could plant two different ones."

She started looking more closely.

"Just make sure they say they do okay in shade. We have lots of trees around the chapel, you know." He held up a finger. "I'll be right back. I'm going to grab a cart."

By the time he returned, she'd narrowed it down to a pink and yellow variegated and a peach.

"Nice." He quickly loaded them, not even questioning her choice, and then nodded back toward other bushes. "Come see what you think of these."

She walked beside him, his arm brushing hers every so often as they dodged other patrons and plants with long branches hanging out.

"Mostly, what we have is plain green shrubs, so I thought it might be fun to mix things up. These leaves have a bit of red to them. We could add those between some of the green ones and then maybe something like this." He pointed to a dwarf-sized evergreen.

She tilted her head as she tried to picture it. "I guess because it would give it a variation in height?"

"Yes." The beaming smile he sent her way had her heart skipping again. What was that about? "That's exactly what I was thinking. Okay. If I did my math right, we'll need about ten of these and twelve of those. Though I wasn't figuring in the roses."

"Sorry. We can put these back." She started to grab one of the pots already in the cart.

He caught her hand. "No. Lennox, you misunderstood. I was just refiguring it out loud. I wasn't complaining. I hadn't even thought about roses, so I'm glad you noticed them. We could even do a couple more, if you like."

"I don't want to mess up your design."

"You're not messing it up. I asked for your opinion because I wanted it."

"Okay." She gave a nod and turned back to the shrubs he'd originally pointed out. "So, how many of these?"

"Let's do ten. If we decide we need more, I can come back another time."

They loaded their selections and meandered their way toward the front, not hurrying. She caught him staring more than once. Why did he smile every time she spotted a new variety of flora she'd never seen before? She couldn't figure him out.

"Do you want some of those? You've reached for something similar about four times now." His voice held a note of teasing, but it wasn't mean.

"Oh, no. You've seen my tiny place. And I'd probably just kill it in the first couple of days." She clasped her hands together to keep from touching anything else, lest he throw it on the cart as well. They were supposed to be shopping for the chapel, after all. And she refused to be beholden to him for anything he purchased outside of that.

"It's not a big deal. And those are really hearty. You'd have to neglect them much longer than a few days before they died." He reached past her, his arm wrapping around her waist for a minute before he could get the pot he wanted.

She held her breath, afraid to move, lest they become tangled up any farther. His warmth against her back was nice, but also unnerving. Did he notice the intimate position they were in? He straightened, the flower procured, and her back was immediately cold, missing his light touch.

"Lennox?" A vaguely familiar voice called her name.

She spun around and her knees went weak.

Ty's hand caught her elbow, giving her support before she even realized she needed it.

Her heart raced, and her breathing quickened.

"Lennox. It's you, isn't it?" Her dad walked toward them, a tomato plant in one hand and a woman slightly older than Lennox holding his other.

"Dad." She breathed the word although it tasted strange on her tongue after not being used for so long. Sure, she'd thought about him through the years, though mostly to berate him for leaving or complain about how he never called. She hadn't used the word "Dad" as an address in over a decade.

He moved as if to hug her, but she stepped back, bumping into the handle of their cart. This wasn't happening, was it? Her dad left them years ago, never to be heard from again. He couldn't be here now, in the town she'd started over in. And especially not with Ty witnessing every agonizing moment of their reunion. Ty had already witnessed too much of her messed-up family.

"It's been a long time, honey," her dad's voice gentled as if he were trying to calm a wild animal. "I'm so glad to see you."

"Twelve years and nine months."

"What?"

Lennox straightened her back, pulling her arm free from Ty's support. "It's been twelve years and nine months since you walked out on us."

The woman with her dad cast him a look of uncertainty.

"Not a day has gone by since then that I didn't think of you and Macy." He reached for her, but Lennox swatted his hand away.

"Lies." She practically spat the word.

"Len."

"No." She jutted out her chin. "No. If you really had thought about us and missed us, you could have checked in. To see how I was. To know how I grew up. So, you don't get to waltz back into my life now and pretend like everything is okay. Because it's not."

She spun on her heel and grabbed the cart and pushed it toward the check out. She didn't need more stress in her life. Didn't she already have enough between helping Sara Beth, worrying about her mom and George, mulling over all the malarkey George had said about God, and the ever-present Ty Dunne? She'd been just fine without her father for over a decade now, and she'd be just fine without him for longer.

"Lennox, please." Her dad's voice gave her pause for a second, but no more. She blinked back unwanted tears and continued walking. Maybe now he'd know the agony of having someone walk away.

Chapter Eighteen

"I really do love her." Lennox's dad's voice pulled Ty's focus off Lennox and back to the man beside him.

The tiny bit of headway Ty had made with Lennox earlier while picking out roses was now shot to pieces. A war raged within Ty over catching up to her hasty stiff-backed retreat or staying to see if there was anything he could do to mend the rift between father and daughter.

"She barely trusts me. She barely trusts anyone." Ty ran a hand through his hair and blew out a stress-filled breath. "I'm not sure it would be wise for me to intervene."

"I understand." Her dad couldn't seem to pull his gaze off his daughter. "Look, can you just give her my phone number? Can you do that for me? Maybe she'll have a change of heart and want to talk. To hear my side of the story."

Ty took the small slip of paper and tucked it in his pocket. "I'll do what I can, but I make no promises. She's been hurting a long time."

"From me." Her dad stated it. "It's one of my biggest regrets in life."

"I'd better go." Ty spun but didn't take a step yet. "If you're a praying man, there's a couple of us trying to convince her of

God's love. Maybe if enough of us pray, we can get through that hard head of hers."

Her dad let out a cynical laugh. "I haven't prayed in a long time, but if I were to start again, she'd be a good reason."

Ty nodded and then rushed to catch up to Lennox. She glared at him as if aware he'd spoken to the enemy. Nothing he could do about it now.

He paid for the plants, and they headed over the bumpy gravel parking lot to his car. As they neared his vehicle, Lennox put her hands on her hips and studied it. What was running through her head?

"Just how are you going to fit all of this in that itty-bitty little convertible?" She pointed back and forth between the stash of plants and the trunk.

"Ever play Tetris?" He smirked. "Watch and learn."

After placing as many shrubs and bushes as he could fit in the tiny back seat, he moved to the trunk and carefully set the rest inside. Perfect. Even enough room left for a few more. She cocked an eyebrow at him, her lips twitching into an almost smile. Success.

But then a glance over her shoulder made her countenance fall once more. Her dad stood across the parking lot. With a gentle touch, Ty grasped her elbow and tugged her around to get into the passenger side.

"I'm gonna return this cart." He didn't even wait to see if she nodded or not. The sooner they got out of there, the better.

"I forgot to ask you." Lennox's dad caught him as he started back toward the car.

Ty barely controlled his frustration. "Yes?"

"Who are you in relation to my daughter?" The words were something any father would ask. Ty couldn't deny having a bit more respect for him after seeing the concern, though it was too little too late.

"We're friends. My cousin and her best friend are getting married this fall, and we're working together on several projects for the wedding." Friends might be a bit more than their true relationship right now, but he wasn't about to take back his words. It was close enough for this encounter. If her dad managed to work his way back into her life, maybe down the road they could figure out the rest. Assuming she let Ty stay in her life too.

Oh, what a mess. "I've got to go."

"Sure. Thanks for any help you can give." Her dad frowned in Lennox's direction and then turned toward a little sedan parked in the other direction.

Ty slid behind the steering wheel and started the engine. "Ready to work?"

"I've already worked today. I was supposed to be *off* this afternoon." Lennox shot him a glare, but it didn't look as wrathful as some others she'd sent his way. "Why were you talking to him again?"

"He wanted to know what our relationship was."

"And you told him ..."

"That we'd been married for five years and are expecting his first grandchild." Ty tried to keep a straight face, but when her skin grew even redder than her hair, he couldn't stop the explosion of laughter.

"You did not!"

Ty whipped around the curves in the road leading out of town. "Of course not. I told him we were friends helping my cousin and your best friend with their wedding plans." Just another mile to the chapel.

"Oh."

"Oh? Was that wrong? I didn't think you considered me anything more than a friend." He waggled his eyebrows. "I can go back and find him if you wanted me to say I was your boyfriend or something."

"No!" She whacked him in the arm. "You're so aggravating."

"*Aww.* And here I thought I was charming." He pulled into the drive and parked as close to the building as possible.

She didn't wait for him to open her door. As he reached it, she was most of the way out. But her shoelace got caught and she tripped forward. He grabbed her elbows and steadied her until she could free her foot. She jerked her arms away from him as soon as she was stable. Much too soon, in his opinion.

"Where do we start?" She leaned over to pull some of the pots from the backseat, and he quickly averted his eyes from the very nice view of her backside.

What had she asked him? Right. "*Um*. Let's get everything unloaded. We'll place each plant close to where we want it. Then, we can just pick a corner and work our way around. I've done a bit here and there, but you can tell it needs more."

"I told you it needed work months ago." She thrust a couple of bushes into his arms.

"Yes, but a couple of months ago, it was still too cold to plant anything. This way, we won't have to worry about the frost nipping our plants while they're settling in."

She rolled her eyes and stomped off with her arms full of greenery. "You said green and red alternating, right?"

"Please." He set the roses on each side of the door and followed her with more pots.

Within fifteen minutes, everything was unloaded and in place. She pulled her gloves apart and moved to slide them on, but he caught her fingers and gave a tug. "Come see what all's been done."

She was hesitant, almost resistant, as he pulled her into the building. Was she remembering the last time they'd been here? He had great expectations this day would go much smoother. Though he wouldn't say *no* if she wanted another kiss.

Not that his hopes were high for such. After her run-in with her father, her emotions had to be running crazy. Ty would give just about anything to read her mind.

She scanned the room. Her eyes zeroed in on the stage, and he barely suppressed a cackle of glee. It was obvious the exact moment she realized the toilet was gone. Her eyes flew to the ceiling, and her breath caught. Yes. She reached out tenderly and pushed against the pew next to her. It held, but just barely.

"Yeah, yeah. Those still need work." Ty pointed at the front of the room. "I have cleaners coming in next week to tackle that mess. Painters after them. Then, new carpet. The window won't be fixed until the end of June. I found a guy who specializes in old stained glass—wanted to make sure we had someone who could do it right."

"Is the window that old?"

"It's from the 1800s. My ancestors brought it over from Ireland." He couldn't stop the pride in his voice.

"Wow." Her awe made it worth it.

"Have I impressed you at least a little?" He tugged the fingers he still held, amazed she hadn't pulled away. Had she been distracted by the improvements, or was she finally okay with the contact?

She yanked free, as if coming to her senses. "I'll not answer such a question. You're fishing for compliments, and you don't need anything else going to that big head of yours."

"So, you *are* impressed." He walked with her back out to the mess of a garden bed.

"What did you have in mind for me to do?" She pointed to the overgrown greenery.

He got down on his knees where he could point to the plants. "See this? I'm going to trim back the established shrubs I haven't already tackled. I did this one last week. For now, you can pull the weeds that have come up through the rocks. Then, we can plant the new bushes in between the ones already here."

"I haven't done a lot of gardening in my life." She pushed the fingers of the gloves down. "Anything I shouldn't pull up?"

"At this point?" He pushed back a strand of hair that flopped over his eyes. "If anything nice was planted here, it's gone wild now. I didn't notice any bulbs or anything popping up this spring. I say let's start fresh. If it's not a shrub or bush, pull it up."

"Okay. Here goes nothing." She clasped a bunch of tall grass and tugged until their roots let go. Evidently, she wasn't expecting to have to use so much force, because when they came up, she went down, landing on her bottom with a little *oof*.

"*Oops*." He offered her a hand, and after a moment, she took it. "Hang on. I think I have just the solution."

A quick rummage through the pile of supplies he'd borrowed from his mom's shed turned up a small cushioned kneeler he'd seen last week—a little worn around the edges, but still better than nothing. He dropped it on the ground in front of her.

"Try putting your knees on that and see if it helps."

"Thanks." She gingerly lowered herself to kneel and tried again, this time maintaining her balance as the weeds turned loose. "And what do I do with these things once I've pulled them?"

"Make a pile behind you, and we'll gather it all up later." He picked up his clippers and walked a few feet to trim a hedge that had grown to look like the Eifel Tower.

They worked in companionable silence for half an hour or so before he couldn't stand the quiet anymore. After all, part of his reasons for bringing her out here this afternoon was to grow closer, and that wouldn't happen if they didn't talk. Plus, his curiosity was about to kill him.

"Want to talk about earlier?" He snapped through an extra thick branch and tossed it behind him.

"Nope."

That went as well as he expected. "You know it helps to talk things out. If you never let out your frustrations, they eat away at you and make you bitter and angry and stressed."

"Well, you should live to be a hundred then, because you can't keep from talking, can you?" Her sarcasm was potent.

"Oh, sure. Blame it on me." He exerted some extra force on another limb. "I'm just trying to look out for you."

"You want to talk? Fine. Let's talk." She chunked a big handful of weeds over her shoulder. "I got off work, looking forward to having an afternoon to myself to unwind and not think about anything, and instead found out that my best friend betrayed me by stealing my car so that I had to ride to a nursery with a guy I don't like where I ran into the man who ruined my life. Which part do you think bothers me most, oh wise one?"

"Len …"

"Don't." She spat the command in his direction. "You don't have the right to call me that."

"Look, I had no idea your dad would be at that nursery. All I wanted was a chance to show you the chapel. And you said at the beginning that you wanted to help. So, I thought I'd give you the chance. If you really don't want to be here, I'll take you home right now. But I thought the fresh air and good clean dirt would do you good."

"Good clean dirt?" She shot him a look full of skepticism.

"Some doctors actually tell moms to let their children go out and get dirty now. I guess people are keeping their children too clean, and it's lowering their immune system. You know minerals and vitamins are found in soil." He shrugged. "I figure it works for adults too."

She wiggled her floral-patterned fingers. "Then, why am I wearing gloves?"

"I assumed you wouldn't want the yuck under your nails. And some of these weeds aren't friendly to skin." He pointed to a prickly looking weed. "I'd recommend keeping your gloves on for pulling out the bad ones, and then we can remove them to plant new ones, if you want."

"I guess that makes sense." She wiped her forehead with the back of her hand, leaving a streak of dirt.

He itched to go over and wipe it off, but that would only get him berated more. At least she'd quit ranting about not wanting to be there. For the moment.

"We're probably not going to get all of this done today. You know that, right?" She scooted her pad down to the next section and leaned over to grab at the grass in the back.

"Yeah. But it's definitely going faster with two of us instead of just me." He finished up the shrub he was at and stood back to make sure the top was even. "I appreciate you being willing to stay, even though it wasn't your original plan. And I really am sorry about putting you in a position to run into your dad."

She straightened and sighed. "I know it wasn't your fault. It's just ..."

He waited. Would she finally open up?

"You know, you were there when my mom was drunk last month. Had to witness that awful side of my life. And today, you witnessed the thing with my dad. It's like ... I don't know. Just embarrassing. I want to be this strong woman who has her act together, but my family can't seem to let me live that life."

"You *are* a strong woman." He crouched down beside her. "I can't imagine the strength it took you to go get your degree and become a partner in a business. You're an amazing teacher. And Sara Beth couldn't function without you in her life. Haven't you basically planned her wedding?"

Lennox giggled. *Giggled.* He had no idea she was capable of giggling. But the sound was glorious.

"Please don't be embarrassed about me seeing your weaker side. Everyone has one. We need them, really. Otherwise, how can we appreciate the strong?" He nudged her shoulder with his. "And, God didn't make us to be here alone. He wanted us to have people around we could lean on when we can't be strong. But He wants us to lean on Him, most of all."

She shook her head. "There you go with the God thing again. George preached at me on Easter, and now you're doing it here."

"I'm not preaching. Though you have me curious about what George said."

"He told me that while my earthly father had left and neglected me, God is a father who never would." She yanked a patch of clover out with more force than necessary.

"He's right." Ty stood slowly, afraid a sudden movement would stop her talking. Because he wanted her to keep talking more than almost anything in the world.

Chapter Nineteen

What could Lennox say? How could she explain to Ty anything running through her head or heart? He'd never understand completely. He was from a complete family, one without all the mess surrounding hers.

"I guess I don't believe God can ... I don't know. I guess I don't believe He can understand me. I mean, He's God. He's never been left or abandoned or dealt with half the things I have. And while it sounds great and all that to say He would love me no matter what, I'm not sure I could trust in a *love* that didn't come from a similar place as I did."

Ty flopped to the ground beside her, his face baffled. "Are you serious?"

Really? That's all he had? She'd tried opening up and letting him see where she was coming from and he questioned her? She chunked a handful of weeds at him. "Of course, I'm serious!"

Before she could throw more dirt his way, he caught her hand and shook his head. "Sorry. That came out wrong. I guess I didn't realize you didn't know."

"Didn't know what?" Did he have an inkling how aggravating he was?

"Didn't know that He was ridiculed and abandoned and rejected and more."

She frowned. "But He's God. Isn't He supposed to be above all that?"

"Well, here's the best part about the story of God—He loved the world so much that He came to earth as a man for a while. He sent part of Himself here in the form of His Son Jesus. And Jesus was literally killed by the people who were supposed to love Him the most."

"Jesus is actually God?" She rubbed a spot on her forehead and then grimaced, remembering the dirty gloves on her fingers.

"It's complicated." He leaned back on his hands and stared up, as if listening for divine help in explaining his point. "Let's just leave it at Jesus was the Son of God and was sent to earth for us. But there's a passage in the Bible where Jesus went back to Nazareth, His hometown, and the people there get so mad at Him that they drive Him out of town and try to force Him off a cliff. And when He was crucified, He asked God, 'My God, my God, why have you forsaken me?' His own Father. That's why I couldn't believe it when you said that God couldn't understand."

"But that's not God." She didn't want to believe what he was saying, even though a prick in her heart told her there was something to it. "That was Jesus. So, how would that make it where God could understand me?"

"Well, for one thing, God is rejected all the time. People don't want to believe in Him, don't want to accept His teachings, don't want to align their lives with His will instead of their own. But beyond that, the Bible tells us that Jesus is our mediator. He's interceding for us with God because He was down here, did live as a human, and does understand all of that."

She couldn't formulate a reply. She needed time to think. Time to process all he had said. Ty must have understood, because he didn't talk anymore. He squeezed her shoulder and went back to trimming the bushes.

It took them another hour, but they got one side cleaned out enough that he said they could plant the new shrubs. He dug the holes. Then showed her how to ease the new plant from the container and open up the roots some so they could work their way into the soil. Satisfaction washed over her as she surveyed their work. Maybe gardening truly was beneficial.

"Shall we go plant those roses before we leave? Something tells me we won't get much more done besides that today." Ty stretched his back.

"Sure."

"You'll probably want your gloves for these. They tend to be a bit prickly." He passed her gloves back to her, and she slipped them on while he worked on a new hole.

Together, they eased the bush from its plastic and into its new home. A few peach petals drifted to the ground as the plant was jostled into place.

Lennox reached through the gnarly branches and picked up a fallen bud. Air hissed through her teeth. She had inadvertently brushed a thorn. Instinctually she jerked her arm back, tucking it close.

Ty was instantly by her side. "Let me see." His touch was gentle on her skin as he twisted her arm back and forth to check the damage. "It's not deep, but I bet it hurts. I might have a Band-Aid in my car."

"I'll be fine. It's not the first time I've gotten a scratch." She glanced up. His face much closer to her than she expected. Close enough to see the stubble of a five o'clock shadow covering his square chin. Something flashed in his eyes, but what? Longing? Desire? Was he about to kiss her again? She did not want his lips near hers—no matter that her heart said otherwise. Her breath hitched, but she couldn't seem to pull away.

"You've got a little dirt." He broke the spell and reached up to wipe her forehead.

Air whooshed out of her lungs, and she blinked a couple of times. "Thanks."

"Sure." He stood and dusted off his pants.

They got the second bush in place with no more injuries, and together they stepped back to survey their work. Much nicer. If the roses were still blooming in September, it would be even better. Sara Beth would approve, wholeheartedly.

"Let's get our mess cleaned up, and then we can call it a day."

Together, they bagged up the pieces of shrubbery and weeds. The few tools were stowed in his small trunk, and the gloves were removed. Lennox leaned against his car and sighed.

"Will the other plants we bought be okay out of the ground?"

"I'll come over and get them in the dirt in the next few days." Ty leaned beside her. "Now that my brother is home from school, I have afternoons off from office work. That lets me come here and work on what I really love."

Lennox glanced at him, truly curious. "You don't love working for your dad?"

"My dad has a different vision for my life than I do. I'd love to work with him as a contracted designer. Instead, he wants me behind the desk in the office, booking all the other contractors, sending out bills, and helping keep him organized. I'm not terribly organized myself on a good day."

"You don't say?" The tease escaped her before she even realized she was going to say it. When had she become comfortable enough with him to be able to pick and poke fun?

"Right. Rumor has it your office isn't that organized, either." He shook a finger at her, a playful grin gracing his lips. "Sara Beth said she had to hunt for ten minutes to find your keys."

"So, it *was* Sara Beth!"

Ty clapped a hand over his mouth. "I promised her I wouldn't tell. That your friendship was more sacred than my plan to lure you out here."

"I won't hold it against her ... much." Lennox winked. "But I also want to point out that I've been learning new moves for some of my classes this week, and what she had to dig through was probably the paperwork and notes we'd all been exchanging to make sure we're offering the classes people actually want. It's not usually like that."

"I believe you."

"So, you don't like office work, but you're still doing it?"

"Someone has to. My dad's business couldn't run without it. And I was brought up working summers there, learning the business inside out. I'm the one most qualified."

"Except you don't love it."

"I guess we can't all have our dream jobs." He shrugged. "Not yet, anyway."

"And what would your dream job be?"

"Like I said, I'd love to be a designer. To help people find what they need to make their homes or whatever look exactly the way they want. That's where I get my pleasure." Ty shifted, his hands deep in his pockets, his shoulders slumped more than before. "But my dad thinks I wouldn't be able to support myself in such work."

They stood in silence. Minutes passed, as if the moment one of them spoke, the camaraderie could be broken.

Lennox ought to be mad at him for dragging her out here, but she couldn't conjure that emotion any more than she could conjure a warm feeling for her father earlier in the day. She wasn't ready for strong feelings, but she was more accepting of the term *friendship* than she had been when they first used it.

"Need help with some of the other flower beds?" Where had that question come from? Hadn't she just been trying to be angry at him for concocting this plan?

"Would you have time? I know your schedule differs daily." He glanced over at her.

"We've switched it up some this week. I'll have Saturday afternoon off too. Hattie wanted a couple of afternoon classes instead of so many early ones." She scratched at a dirty spot on her arm.

"I wouldn't turn down more help on Saturday, if you're willing."

"Sure. I can come. Gotta make sure this place looks as good as we can, right? For Sara Beth."

"Right. For Sara Beth." One corner of his mouth turned up, as if he didn't believe her story. "What time should I pick you up?"

"I can drive, you know."

"I know." He faced her more fully. "But if I pick you up, I get to spend that much longer with you."

Her heart flipped. As crazy as it was, the sweet words did something to her, something she wasn't sure she was ready for. She reached through the open window of the car and pulled out her planner. "Let's see."

"Wow. Color-coded and everything." He leaned over her shoulder.

"It helps me know what to expect each day." She ran her finger down the spot for Saturday. "I should be done around two."

"Works for me."

She penciled it in and then pulled out her phone and opened the calendar app.

"What are you doing?"

She quickly typed it in as an appointment and set a reminder. "Making sure it's in my calendar on here too."

"You have two different calendars?"

"Three."

"Three?" He pushed his sunglasses up on his head revealing his wide eyes. "Why?"

"One on my fridge at home. This one on my phone reminds me the day of. And the planner lets me have the overall picture. See?" She held it up to a different page. "It has not only weekly pages but also monthly, so I can see the whole month at a time. Oh, and there's one on my desk at work too. So, four."

"That's intense."

"Not really. I learned a long time ago that if I didn't have backups, things fell through the cracks."

"I'm impressed."

"Thanks." She put her bag back in the car. "Can you take me home now? I don't know about you, but I need a shower."

He sighed but then smiled. "Okay."

The ride back to town was quiet, but not uncomfortable. The chapel was only fifteen minutes from the city limits and not quite half an hour to her place. She closed her eyes and tried not to think about the fact that her estranged father was somewhere in their small town.

"Don't suppose I could talk you into dinner?" Ty's question interrupted her thoughts.

"Hm? No. Not tonight, Ty." She opened her eyes and discovered they were already at her apartment complex.

"All right. Another time." He caught her arm before she could get out. "I'm not going to pressure you to do something with this, no matter what, but ... just in case."

She frowned. What was he talking about? He pulled a small slip of paper from his pocket and passed it to her.

A phone number. She didn't recognize the area code. And she already had Ty's number, so it wasn't that.

"Your dad gave it to me before we left. He wanted me to pass it on."

She grabbed each side and moved to rip the slip in half, but Ty caught her hands.

"Don't do that yet, okay? I'm not saying use it, but don't burn the bridge, either. Think about it for a while." His voice was quiet, like he was calming a wild animal. Considering her emotions roiling inside, he was.

"It's my choice, Ty." She ground the words out between clenched teeth.

"Just don't do something you'll regret."

Tears burned behind her eyelids, but she blinked them back. "He burned this bridge when he walked out twelve years ago. He doesn't get to try and build a new one."

She placed her right hand on the door handle, ready to retreat inside. She would not show herself more susceptible. He'd seen enough of her weak side.

"Lennox, please." Ty waited until she turned her face his way. "Don't do this in a fit of anger. There may come a day when you wish you had this number."

"Not today."

"Should I hold onto it until you're ready?" He squeezed her fingers beneath his.

She shook her head. "No. You don't need to be involved any more than you already are. I'm sorry he put you up to this."

"I'm not." He slowly released the pressure he was applying to her hands. "And just so you know, I took a picture of it, so I could still get it to you later."

She banged her head back against his leather seat. "Incorrigible busybody."

"You'll learn to appreciate me someday."

She huffed out her exasperation.

He came around and opened her door while she pondered whether to rip the paper to shreds and be done with it. "I'll see you Saturday. Thanks again for your help."

"Like I had much choice." She couldn't be as gracious about it now. Not knowing he'd helped the enemy.

"Bye, Lennox." He dropped a kiss on her cheek before she could protest. He slipped into his car and waved to her. She wanted to stomp her foot, but he wouldn't see it, and it would probably only hurt her more. That man!

She pulled her phone out and sighed. She needed to do one more thing before she could call it a day. Someone else needed a head's up that her father had come to Park Haven.

Chapter Twenty

Awhole Saturday afternoon with Lennox. Nothing sounded more perfect to Ty. He drummed his fingers on the hood of his car where he waited for her to finish work. Just past two. She should be out any minute.

The door opened, and his heart skipped a beat.

There she was.

Ty was coming to appreciate how his whole body came alive when Lennox was around. As if a piece of him was missing when she wasn't nearby.

"Oh." She stopped and glared between him and her vehicle. "Did we agree on you picking me up?"

"I thought it was understood." He stood and dusted off his backside.

She twisted her sunglasses around and around as if it helped her think. "But my car."

"I can follow you home, and we can leave from there. Or we can swing by here on our way back." He wasn't about to give up his chance to spend every moment he could with her. And if they drove separately, that was over half an hour they'd be apart. Not to mention the trip back to town.

"This is ridiculous."

"Agreed. Get in, and we'll work it out later." He nodded his head toward the passenger side and went over and opened the door.

She cocked one hip, her fist against it. He lifted an eyebrow, resisting the urge to tell her how cute she was right now. When he didn't back down, she huffed, rolled her eyes, and stomped over to slide in. He controlled his grin of triumph—mostly.

"You're still incorrigible." She muttered as she buckled in.

"And yet, you're here, aren't you?"

"It's for Sara Beth."

"Uh-huh." He pointed the convertible toward the outskirts of town.

Her phone started playing the Shirelles' "Mama Said." She snatched it out of her bag and answered so quickly he figured it must be a call she'd been waiting for.

"Mom?"

He couldn't hear the voice on the other end. Only muffled snippets let him know Faye was talking.

"I've been trying to reach you for two days. Did you get my voicemail?" Lennox faced her window so he couldn't see her expression, but her tone sounded tight and worried. "Right. Yeah. I need to warn you about someone I saw the other day."

Her mom must be talking again. Was Lennox just now getting to tell her mom about running into her dad on Thursday? He glanced her way, but she continued to avoid his gaze.

"No, Mom. Listen. I saw your ex-husband."

Silence.

Lennox glanced over at him and then quickly back in the other direction. "Mom?"

Muffled talking.

"What? What? No, I don't want to come over. What's there to talk about?"

Lennox must be regretting having this conversation with him nearby, but he couldn't exactly get out of the car while driving. Just a few more miles to the chapel.

"No, Mom. I can't. Not tonight. I'm with ... a friend."

The voice on the other end got a bit louder, though not loud enough for him to make out exactly what was said.

"What? Why would you assume it's Ty?" Lennox shot him a guilty look he couldn't quite translate. "No. No, he doesn't want to come to dinner too."

Ty ripped the phone from Lennox's hand before she could stop him. "Ms. Malone? Hi. It's Ty. We can do dinner tonight. What time do you want me to bring Lennox over?"

"Ty!" Lennox hissed, and he quickly switched the phone to his other hand.

If a police officer were to catch him, he'd get a ticket for sure, but it was worth it.

"Ty!" Faye's voice was practically giddy. "We'd love that. How about six-thirty?"

"See you then." He passed the device back to Lennox despite the glare she shot his way.

She wrapped up the conversation as he pulled into the parking lot. "Yes. Evidently, I'll see you later."

He stepped back as she climbed out of the car. Her face was a thunderstorm of anger and frustration. Had he gone too far?

"Give me something to hit." Her words came out between clenched teeth.

He offered a bicep. She tilted her head, as if wondering if it was worthy to take her anger. Then, she pulled her fist back and punched him without holding back. He grimaced, but so did she.

"What's that?" She shook out her hand.

"What?" He rubbed the spot she'd walloped.

"There's muscle in there."

He couldn't help it. He bent in half, laughing so hard. She gave him another shove.

"I'm sorry." He gasped the words between the remaining chuckles. "You were just so aggravated at the fact I had muscles. It was funny."

She shook her head.

"I have a weight machine in my garage." He rolled his sleeve up to his shoulder and flexed. "I may be thin, but it's all toned."

Her eyes widened before she slid her sunglasses into place where he couldn't read her expression anymore. But for a minute, she'd been impressed. Perhaps he'd earned back a little of the whatever they had growing between them—though maybe not enough to make up for what he'd lost by agreeing to dinner tonight. Ah, well.

"Let's get to work. Since we have to leave in time to be at Mom's by six-thirty." Her voice was petulant, and he snickered again as he followed her around to a side of the building that hadn't been worked on yet. "You got more of it cleaned out." She pointed to the side under the stained-glass window.

"Yeah. I came over yesterday afternoon for a while. It wasn't nearly as much fun as Thursday when you worked with me."

She shook her head and pulled on the gloves he tossed her. "Right."

"I'm not sure about this side. He may have to put a ladder or something in it to work on the window."

"When did you say that was happening?" She yanked a handful of weeds from the bed.

"Late June. He had a couple of other projects to finish up first and wanted to make sure he could focus on this one with nothing else going on, considering how old the window is." He reached up and patted the bottom of the glass.

"I guess that makes sense. You said your family brought it over from Ireland?" She glanced up at it.

"Yeah. The building it was originally made for in Ireland was destroyed, but my ancestors somehow saved this beauty. When my great-great-whatever-uncle moved here after breaking off from the rest of the family—"

"The mobsters?"

"Good memory." He shot her a smile. "Yes. Anyway, he was a preacher and carried the window to Tennessee with him. After he arrived, he realized the need for a church out here where so many farmers lived. They all came together to work on this chapel. Near the end, he convinced them to put the window in, incorporating a piece of his old homeland into his new."

"Wow. And when did they build it?" She shot a look of awe toward the structure before them.

"1927." Ty gazed up at the beloved building. "So, around a hundred years ago. It's the oldest building out here except for the original cabin. But that was only good for cousin sleepovers growing up—when we didn't mind having to go out to the outhouse at night. The cabin was torn down a few years ago, so now I just focus on the chapel. For Sara Beth and Brian."

Lennox's lips twitched.

"The stones are all original, though I think it's been patched up a few times through the years. The little classroom wing came in the eighties. Along with the updated restrooms, which led to the plumbing problems."

He might not be able to see her eyes, but he could spy the grin on her beautiful mouth. Maybe he hadn't messed up too much earlier. He itched to ask her how she was dealing with her dad being in town, but a niggle of wisdom cautioned him against it. He'd probably learn more by listening at dinner tonight.

They worked in mostly silence for a while, only talking about what they were working on or inconsequential things like the weather or their jobs. After a couple of hours, they'd finished cleaning out most of the flower beds. All that was left was digging holes and putting in the new shrubs.

"Whew!" Lennox swiped a hand across her forehead. "Mom isn't going to want us to come tonight if we look and smell like this."

"Do I stink?" He pulled his shirt up to sniff it and wrinkled his nose. "Maybe a little, huh?"

"Just a bit." She laughed. "It might serve Mom right if we show up like this. That's what she gets for insisting on us coming without knowing what we were doing to begin with."

"True." He stuck his shovel in the dirt. "Or we could run over to my house and clean up."

"Um ..."

"It's just right there." He pointed through the trees to the white farmhouse on the edge of the property.

"That's *your* house?" She leaned over and shielded her eyes from the sun.

"For now." He dusted his hands off. "It was the house Great-great-grandpa Brendan built shortly after the chapel. It's stayed in the family all these years too. Gran Nancy lived in it up until a few years ago when she needed more care and moved to Park Haven Assisted Living. Since I'm the oldest grandchild, Gramps offered it to me. I've always loved that house."

"Why *for now*?" She frowned and turned her attention his way. "Won't you always be the oldest grandchild?"

"Yeah. Gran mentioned Easter weekend changing her mind since I won't be the first married."

"So?"

"Gran has been on a kick lately, pressuring us all to marry young and start our families." He shrugged. "Live up to our potential. As if marriage is the pinnacle of life."

"Wow." She shook her head. "I thought my family was messed up."

"Hey, now. We're not comparing the craziness of our families. Every family has its own personal brand of craziness, and it's not a competition. But still ... I think Gran has a bit of that mob attitude in her, whether she admits it or not. Anymore, she's pretty strict about having things done her way or not at all. Funny, since she's the one who married into the family."

She giggled, and the sound did his heart good. "Now I have this mental image of a little old woman in a pin-striped suit."

He laughed with her. "We better clean up so we can hit the road. Can't let your family down as much as I'm already letting mine down."

Her hand caught his arm as he turned. "I don't believe for a minute that you're letting your family down. And, if they think you are, then they're not looking at you closely enough."

A lump caught in his throat. *Wow.* She was going soft on him, and he wasn't sure what to do about it. But he wasn't about to wish it away. Instead, he pulled her into a hug, whether she wanted one or not.

"Ty?" Her voice was muffled in his shoulder.

"Hm?"

"You really do stink." She pushed him back with a smirk. "Let's go."

"Okay. Sorry. Maybe I'll snag another hug again later after I've washed some of this off." He wiggled his eyebrows at her and then helped her grab her bag. Had he cleaned up his mess from breakfast this morning? Too late now. Time to let her see a little more of his private life. Maybe it would soften her up even more?

Would she like the antique furniture mixed with modern design he used in his decorating style? The hardwood floors? The old farmhouse-style sink in the kitchen? Why did it matter so much if she did?

Because she'd worked her way into his heart, and now he couldn't picture anyone else in that spot. He just had to hope against hope she really was softening toward him. Because if she wasn't, his life could end up very lonely.

A thought best saved for later. Now, he needed to scrub off some of the sweat so he could meet her mom again—this time with less alcohol involved, he hoped. For his sake and for Lennox's. Either way, he'd support her through it as much as she allowed.

Please, God, let her let me in.

Chapter Twenty-One

Walking into Ty's house was like opening a door into his brain. While the history had been preserved in the wood floors and beautiful moldings around the ceilings, he had brought the modern world in too.

A large painting took up the wall over the fireplace, and on looking closer, she could see it was of the chapel, the sunlight streaming down on it as if the artist considered it a blessing of God. A few knickknacks were arranged around books in the built-in bookshelves. Two comfy-looking striped chairs, the colors perfect to complement her own sofa, stood waiting for people to curl up and spend a quiet evening together.

Where had that come from? Lennox hadn't meant to, but she'd pictured herself and Ty as those people. That was new. She'd never been able to imagine herself in a relationship that close before.

"So, your options are the bathroom down here or a bedroom upstairs." Ty's voice pulled her back to reality. "If you want to have water to remove some of the filth, the bathroom might be a better option."

"Whatever's easiest." She was almost afraid to go much farther into this home lest she have even crazier ideas.

"Okay." He leaned into a small powder room off the hallway and flipped the light on. "Your changing room awaits, my lady."

"Thanks."

"Sure. I'm going to hop upstairs and grab a clean shirt, at least. If you get done first, make yourself at home."

That's what she was afraid of. She edged past him and shut the door for a little privacy with her out-of-control thoughts. One thing was for sure, she needed to get them under control before they got to her mom's house. No way did her mom need more fodder for pushing a relationship that didn't exist.

The bathroom had a pedestal sink Lennox guessed was original to the house. Small wire baskets held extra toilet paper, washcloths, and other things one might need in a neat arrangement over the toilet. A sign on the other wall read, "Hope everything comes out okay," in a nice cursive font. That might need to go.

And there she went again, imagining herself living in this house. She splashed some water on her face, hoping to bring her brain back into working order. A quick rummage in her bag turned up a shirt that wasn't as filthy and a pair of jeans. That would work. A comb through her hair and a quick spray of her floral perfume, she was good enough for dinner at Mom's.

Lennox opened the door and almost walked into Ty. He caught her elbow with the hand that didn't hold a travel mug. His hair was wet and combed back neatly. Had he washed it in the time she'd taken to freshen up? How long had she been in there?

She pressed a fist to her heart, willing it to slow back down. It was going crazy from being startled. Nothing else. Because there couldn't be anything else.

"Thought you might need a pick-me-up." He held the mug out.

She took a sniff. "Green tea?"

"You intrigued me with all those flavors you listed. I figured it wouldn't hurt me to try some." He gave a shrug.

"Thank you." She breathed in the sharp scent, letting the tea calm some of her frazzled nerves.

"Sure." He nodded to her bag. "You all set? Anything else you need before we head out? I don't promise to have everything a girl might need, but I like to think I have the necessities."

"I had everything I needed. Thanks." She took a sip of her tea and found it steeped to perfection. "Let's get this over with."

"Oh, come on. It's not going to be that bad, is it?" His hand rested at the small of her back as he escorted her out. There was something so right about the gentle pressure, the heat of his fingers radiating through her shirt. Yet, she didn't want it to be the new normal in her life. She hadn't changed. She didn't believe in love. She'd probably just had too much sunshine this afternoon.

"Remember how to get there?" She buckled as he started his engine.

"Yes, ma'am." He gave her a wink. "Let's go prove to your mom we're friends."

"And nothing more."

"What?" He clutched a hand to his chest as if wounded. "But I wanted to be *best* friends."

"You know what I meant."

"I do." His words almost sounded sad, but she couldn't let it affect her. Friendship was all she could offer, and it was more than she'd expected when they first met.

George's truck was parked next to her mom's trailer when they pulled in. *Great.* Just what she needed tonight. Another Bible-banger to witness as she spoke with her mom about the dad who left them a dozen years before. And after what Jane told Lennox about George on Easter, she wasn't sure she wanted him to meet Ty, either. One more worry to add to her list.

"It won't be as bad as you think it will." Ty broke into her musings. She turned his way, and he added, "You look like you're about to head into a firing squad."

"Not necessarily that bad, but I have a feeling I won't like the talk around the dinner table." She pressed a hand to her stomach.

The front door opened, and Mom waved. No turning back now. She'd been seen. Ty had come around and opened her door when her attention was diverted, and she had no choice but to take his hand and be helped out. He squeezed her fingers before letting go and following her up the stairs.

"Such a gentleman." Mom greeted Ty before she even acknowledged Lennox. "Come on in here. I've been wanting to get to know you better."

"Has Lennox not brought friends over for dinner before?" Ty gave his best smile, and Lennox couldn't decide if she wanted to bless him for using the term *friends* or throttle him for all the charm he poured on.

"Not often." Her mom wove her arm through Ty's and led him into the kitchen. "But we're just so glad you're here."

"I'm glad to be here too. I'm looking forward to getting to know Lennox better through her family." Ty really was going too far this time.

"Come on in and meet George." Her mom didn't even look back to see if Lennox followed. Wasn't the point of this dinner to discuss Dad being back in town? The way her mom acted, you'd think it was an engagement party.

"George?" Ty offered his hand as the older gentleman stood from the table. "How are you, man?"

"Wait." Lennox gawked at their warm man-hug. "You two know each other?"

"We worship with the same congregation." George gave her a smile and reached over to squeeze her shoulder. "Ty also helped me with some work I had done on my house last year."

"Everything still holding up?" Ty asked. How was he so comfortable in this situation?

"Perfectly. Your men did great work."

"Sit, sit." Her mom fluttered around the table, making sure

Ty and Lennox were seated next to each other. "We don't want the food to get cold."

Ty's hand somehow found hers under the table and gave her fingers a squeeze. "Sorry we're later than we promised. When we got done, we needed to clean up a bit."

"No worries." Her mom waved the excuse away. "After George offers the blessing, you'll have to tell us what you were doing." Her eyes gleamed as if her mind were conjuring ideas Lennox would never approve of.

Ty captured her hand in his while George's prayer wafted over them.

"Lord, we thank you that you've blessed us with this time together. Give our words grace and love so we can have a good conversation. Give us peace about the situation. And we thank you for this feast in front of us. In Jesus' name, Amen."

"Amen." Ty gave her one more press and then released her hand to accept a bowl of peas from her mother.

"So, what were you up to this afternoon?" George accepted a pork chop and then passed the platter to his right.

"We've been doing some work out at the old Park Haven chapel. It's fallen into disrepair through the years, and we're trying to bring it back to life for Sara Beth and Brian's wedding." Ty spoke easily, as if he'd known these people for years instead of moments. Of course, that might be true in the case of George. How did she not foresee this happening?

"I didn't know you knew about construction, Len." Her mom finally acknowledged her.

"I don't, actually." Lennox plopped a spoonful of potatoes on her plate with more gusto than necessary. "I was helping him with the flower beds. That's how I ran into Dad the other day. He was at the nursery the same time we were."

"Oh?" Her mom's face gave nothing away, but did her shoulders tighten? "Did he say what he was doing in town?"

"No. I didn't really give him a chance. He started to say something about how he'd missed Macy and me every day since leaving." Just thinking about it brought the ire up into Lennox's throat again. The audacity of her father thinking she'd believe such a falsehood was astounding. "I called him a liar and then, left."

Her mom exchanged a look with George that Lennox couldn't interpret. What was going on? And why wasn't her mom just as angry?

Lennox tossed her fork aside, the little bit of appetite she'd had all but gone now. "Did you know he was in town?"

"No!" Her mom cut her hands through the air. "Not until you called. I've just been ... working through ... some of the stuff having to do with your dad, so I guess I've already moved past a lot of the anger and hatred I had for so long."

Lennox frowned. "What?"

"Faye agreed to go with me to some counseling sessions offered by the church." George reached over and rubbed her mom's back. "She's been going back to the beginning, looking at things with a clearer head, trying to get more control over her life. She hasn't had a drink in over a week now."

Her mom, the woman who'd spent the last twelve years blaming everything on her dad, the one who turned to men and alcohol to solve her issues, suddenly didn't need any of it? Had the church brainwashed her? How could she forgive him? He hadn't even apologized.

"So, if you saw Dad tomorrow, you'd be okay? Just like that? Everything he did or didn't do is just water under the bridge?" Lennox's heart rate accelerated and tears burned her eyes. "Because I can't do that. I can't forget so easily."

"Lennox." Her mom started to rise, but Lennox shook her head.

"No, Mom. No. I don't understand. I'm not even sure I want to. He. Left. Us. Didn't even check in. Didn't remember our birthdays. Or send money to help with anything. How is that okay?" Lennox pushed back and held her hands fisted next to her legs. "It's not okay."

"But honey. You need to know something." Her mom visibly swallowed and lowered her head. Was she guilty? "He did try to keep in contact the first couple of years. I ... I sent everything back to him unopened."

Lennox's heart clenched tighter. *What?* Her father had tried to stay in contact, and Mom hadn't let him?

Ty reached over and put a hand on her shoulder, but she jerked away. This was worse than she'd expected. She stood and headed out to the deck. She needed air. She needed to be away from the deception. Away from the woman who'd made her life miserable all through high school and now admitted it could've been a little bit better.

Her whole world was a lie. All these years, she'd believed the stories her mom told them. She'd gone along with the anger and blamed everything on her dad leaving. Now, she wasn't sure what to believe.

Not five minutes after she'd stepped out, the door opened and shut behind her.

"I don't want to talk about it, Ty."

"Well, I'm not Ty." George's easy voice drifted to her from the door. "Just someone else who's worried about you. Ty's actually trying to comfort Faye."

"That seems a bit backward." Lennox rubbed her forehead. "Her boyfriend out here with me and my ... friend in there with her."

"Friend, huh?" George's eyes practically twinkled as the smile wrinkles around them crinkled. "Okay. We'll go with that for now."

"Not you too."

He held up his hands in surrender. "Okay. No more talk about Ty. I'm more interested in making sure you're okay."

"How can I be okay with any of this? None of it is the way it's supposed to be." Lennox flopped her fists against her thighs. "Supposedly, marriage lasts forever, and no one should leave, but my parents proved that wrong. Supposedly, a mom should look out for her children's best interests. Instead, mine hid the fact that my dad reached out after he left. She fed my belief that everything wrong with our lives all this time was his fault. I don't know what to think anymore."

George nodded and came over to lean against the railing with her. "It's a lot."

"That's all you've got?" Lennox shot him a look that was probably more disdainful than it should be.

"Well, I've learned that sometimes, even if you think you should say something, it's better to wait until the person is ready to hear it." George's words were soft, not angry nor disapproving. Just letting her know he wanted her to have however long she needed to come to grips with all the changes that had happened in her life this week.

"Does Macy know?"

"Faye called her earlier. I think she reacted a lot like you did. But she's even less ready to hear some of this than you." George scratched his mustache. "She was fed the lies three years longer than you. You had college and started your own life. Macy doesn't have the same kind of support system as you do with your friend Sara Beth and your *friend* Ty."

"Ready to hear what, George?" Lennox shoved her hands in her pockets to keep from punching something. "To hear that my mom has forgiven a man who hasn't even asked for forgiveness?"

"Your mom and I have been studying for about six weeks now. And while I can see her growing in her knowledge of God and what He expects from His people, even I was amazed at her willingness to do that." George stared up into the sky—not that much was up there to see besides a few clouds.

"Why would she do that? What's in it for her?"

"Peace."

The word was powerful. Peace was something Lennox hadn't had much of lately. Had she *ever* had it? Maybe as a very young girl. Before everything fell apart.

"How can she do that? Surely your God, who knows

everything, wouldn't expect her to forgive all she's been through." Lennox pulled her hands free again and crossed her arms over her chest.

"On the contrary—it's exactly what God expects."

"He's so heartless?"

"No." George shook his head. "He's so loving."

"That doesn't even make sense."

George was quiet for a few moments, as if trying to find the right words. Finally, he turned to her and gave a little nod. "We're all supposed to be striving to be more and more like God. To that end, we're supposed to follow His example."

"And you're telling me He's forgiven people who didn't ask for it?" Lennox thought about what Ty said on Thursday about Jesus being neglected, ridiculed, and even murdered by those who were supposed to love Him. But surely, He wouldn't have forgiven them, would he?

"Well, He forgives me. And you, if you accept it."

"Me? What have I done?" Lennox wasn't a bad person.

"Every time we sin, we're basically telling Jesus that we don't care that He died for us. That we don't need his sacrifice. That we don't want His grace or mercy or love." George bobbled his head. "If that doesn't require forgiveness, I don't know what does."

Movement on the other side of the door caught Lennox's attention. Ty stood there, worry written across his face. George nodded and gave her shoulder a pat.

"Think about it." He walked back in, said something to Ty, and then disappeared around the corner, probably to find her mom.

"You okay?" Ty joined her at the railing.

"Should I be?"

"No."

"Good, because I'm not."

He nodded and leaned on his elbows. "You want to leave?"

"I think so. I can't do polite conversation anymore tonight. Too much to process."

"Okay. I'll go let your mom know and meet you at the car." He didn't even question her or push her to wait. What kind of man was he? She was learning, but wasn't sure she completely believed it.

Lennox walked around the double-wide and got to Ty's car just as he came out. He quickly opened her door and helped her in before going around to his side. He headed out of the trailer park and back toward Twisted Barre.

"I could drop you at home if you'd rather not drive." His words were soft and compassionate.

"I'm okay to drive, Ty. But thanks."

"Right." He stilled her before she could get out, ran around, and opened her door. "Please take care of yourself."

"I will." She nodded. Why was his gentle squeeze at her elbow, his waiting until she got her stuff situated in her car, his offer to drive her around so moving? Why did it make her want to cuddle up into his arms and cry until all the tears were gone? When had she ever let herself be so vulnerable? Not in years.

"I better get home."

"Sure." Still, he stood there. "I'm praying for you."

She swallowed an unwanted lump in her throat. "I figured."

He chuckled. "Good night, Lennox."

Ten minutes later, she let herself into her apartment. She'd always been comfortable here, but tonight, part of her wished to be back at a house built in the early 1900s, sitting in a chair in front of the fireplace, letting a man with warm brown eyes distract her from everything in her head. Thoughts of forgiveness and love and a God bigger than it all.

But how could she forgive? How could she accept that she needed forgiveness, too, when she didn't feel like she'd done anything wrong? How could she regain some of the distance that had closed between her and Ty this week? She needed distance, or her heart might decide her brain was wrong and love was real—a possibility she'd never considered before.

Chapter Twenty-Two

Two weeks.

Ty hadn't seen Lennox in fourteen days, and he couldn't wait any longer. He'd tried to give her space. Tried to give her room to think and figure out everything happening in her life. But it had taken everything in him to even let her drive herself home that night. He'd longed to wrap her in his arms and find a way to make it all okay. Deep down, he was aware he wasn't the one who could fix all her problems, but still ... he yearned to do something more than the prayers he sent up daily. Multiple times a day.

So, today being a Saturday, he changed into athletic clothes and headed down to Twisted Barre—fifteen minutes early—to try out a certain kickboxing class again. Any excuse to see the instructor. Brian had confirmed this part of her schedule hadn't changed.

Lennox studied her phone as she walked in, probably pulling up the music for this session. She didn't even notice Ty in the corner as she plugged in the device, adjusted something, and then turned. She froze, her gaze colliding with his. He barely controlled the full-out belly laugh wanting to escape—her expression was utterly astounded.

"Good morning." He leaned over to stretch out his calves, remembering how much they hurt after the last time he did this class.

"Good morning." She started her own stretches, but continued shooting glances his way.

"Hey, man." Brian clapped him on the shoulder as he took his normal spot.

Sara Beth wrapped him in a hug. "I'm so glad you're here this morning. I need to talk to you about my bouquets and boutonnieres. I thought I knew what I was doing, but now I'm panicking. And we're just under three months out."

He returned her side squeeze. "You know I'm glad to help."

"I love all the different flowers you helped Lennox pick." Sara Beth moved from him to her friend and hugged her too.

The girls spoke quietly for a few moments, Lennox frowning and shaking her head, as if it was a topic she didn't want to discuss right then. Considering everything that had happened in Lennox's life in the last month, Ty could only imagine. He quickly averted his eyes when she glanced his way, focusing on making sure his shoes were tied tightly.

Sara Beth pressed once more, but Lennox motioned to her watch. He figured it was probably an excuse to stop the conversation more than a worry about being late. She turned on the music as a slightly pouty Sara Beth took her place.

The high-energy routine had him breathing hard and sweating in no time. He didn't mind, though. Because even if Lennox didn't say anything beyond the greeting she'd given him earlier, at least he'd seen her. He hadn't expected her to be a puddle of emotions or skin and bones or anything drastic like that. But it was still reassuring to see her carrying on with her normal life—at least on the outside. No signs of extra dark circles under her eyes. No lines of fatigue or worry. Not right now, anyway.

He followed her lead, punching and kicking his way through the forty-five minutes. The cool-down part at the end was nice, but almost too short. His heart still raced as the music completed and everyone gathered their things. Although that could also be because he hoped to catch her and talk for a few minutes.

Sara Beth beat him to it. "Len, I want your input on flowers too. Think you could spare an evening sometime soon?"

Ty wrapped his towel around his neck and observed from where he stood, almost afraid if he moved closer, he might spook her.

"Maybe." Lennox gave a shrug and noncommittal attitude, although her eyes darted his way before returning to her friend. "I'm not great with things like arranging flowers, though. You might be better off sticking with Ty."

"But I want you to be part of it too. Even if all you do is give your approval." Sara Beth squeezed Lennox's arm. "Please think about it?"

"I'll think about it." Lennox gathered her phone and water bottle.

Sara Beth turned her Southern wiles on Ty. "You've got to help me convince her."

Ty shook his head. "No. You know better than I do that Lennox won't do anything she doesn't want to. Give her time to think about it. We don't need to finish those arrangements yet. There's plenty of time."

"What good is it to have you as our best man if you won't help me get the maid of honor involved?" She smirked. "Let me know, will you?" She grabbed Brian's arm and walked out of the room, leaving the two of them as the last ones.

"I wasn't expecting you today." Lennox avoided his gaze.

"I wanted to see you." He swallowed. "I missed you." Crazy as it sounded, considering they'd only seen each other a grand total of about seven times. Still, those encounters had been enough to hook him.

She huffed. "Oh, please. Missed me? You barely know me."

"I might know more than you think."

She glanced away, but emotions flickered across her beautiful face as if she remembered exactly how much he did know, having seen her in several awkward situations.

"I know you love roses and sunshine and green tea."

A soft chuckle came out, and she glanced his way. "What girl doesn't love roses?"

"Some girls prefer sunflowers or daisies or even lilies." He cocked his head to the side. "You work hard and don't give yourself enough credit. You don't want to love your family, but you do. You detest that I'm here right now, but are also secretly glad."

"Good grief." She flicked her towel at him and started walking toward the exit. "You don't know me at all, do you?" Yet, something in her voice said he might have been closer to right than wrong.

"So, help me get to know you better."

"I told you. I don't want love. I don't want a relationship." She held up a hand, as if knowing he was about to protest. "Don't push me on this."

"What happened to friendship?" He folded his arms across his chest.

Another girl poked her head in the door. "You about done in here, Lennox? I have a class in ten minutes."

"Yep. We're leaving now." Lennox walked through the doorway and headed toward the back of the building.

He followed, whether he was supposed to or not. "You didn't answer my question."

"You shouldn't be back here." She shot him a dirty look before stepping into what must be her office.

He let out a slow whistle as he took in the stacks of paper and the messy desk. "You make my office space look good."

"I've had a few things on my mind." She ran a hand through her hair, leaving several pieces in the front going every which way.

"I know." He remained in the doorway. "Lennox, seriously. Are you okay?"

She lowered herself into her chair, still more graceful than he could ever hope to be. She moved a few stacks, picked up a couple of pencils and dropped them in a cup, and threw away some trash. He came in and perched on the edge of the sofa on the other side of her desk.

"The gardens look good around the chapel." Maybe a change in subject would help. "Thanks again for helping with that. I might still be working on it without your assistance."

"Oh, please." She rolled her eyes. "We both know my help wasn't that much. I only did what you told me to."

"But everything you did, I didn't have to." He shot her his favorite grin, the one that usually made girls blush.

"Everything else on schedule out there?" She twisted a paper clip into a shape that would never hold anything together.

"Going great. Paint is going up this week. The carpet is being laid next week. And then the window guy comes the week after that."

She nodded, but didn't seem very into their conversation.

Time to test her attention. "Since the painters were there anyway, I asked them to make all the pews sky blue. I thought it would look good with the greens and yellows in the window."

"Mm-hmm."

"And maybe we could talk Sara Beth into hanging fake monkeys from the rafters."

"Probably."

Time to shock her back to her senses. "Lennox, do I need to kiss you again?"

Her head jerked up, her eyes wide. "What?"

"There you are." He leaned forward. "Have you heard a single word I've said?"

"Something about everything going well in the chapel." She shrugged. "You made it very clear you didn't need my help to do anything out there. Besides pulling weeds. And like you told Sara Beth, we've still got plenty of time before the wedding."

He leaned back again, folding his arms back across his chest. What was he going to do with her? The temptation to carry out his threat of a moment before was strong, but she wasn't ready. He sighed.

Her eyes met his fully for the first time that day. "I'm disappointing you." She frowned. "I seem to be doing that a lot lately with different people."

"Why do you say that?"

"Mom's been on me to talk to my dad. George hasn't said anything else since that night two weeks ago, but I can see it in his face. He looks at me like he's expecting more. Earlier, Sara Beth was put out with me for not just going along with her plans even though she knows about my dad being back. Macy thinks I need to be more on her side—which is the opposite of Mom." She blinked a few times. "And now, you."

"I'm more worried, not disappointed." He shifted again. "I want to be able to help, but don't know how."

"I don't think you can." She threw the now mutilated paper clip in the trash. "Unless you've got something to distract me from it all."

His heart leaped. Had she really just suggested them spending more time together? As much as he loved that idea, if she simply let herself be distracted from the situation, she'd never work up to facing and handling it. What to say ...

"I'm afraid I don't have anything right away. Nothing more than maybe you going to dinner with me tonight." Her wrinkled nose didn't surprise him. Okay. Moving on. "But you're more than welcome to come out in a few weeks when the guy works on the window. It might be fun to see how he fixes the crack."

She nodded. "It might. It's a gorgeous window." She pulled her planner over. "What day?"

He tapped the calendar app on his phone and tried not to be disappointed when he realized it was a day she usually worked mornings. "Wednesday after next, around ten."

"When you say *around ten*, does that mean he's like you and shows up half an hour late?" She shot him the first smile he'd seen on her face in far too long.

He waggled a finger in her direction. "I would like to point out, for the record, that I was fifteen minutes early this morning."

"Okay, okay. Truce." She tapped a pencil against her planner. "I might be able to switch up my schedule. I'll talk to Hattie and Presley and see what they think. We try to be a little more flexible during summer. And we've been training a girl to be able to sub for some of our classes."

"Sounds good." And it did. Except it meant he probably wouldn't see her for another week and a half unless he came to her class again next Saturday. He might. Because ten days sounded like forever. "So, no to dinner tonight?"

"Don't press your luck."

He stood and gathered his stuff again. "Right. I guess I'll see you another time, then."

"Thanks, Ty." She moved over to stand by him as he lingered in the doorway. "I know I'm a mess right now. Who am I kidding? I'm a mess most of the time."

"But a beautiful one." He pressed a kiss to her forehead before he could stop himself. "Please let me know if you need anything between now and then."

Before she could utter a protest or complaint, he headed down the hallway toward the front door. The meeting hadn't gone quite as well as it could have, but it also hadn't gone as badly as he'd braced himself for. Next time, he'd work on her for Sara Beth too. Any excuse to see her more was a good one. Yep. He was completely addicted.

Chapter Twenty-Three

"I told you I could drive myself." Lennox could not believe the nerve of Ty showing up to pick her up this morning. "What's the point of having a car if you never let me use it?"

"If we take separate cars, we'll waste time." He twirled his keys around his finger.

"What on earth does that even mean?"

"It means, my dear, that I'm driving you because I like your company. And this gives me at least an hour longer in your presence than I'd get if you drove yourself." He gently clasped her elbow and steered her toward his convertible.

She planted her feet. "I ought to drive myself anyway. You're obviously reading too much into this ..." She pointed her finger between herself and him "... whatever we have."

"Friendship?" He shot her that annoying little half-grin and tugged just enough for her to take a step. "I believe we said we're friends, did we not? And friends spend time together."

"*Ugh.*" She tossed her purse into the vehicle and slid into the low seat. "You're so frustrating."

"I'll add it to the list."

"What list?"

"Incorrigible, annoying, frustrating. I can't remember. Have you used any other terms of endearment for me or just those?" He started the ignition and pulled out in one smooth motion.

"Well, we know we can't add humble." She took a deep breath. In truth, she'd been looking forward to this morning. While she was loath to admit Ty was right about anything, the chapel grew on her the more she visited it. There was something about sitting in a building over a hundred years old, surrounded by history and beauty. It calmed her. But she didn't like not having the option of leaving whenever she wanted to.

"How long can you stay this morning?" His question made her wonder if he could read her thoughts.

"I took the whole day off. The girls insisted—I haven't taken a vacation day since the beginning of the year."

"And no dinner with your mom scheduled for tonight?" He smirked, obviously teasing.

"No. She hasn't discovered I'm with you today, so no forced dinner with my family." She rolled her eyes. "To listen to her, you'd think you were the be-all-end-all of the modern gentleman and that we should get married the same day as Sara Beth and Brian."

"Maybe you should."

"Marry you?" She scooted a little farther from him, even though the idea wasn't quite as repulsive as it had been two months earlier.

"Listen to your mother." He waggled his finger in her direction. "Isn't the old saying *mother knows best*?"

"Not this time, thank you very much."

"You don't think I'm the be-all-end-all?" He pouted his lips in such a ridiculous expression that a giggle escaped before she could hold it in.

"Like I said, you're not humble."

His tires crunched over the gravel of the parking lot, and he pulled as close to the front of the building as he could. Her roses were in full bloom. And why was she mentally referring to them as hers? Once the wedding was over, she'd probably never come out here again.

She walked over and breathed in their heavy aroma, closing her eyes. Between the sunshine beating down on her back and the songs of birds and cicadas, everything that had happened over the last few weeks lifted from her shoulders for a moment. Ty's hand rested on her arm, and she opened her eyes.

"Okay?" His brown eyes searched hers.

"Just smelling the roses and enjoying the peace of this space."

He smiled. "I understand. Want to see the inside?"

She nodded and followed him into the cool interior. The carpet along the aisles changed the whole look of the room, quieting their steps as they walked toward the front. She reached out and touched the end of one of the recently polished pews. Gone were the stains and mold and odor. Instead, everything appeared clean and fresh. Everything but that crack in the pane of stained glass.

"Anyone home?" A gruff voice called from behind them.

"Here," Ty answered and left her side to meet the man who must be here to work on the window.

Lennox gave a gentle shove to one of the pews, but it didn't budge at all. She tried twice more, and when she got the same results, she lowered herself onto the smooth wood. Hadn't Ty mentioned painting these? Surely, he wouldn't do that. It would ruin the vintage vibe of the place.

"Just let me know what you need. Here's my main concern." Ty pointed to the broken glass. "But I want you to look the whole thing over, make sure the cames are tight enough, and that there aren't any other problems I don't know about. This window is very old and pretty important to my family."

"Sure thing." The gentleman had a couple of teenagers with him, possibly his grandsons. He set up his ladder and climbed up to examine the structure.

Ty slid onto the bench beside her, his arm going around her shoulders. She glanced his way, but didn't move away from his touch. Fortunately, the glazier didn't seem to mind having an audience, although one of the teenagers kept looking her way and blushing.

"Tell me about the window again." Lennox broke the silence that had fallen between them.

"It was made in the 1800s, in Ireland for a little church where my family was from." Ty's voice almost took on an Irish lilt as he talked. "The building was destroyed, but somehow the window survived. When my family decided to come to America, my great-great-great-uncle Patrick Dunne packed the glass up in quilts and anything else he could find to cushion it and brought it with them.

"It stayed in storage for a long while, as the family established themselves in Illinois. But as quite a few members became involved in mob activity, Patrick was ostracized. He was too ... Christian, for lack of a better term. The gangster side of the family basically disowned him. He moved here to Tennessee to get away from all of that, and he brought the family window with him, still not knowing what he'd do with it."

"And the mobster members of your family simply let him take it?" She was intrigued more than she wanted to admit.

"I don't think they cared about it like he did." Ty slumped down a little farther in the pew, as if getting comfortable for a long tale. "Anyway, Patrick settled here and discovered a need for a church. It took him several years, but he began services, meeting in the schoolhouse for a while, and finally gathered enough money and supplies to start building."

"He built this?" She frowned. "By himself?"

"Quite a bit of it." He chuckled. "The locals helped when they could. And then he had more help. That's where my great-great-grandfather Brendan comes in. He left mob life after his teens. When his brother caused trouble that got him killed, Brendan escaped down here to Uncle Patrick to lay low. He married his girl Evangeline and brought her with him. They arrived in time to help install the window. And then, they were the first couple to have a wedding here."

"Really?" Lennox moved her attention back and forth between him and the work being done. "Wait. If they were already married, why did they need a wedding?"

Before Ty could answer, the worker let out a soft curse and glanced over at them. "You're not going to like this."

Ty jumped to his feet, and Lennox followed, curious what was wrong.

"See this?" The man pointed to the casing. "The wood's rotten clear through in several spots. I'm going to have to take the whole thing out and repair it before I do anything else. Otherwise, you're going to run into more problems than just this little crack. If the wood gets any weaker, it could drop the whole thing and shatter it into a million pieces."

Lennox's breath caught in her throat. That would be a true tragedy. She couldn't even imagine this place without the sparkling Celtic cross at the front.

"How can we help?" Ty squeezed her arm as if he understood she needed the reassurance. Surely, he was just as disheartened as she was, if not more. After all, this window was part of his family history.

"When I get ready, I'll have my boys on that side of the window and get you to help me on this side. Between all five of us and my equipment, it shouldn't be a problem. But we'll have to put a tarp over this hole. I'll take the whole piece back to my shop, where I have my supplies more readily available, and let you know when I can get it back in place. Shouldn't take more than a week or two."

Ty nodded. Lennox held her breath as the man used various tools to ease the casing away from the walls. Every time the ancient wood splintered or cracked, she had to control herself to keep from gasping. Her heart raced as the glazier brought in several pads to brace the glass and hooked up some make-shift pulleys to help bear the weight. As they eased the window down into their arms, she couldn't help but think it was heavier due to the history embedded in it.

After the contractor loaded up the fragile piece of antiquity, he tacked the black tarp into place on the outside of the chapel and drove off. The interior was dark and dreary without the sunlight streaming in through all the colors—the windows along the side of the building were not as vibrant. Lennox rubbed her hands up and down her arms as she stared at the empty space.

"Hey, come look at this." Ty was up front, staring down into the space in the wall where the window had been.

"What did you find?" Lennox jumped the stairs in two steps and lifted to her tiptoes to see what he was examining.

"Does it look like there's something down there?" He pulled out his cell phone and used the flashlight feature to illuminate the crack.

"Yes." She tried to reach, but it was about a foot too far. "Give me a boost."

"Don't have to ask me twice." He wiggled his eyebrows.

She swatted him, but accepted his hand and bent knee to step onto. From that angle, her arm could reach down farther. Her fingers brushed cardboard, slipped off, and then caught hold of just enough. She tugged it free and lifted it out.

"What do you think is in here?"

"Let's find out."

The tape practically disintegrated in their hands as they pulled it from the top. Inside was a veritable treasure trove. Ty lifted out a watch and some sort of charm bracelet, then two more pieces of jewelry.

She ran a finger over the filigree on the front of the smaller gold round piece. The larger one was more of a silver color, although it had tarnished some through the years. Ty pressed a switch and opened the silver circle to show a timepiece.

"Hey, look. There's one more thing." A piece of folded paper, yellowed with age, was tucked in the bottom of the box. He skimmed the words and then looked at her, his eyes slightly wider.

"This is from Gramps and Gran back in 1970. Right before they got married."

"What does it say?"

He sank down on the top step and ran a finger down the words. "It tells the story of the pieces. The Army watch was Gramps's. But his time in the Army wasn't a good one, and he wanted to leave the terror behind him. The bracelet was Gran Nancy's—well, actually, it was her mom's. But also had bad memories attached to it."

Lennox waited while he skimmed more of the letter.

"The pocket watch was Great-Great-Grandpa Brendan's. Something his dad gave him to remind him to stay true to his family—though seems he meant it to tie Brendan to the mob. Brendan hid it in the window casing when he came down here as a symbol of him leaving that behind."

"If the watch belongs to him, do you think this might be hers? What did you say her name was? Angela?" Lennox worked at the small clasp on the locket.

"Evangeline." Ty leaned closer as the metal released and showed a faded picture of a family. From the styles of clothes, it must have been taken around the 1920s.

"Do you think that's her?" Lennox tapped the young girl in the photo.

"I'd say it's a fair chance." Ty stood and tugged her up with him. "Come on. Let's go check something."

"What?"

He pushed open a door into a room packed with furniture and junk. She followed him into the musty interior, pinching her nose against a sneeze as he stirred up dust.

"What is this place?"

"For a few years, it was a classroom, but over the past decade or so, it's turned into more of a storage wasteland." He moved a few boxes and pushed through several stacks of what appeared to be Sunday school material before letting out a triumphant yell, "Here."

He settled an old book on top of a stack of chairs and brushed off the layer of filth.

"And this is?" She leaned over to see the words written on the pages he turned to.

"A register of all the marriages that started in this chapel." He ran his fingers over the writing as if it were as holy as the Bible. "And, as far as we've been able to research, none of the marriages has failed. No divorces."

She frowned up at him in shock. "There's no way you could know that. This goes back a hundred years."

"It does. Here's the listing for Brendan and Evangeline Dunne." He tapped the very top line. "But you've got to remember that my family has been in charge of the upkeep of this place the whole time. And Park Haven is a small town. It's not hard to keep track of the couples in a community where gossip travels faster than my car."

"Obviously, my parents' names won't be on this list." She resented the bitterness in her voice.

"Were they married in Park Haven?" He ran a hand over her hair.

"No. Mom didn't move us here until ninth grade, remember?"

He didn't move his hand, and she looked into his eyes. So much was there. Some of the things she sensed were easier to accept than others. He cared about her. But she didn't want to accept it. She couldn't. Even if she might be led to believe in love, she couldn't be part of it. It didn't work. Not in her life.

The longer he kept his gaze on her, the longer she wondered if he might want to kiss her again. This time it wouldn't catch her off guard. But she also didn't want it any more than the last time. She had nothing to offer in return. She moved back and broke the trance that had settled over them.

"So, why would they have hidden their watch and locket in the walls of the chapel? You said they helped build it, right?" She fingered the metal pieces once more.

"They did. I know they left Illinois in a hurry. And basically, were cut off from their families at the same time. If we're to believe the letter, this was the way they symbolized giving up their pasts and moving ahead with their new future together."

"You probably like to watch rom-coms, don't you?" She flipped him a raised eyebrow.

"Better believe it." There went that half-grin again.

He might believe in romance and love and marriages that lasted, but she couldn't wrap her mind around it. In her history, those things simply didn't exist. Though, the longer she spent with Ty Dunne, the more she found she wished she could believe in them too. Because they made for a much better story than the one she'd lived up to now.

Chapter Twenty-Four

He'd done it. He'd talked her into helping Sara Beth arrange her flowers. Sure, it took him a few weeks longer than he'd hoped, but it was still the first half of July ... barely.

"Why am I here again?" Lennox held up two different sizes of artificial sunflowers and looked back and forth between them.

"Moral support." Sara Beth passed her a tin of cookies. "Here. Fortify."

Ty snitched a treat before Lennox could even get her hands into the container. "Thanks. I needed this." He bit off half of it in one bite.

"Pig," Lennox muttered.

"Oink." He shot her a wink. "Hand me the smaller one."

"Smaller cookie?"

"Flower." He pointed to her hands. She passed over the one to her left. His fingers deftly added a few red and orange leaves and another few sprigs of filler before wrapping it with the sticky green floral tape. He added it to the pile of finished boutonnieres and corsages. "How many more do we need?"

Lennox leaned forward at the same time as he did, and their heads bonked. She jerked back and rubbed the spot, scowling at him. He offered a placating smile, then reached over to pull her head down and plopped a kiss where she'd been bumped. The fruity smell of her shampoo filled his nostrils, and he breathed in deeply before letting her go again.

Sara Beth smirked as she glanced between the two of them. "Did I have the number on the list?"

"Yes." Ty held up a finger. "Hang on." Once more, he leaned forward and scanned through the detailed sheet on the floor between him and Lennox. "Okay. Looks like one more boutonniere and two more corsages. We're getting there."

"Sure. All we have left are all the bouquets and decorations for the wedding itself. No big deal." Lennox's voice was full of uncertainty—something Ty hadn't detected in it much before. Was she really that concerned about her lack of flower-arranging skills?

"Oh, Lennox. Look at this. What do you think about wearing a crown of flowers?" Sara Beth held her phone up to show a picture of a bridesmaid with flowers adorning her hair.

"No." Lennox sliced her hand through the air. "You're already pushing it with the dress and crazy high heels. Sara Beth, you're my best friend, but we have to draw the line somewhere."

"Oh, come on." Sara Beth shot her a puppy dog expression that only really worked on Brian. "I mean, you can retaliate and put me in whatever you want when I get to be a bridesmaid for you."

Lennox started choking on the sip of tea she'd just taken. She pounded her chest and tried to catch a full breath again. Obviously, that assumption had caught her off-guard, although Ty couldn't object too much to it. Especially if he got to pick the groom.

"You okay?" Ty glanced over at her. He could tell exactly what was running through her head and probably what had prompted Sara Beth's statement.

"Fine." Lennox took another drink. "Sara Beth, you know I'm not getting married. What a ridiculous thing to say."

Ty had hoped after Lennox learned the story of Brendan and Evangeline in the chapel and witnessed the list of marriages that *hadn't* failed, maybe she'd be more optimistic about the idea. But it had only been a few weeks. And she had a lot on her mind dealing with her mom and dad. She'd mentioned something when they first arrived about her sister Macy having a rough time, as well.

"Something tells me you're going to change your mind." Sara Beth glanced back and forth between Ty and Lennox once more. "I think Ty is growing on you."

"Maybe like a mold or fungus." Lennox wrinkled her nose.

"Hey. She didn't deny I was growing on her. I'll take it." He stretched out one of his legs that had been folded under him, and his foot bumped into hers. She peered up at him, but he pretended not to notice.

"I think I found sort of what I want, Ty." Sara Beth showed him a picture. "What do you think? Can we pull it off?"

"Yes. And I have a great idea to make it even more special." He reached around behind him, his toes brushing against Lennox's feet and sending a spark of something warm up through his legs. Yet, he still didn't show any sign to acknowledge it had happened. Maybe if he acted nonchalant, Lennox would leave it, and he could keep playing accidental footsie with her.

"*Ooh*. What do you have?" Sara Beth leaned his way to see what he was pulling from a messenger bag.

"Because you're marrying into an Irish family, how about a few shamrocks scattered in? And a bit of Irish lace to go around the stems." He held them out to Sara Beth, and she bounced where she sat.

"Perfect!"

Lennox even gave him a small grin as she diligently admired her friend's excitement. "I remembered your family was from Ireland, but I guess I didn't realize you held to all their traditions."

"We don't always, but I love the history of it. And I love being able to incorporate some little things like that. They won't stand out or anything, but they'll be special for Sara Beth and Brian."

"You'd be such a great design consultant." Lennox's words shot something through him he couldn't define. Was it pleasure or remorse or somewhere in the middle? "You're great at the details."

He quickly swallowed the lump of whatever it was. "You sound shocked."

"I admit, when I first met you, I never would have imagined you could pay attention to things like that. You came across as much more of a free spirit, doing whatever whim happened to catch you at the time."

"First impressions aren't always reliable, you know."

Sara Beth's phone chimed. "Oh. I need to call Brian. Back in a jiff."

Ty dug through the flora scattered all over the floor around them, picking out sunflowers and other smaller blooms he thought would work for Sara Beth's bouquet. He'd start with hers and then move on to the bridesmaids'. His fingers brushed against Lennox's as she started to hand him one that was out of his reach. Once more, that warmth moved through him at the simple contact.

"Thanks." His voice came out a bit gruffer than he'd planned.

"You're welcome." Lennox glanced over her shoulder and then back at him, her fingers twisting together, as if she were unsure about something.

He stilled and leaned over until he could meet her downward gaze. "What's wrong?"

Lennox visibly swallowed, hesitated another second, and then another. "Mom set something up and wants me to come."

"She's not trying to set you up with someone else, is she?" Ty gave a half-hearted laugh, trying to lighten the mood. "I thought I'd won her over."

"Oh, no. Nothing like that." Lennox rolled her eyes. "She's completely sure you're the one for me."

Ty reached over and lifted Lennox's chin so she'd look at him instead of everything else. "Then, what?"

"She's somehow found my dad's number and invited him for dinner one night next week."

Ty swallowed quickly. He knew exactly how Faye had found his number, but he wasn't about to say anything. He was still second-guessing that decision.

"She wants me to come. And Macy, although I wish her luck there. Macy ..." Lennox shook her head. "Macy isn't handling this nearly as well as I am, and I feel like a constant wreck."

"No one could tell by looking at you." Ty waited, wondering how to help. "Will you go?"

Lennox turned her face away, but her expression was full of longing and uncertainty and fear and hurt. If only he could wipe it all from her life and replace it with nothing but happiness. But until she dealt with this, there was no way she could move past it. And he couldn't make her do it, no matter how much he wished he could.

"I don't know." Her answer came in a whisper. "I don't know if I can."

It was a huge risk, but he took it anyway. "What if I came with you? Moral support?"

"No." Her blue eyes met his, wide with something he couldn't define. "Mom already thinks you and I are closer to each other than we really are. And it would just add more awkwardness to an already awkward situation. I don't think that's a good idea at all."

"I don't want you to have to go through it alone." Ty reached out and stilled her fidgety hands. "Think about it. You have my number in your phone. I'll go. No need for advance notice. You text, and I'm there."

"Ty ..." She hung her head, but didn't pull away.

"Don't give me an answer tonight. Just say, *thank you*." He squeezed her fingers. "It's what friends do. They support each other."

"Sara Beth offered to go too, but she actually knows even less about the situation than you do." Lennox's words caught him off-guard. He knew more than her best friend? What did *that* mean in the scheme of things? Only that he'd spent more time talking to her lately? Or that he'd been there when she first discovered her dad was back in town? Or nothing at all?

"So, Sara Beth wouldn't be a great option to go. Please, let me do this for you."

"Hey, guys. Sorry about that," Sara Beth's chipper voice broke in before he could get a final answer. "Oh. Am I interrupting something?" Her gaze moved back and forth between them, lingering on their clasped hands.

"No." Lennox quickly pulled free from his embrace, and he missed the contact immediately. "Ty was grabbing a flower I had picked up, and it scratched my finger. That's all."

The excuse sounded weak even to his ears, but he'd play along if that's what she wanted. "Yeah, I can't seem to stop injuring her tonight."

"Uh-huh." Sara Beth appeared skeptical, but sat back down.

"So, what do you think of these for your bouquet?" Ty held up the bundle of flowers he'd set down when Lennox started opening up to him. Had that really just happened? A glance in her direction showed her mask mostly back in place, but the earlier emotions lingered around the edges of her eyes and mouth. If only they'd had a few more minutes!

"Perfect!" Sara Beth helped hold the flowers, and he wrapped them with the burlap before adding the lace around the outside.

His toes wiggled against Lennox's foot, and her head jerked up, but he kept his expression natural, hiding the mirth bubbling underneath. How long would she let him continue to do such things? He pressed his luck already, but couldn't help it. The longer she didn't pull her own toes back, the more hope he held of growing even closer.

Was there a more real possibility? The fact that she even considered going to dinner with her dad showed she'd at least been letting some of what he and George had talked to her about sink in. Maybe she'd let the rest work its way into her heart. Because even more than wanting her to let him love her, he wanted her to let God love her. And the best way to starting a relationship with a Heavenly Father would be to make peace with her earthly one.

He sent up a few more prayers and hoped against hope that he'd be allowed to accompany her to the family dinner next week. Maybe it was cruel, knowing her mom had set her hopes on him winning Lennox's affection. But the love he'd only thought might grow had gained a momentum he had no control over. And if there was any way, he wanted to be at her side to help her through such an emotional upheaval.

He met her gaze and winked as he worked on her bouquet. It was probably a good thing she wouldn't be wearing flowers in her hair at the wedding. There was only so much temptation a man could take. And he was reaching his limit in a hurry.

Chapter Twenty-Five

Lennox barely controlled a scream when she found Ty's red car parked in front of her mom's home. She crunched over the gravel and poked him in the chest. "I told you not to come. How did you find out when this was happening?"

Ty rubbed the back of his neck. "Sara Beth let it slip yesterday."

"Some best friend she's turned out to be." Lennox kicked at the rocks under her feet and then winced as one sliced into her toe exposed by her thong sandals.

"Did you just stomp your foot in a little fit and hurt yourself?" Ty's easy grin wouldn't work on her today. She was in no mood for his nonchalant attitude.

"Please, just go."

"All I want to do is be here to support you through this. Why won't you let me?"

"Because …" She dashed a hand over her face. "Because it's embarrassing. It's humiliating to have you witness every awful thing about my family."

"Why is it embarrassing?" He placed a hand on her shoulder and dipped his head to look into her downcast eyes.

Why was it embarrassing? It shouldn't be. It shouldn't matter at all what he thought of her. And yet ... Oh, no. No, no, no. He'd gotten to her. He'd worked his way under her skin and was dangerously close to her heart. This was not good at all.

She blamed Sara Beth and her eternal optimism that everyone in the world should find love like she had. And the fact that her so-called best friend kept finding ways to throw her together with Ty. Who turned out to be not as awful as she'd originally thought.

Then, he showed her that stupid book full of names of people who stayed married after having their wedding in the chapel. Which raised her optimism level for Sara Beth and Brian. And made her wonder if the chapel could work its magic on her, too, assuming she ever got married. Maybe it could help her break the curse of bad relationships that ran in her family.

She needed time away from all this talk about love and marriage. Maybe she could just avoid Ty and Sara Beth until the wedding. Except that wouldn't work because the ceremony was less than two months away now. And that meant Sara Beth would want her to think about it *more. Ugh.*

"Len?" Lennox's mom interrupted her turmoiled thoughts. "You guys coming in? George says the meat's almost ready."

"Oh, good. George is here too. Let's just invite the whole county, while we're at it." Lennox mumbled under her breath as she walked up the stairs. She didn't bother trying to tell Ty to leave again. Something told her neither he nor her mother would let that happen now. Instead, she pretended to ignore him, a task harder than it should be because his hand hovered at the small of her back, radiating warmth through her that she wanted and didn't want all at the same time.

Macy stood in the corner of the living room, her arms crossed, a scowl across her normally pretty face. "I didn't realize you were bringing a boyfriend."

"He's not my boyfriend." Lennox narrowed her eyes.

He reached his hand out to greet her sister, and Lennox's back immediately felt cold. "I'm Ty. Just here for moral support."

"Moral support, huh? Whatever she wants to call it." Macy scoffed.

"Where's Jared?" Lennox refused to take the bait. If her sister wanted a fight, she could take her anger out on someone else. Lennox had enough battles of her own without adding more.

"He left a couple of weeks ago." Macy studied her fingernails.

"I'm sorry, Macy." Lennox truly meant it. She didn't understand her sister's relationships, but that didn't mean she wished for them to fail, either. "Where's Dad?"

"Out back with George. I think he just couldn't stand to be in the same room with me." Macy's shield fell back into place. "After all, he hasn't wanted to be around me in a dozen years. Why start now?"

"Mace—" Lennox reached out toward her sister, but Macy jerked away, the anger in her eyes potent. If Lennox thought she struggled with all of this, it was nothing compared to how Macy was handling things.

"Meat's on." George came through the door from the deck, a plate of grilled chicken in his hands. Her dad followed right behind with the same girl Lennox saw at the nursery.

"Just in time. Everything else is ready." Her mom waved from the dining table. "I'm glad you could join us, Ty, even though Lennox forgot to mention you were coming. I had hoped, anyway."

Lennox opened her mouth to protest, but Ty's answer beat her to it. "I wasn't sure my schedule would allow it, but it worked out yesterday, so here I am. Silly me, I forgot to tell Lennox I was coming."

Lennox sent him a look she hoped he could interpret as *you'll pay for that later*. Sure, it was mostly true. It hadn't been in his schedule until her loud-mouthed friend let the information slip. And he hadn't let her know, because if he had, she would never have agreed. Were all men so slimy and manipulative? No. George turned out to be okay—except for his preachiness.

Everyone moved to the table, Macy insisting on the chair

farthest from their father and his girlfriend. Lennox ended up across from him. George and Mom took either end. Ty grabbed her hand while George led them in prayer. She didn't pull away although it wasn't a great idea for her to start leaning even more on him. He was becoming much too much of a fixture in her life as it was.

The table remained quiet for the first ten minutes of the meal except for the *please pass* comments and clinks of utensils hitting plates. Then, Dad cleared his throat and took a drink of water, obviously gearing up for a speech of some sort. He exchanged a glance with Mom, who nodded back at him. It was the most civilized interchange Lennox could remember them ever having.

"When your mom suggested this dinner tonight, I wondered at the reasonableness of it. After all, when two people have the history Faye and I do, it's not always easy to rebuild bridges burned years before." Dad fiddled with the edge of his napkin, looking anywhere but at his daughters. "As much as I wanted to come back and reconnect with you girls, I wondered if I'd hurt you too much to be able to make that happen."

Macy leaned back in her seat, arms crossed over her chest. Ty's hand came over to rest on Lennox's shoulder, offering as much of his strength as she needed. Mom and George remained silent, their expressions open.

"When I started dating Sami, she chided me for not trying to reach out more than I had through the years." Evidently, the woman with Dad was his girlfriend. It didn't surprise Lennox much, although it was a bit awkward considering Sami couldn't be much older than herself.

"So, more than never. Got it." Macy's snide comment sent a guilty expression over Dad's face.

"I failed in more ways than I probably know. I realize that now. I decided that if we couldn't be a happy family, then we shouldn't be a family at all. I know now how selfish that was of me. Honestly, I should have tried to make amends before now, but every time I considered it, I figured you were better off without me."

It wasn't true, although Lennox could understand how hard it would be to face a past you'd left behind. That was one of the reasons she despised this trailer park. Didn't want to be here tonight, either. If she ignored the past, maybe it would go away.

"Anyway, I want to say I'm sorry for … for all of it. Your mom just about knocked me over when she told me she'd forgiven me. I couldn't believe in such grace. Still can't totally fathom it. But it seems she's found a better man than I am to spend her time with lately." He shot George a look, although Lennox couldn't decide if it was one of envy or approval. Then, he turned his attention to her and Macy. "I only hope that sometime down the road, you'll be more open to trying to have a relationship with me again. I don't deserve it, but I would like to try."

Macy shoved back from the table, her chair falling over from the force of it. "You're right—you don't deserve it. You don't even deserve to be here right now. You ruined our lives. We had to move to this tiny little Podunk town, go to a school where people made fun of us for our hand-me-down clothes, live in a trailer park, and scrimp and save for every penny. Too bad for you if you feel sorry about it now. It's too late to fix it."

Faye went after Macy as she stormed from the room. Lennox's fingers shook too much to use her fork, so she set the metal down on the table and clasped her hands in her lap. Part of her agreed with every word Macy had said. She detested those memories too. But she hadn't been terribly attached to where they'd lived before. And it wasn't like they'd been much richer then, either. Plus, Park Haven had given her Sara Beth.

"I suppose you feel the same way." Dad ducked his head and picked at the few pieces of lettuce remaining on his plate.

"No." The answer surprised Lennox, but she didn't want to take it back. She was tired of holding on to the pain and hurt and bitterness. She didn't want to be as hateful and cold as her sister was tonight. Though she also didn't know how to be as forgiving as her mom.

Dad's head jerked back up as Ty squeezed her shoulder. "No?"

"I don't feel exactly the same way Macy does." Lennox shrugged. "Don't get me wrong. I don't like the fact that I had to grow up the way I did. And I know all three of us have a lot of baggage we still need to find a way to get rid of. But it's too heavy to keep carrying around."

"Does that mean you forgive me?" Dad's voice broke, and his eyes filled with tears.

Lennox swallowed, caught George's eye, and swallowed again. George would want her to. He was probably halfway hoping all his little talks had touched her enough to be able to. But could she?

"I ..." She glanced at Ty. His hand dropped to cover her fidgeting fingers, infusing them with his strength, as if to say he'd support her no matter her answer. Who was this man, and how did he fit into her life? *Could he fit into it?* That was a question for another time.

"I want to." She did, although she still wasn't sure exactly how to go about it. "But it might take some time. And please don't expect everything to be okay automatically. There's a lot of history to overcome here."

Dad gave a nod. "It's more than I hoped for."

Mom came back in the room and sat once more, but her eyelashes were damp, and there was no sign of Macy. "I think I might have lost her for good this time."

"Where did she go?" Lennox's heart raced at the thought of her sister never coming back. Sure, they didn't get along well, but she didn't want anything bad to happen to her.

Mom shook her head. "I'm not sure. I thought I had time to be a better mother, but I was so wrapped up in my own grief and self-pity that I neglected you girls. And I wasn't a great example, either, drowning myself in alcohol and boyfriends."

"Neither of us did a great job, did we?" Dad reached over and covered Mom's hand. "I'm sorry this didn't go as well as you wanted it to. As well as either of us hoped. Although, maybe at least a little good came from it." He shot a grateful smile Lennox's way, and she was taken back to when she was a little girl and lived for receiving that grin.

"What?" Mom's head darted up, and then glanced between her and Dad.

"Lennox says she wants to work toward forgiving me." Dad's voice cracked, and a lump grew in her own throat at the emotional conversation.

"Sounds like it's a good thing we have chocolate cake." George pushed back and headed for the kitchen. "I think this is just what we need."

"My favorite." Lennox and Ty said at the same time. He chuckled as he helped George pass around plates of the rich confection. Some of the awkwardness lifted as everyone settled into dessert and small talk.

No other heavy subjects were raised, but that was okay. It would take time to work through all the repercussions. And Macy wasn't mentioned again, although she was obviously on everyone's mind. When enough time passed that Lennox was comfortable leaving, she didn't step into a hug with her father, but accepted a squeeze of her hand.

Ty walked out with her, his hand once more hovering over the small of her back. Why was that becoming something she anticipated? She should step away, increase the distance. And yet, she couldn't.

"I'm proud of you." Ty whispered the words in her ear, and her heart tripped several beats as a wave of warmth washed through her.

"I didn't do anything."

"You went in there open to having a real conversation and even agreed to work toward reconciling. I'd say that's something." He stood close, his head only inches from hers.

"I'm just tired of thinking about it. I don't want to have to be upset by those memories anymore. I don't want to carry around the baggage of disappointment and hurt and anger."

He pressed a kiss to her forehead and wrapped her up in his arms, her head nestling perfectly into the hollow under his chin. Security and comfort and something else filled her, and she stilled, enjoying the sensation. So much for maintaining distance between them.

"I think you're possibly on the way to more than just forgiving your dad." Ty gave one more squeeze and then stepped back. Cold settled over her despite the heavy July air that kept it hot even after the sun went down. "I'm still praying for you."

"Thanks," she choked out the word, knowing she wouldn't be able to argue with him even if she could coherently come up with the right words.

"I'll see you Saturday in class." He ran a finger down her cheek and then moved to open her car door.

How did he do that? How did he show up unwanted and then make it so she yearned for him to stay longer? How did he stir emotions inside her that she thought didn't exist—couldn't exist? And how was she supposed to keep fighting a battle that appeared more and more like she was losing?

Chapter Twenty-Six

How many months had it been now? Ty couldn't even remember, although it had to have been at least four ... maybe five. And finally—finally, Lennox texted him.

Granted, her message was short. Nothing more than letting him know she had his tux for the wedding, and he needed to come pick it up. But still ... She sent him a message so he finally had her number. Progress.

When should I get it?

I can bring it to class on Saturday.

No. That wouldn't work. If they did it that way, he had no excuse to see her more than the forty-five minutes she taught. She'd been avoiding him again ever since that dinner at her mom's house almost a month before. Had she somehow found out his part in all that?

Here he was, sitting in her parking lot, debating. This was her night off. She was home.

Would she shove the garment bag out the door and slam it in his face? Or could he talk her into dinner or something? His

197

hopes were on the latter, although it wouldn't surprise him if the first happened. She was skittish, as if fighting her biggest fear. And for some strange reason, that fear was love. A man could dream.

Ty ran his fingers through his hair. Did the length still bother her? He'd promised his mom to get it cut before the wedding in two weeks. But the haircut would be more to impress a certain bridesmaid than to get his mother off his back. A quick rap at Lennox's door, and he waited.

A few moments passed. Did she regret agreeing to let him pick it up here? Then, the sound of the locks, and there she was, peeking through the crack. Soft light bathed her from behind. She gave a tentative smile, which quickly vanished again, as if she hadn't meant for it to sneak out in the first place.

"Hi."

She nibbled her lower lip, still not opening the door wider. "Hi."

"You said I was supposed to get my tux." He raised an eyebrow. "Unless you just really like my clothes hanging in your closet."

"Oh ..." She straightened, face flushed red, and motioned him in.

As he stepped over the threshold, something started beeping in the kitchen.

"*Argh!*" She hesitated a moment, staring at him before dashing toward the sound. "Don't move!"

He closed the door and wandered toward the smell of something burning. She pulled a pan out of the oven, her face crumpling at the black mass of whatever it had once been. Cookies?

"You okay?"

"No, I'm not okay. And you were supposed to stay by the door." She pointed a finger at him even as she slumped to her floor.

"Bad day?" He came and sat beside her on a rug decorated with coffee mugs.

"Yes. No. I don't know." She pressed her palms to her forehead. "I was doing okay, but just off the whole day. So, I thought maybe some yoga and cookies would help. Except I got so involved in the yoga that I forgot the cookies. And evidently, when I set the timer, I didn't pay attention to the fact that I hadn't reset how long it was for."

"I have an idea. If I leave, will you let me back in again?" Ty studied her, waiting for rejection.

"Do I have a choice?"

"Lennox."

"Yes." She finally met his gaze. "Go do whatever it is you think will fix this."

"I promise to be as quick as I can." He pressed a kiss to her forehead before sprinting down to his car once more.

The Cookie Jar closed in half an hour but was only three blocks away. He could make this right. He would.

The girl at the window gave him a less-than-welcoming smile, but agreed to let him have everything left for twenty-five percent off since they were about to close. He took the box of three dozen cookies and forced himself to be good all the way back to her apartment. Besides, in this dim interior, he might accidentally grab an oatmeal raisin, and that would never do.

Lennox's eyes widened as he held the confections in front of her. "Wow. Where did you get those? They're huge."

"My favorite spot, The Cookie Jar. I just happened to catch them right before they closed, so they sold me everything left at a discount."

"You're insane." She dug through until she pulled out a chocolate chunk. "But right now, I don't even care."

Progress.

He followed her to the kitchen once more, and discovered the earlier mess already cleaned up. Two mugs stood on the counter with steam rising from the top. He grabbed his own cookie, a frosted sugar, and accepted the beverage from her.

"Thank you." He leaned against the counter and breathed in

the now-familiar smell of green tea. He'd drunk a cup every day after finding out she liked it, and the flavor had grown on him. Somehow, she'd known he would prefer the blueberry instead of plain or ginger.

"You're welcome. And thank you too. I wasn't up to trying again with the cookie-making tonight." She munched for a few minutes in silence, although he caught her peeking at him a few times.

"I meant to ask you to go to dinner, but I like the idea of cookies better." He grabbed another.

"Probably not a great meal choice if I'm going to fit into that dress in a few weeks." Lennox brushed crumbs from her fingers.

"As much as you work out?" He shook his head. "You'll look as gorgeous as ever in that gown."

She shot him a skeptical look.

"I know a tux that can't wait until it can step onto the dance floor with your dress."

Her eyes widened again. "Dance!"

"We're Irish. Of course, there will be dancing." He shrugged and grinned.

"Like, step?"

He chuckled. "No. Although I do have a few cousins in step dancing groups who perform in various places. Most of us don't know how to do anything that fancy."

"I don't know how to do anything at all." She rubbed her hands over her upper arms.

"But you teach ballet, don't you?"

"No. I teach exercise routines that use ballet positions. Totally different. And it's not like I could just go out and do a ballet dance at a wedding." She paced in front of him, but he caught her hand and stilled her on the second pass.

"Have you broken in your shoes yet?"

"My shoes?"

"For the wedding."

Her nose wrinkled in the cutest way. "No. I haven't had time."

"Go get them and my tux." He pulled his phone from his pocket and did a quick search through his music choices. *Perfect.*

She walked back in with the garment bag in one hand and her strappy sandals dangling from the other. "And what exactly are we supposed to do with these?"

He held up a finger. With a quick zip, he opened the bag and pulled his coat from it. Nice. It settled around his shoulders, but wasn't nearly as suffocating as he'd expected. Then, he steered her to the sofa and knelt before her, buckling each shoe into place as if he were Prince Charming and she his Cinderella.

He rose to his feet and offered a hand. She hesitated a moment, uncertainty written all over her face. But he wouldn't push her or pressure her. She needed to trust him all on her own. Finally, she tentatively reached her fingers his way and accepted his help.

He eased one of her hands to his shoulder, and the other he twined their fingers together. Her waist beneath his own hand fit as if notched for that purpose. His phone played a slow song, one Brian and Sara Beth had chosen for their reception.

"My family isn't too fancy. And from what I can tell of Sara Beth's, hers isn't, either. But I can teach you a few simple steps. First, though, you need to relax. Feel the music's rhythm."

Her eyes close as a little of the tension eased from her frame.

More progress. When they'd first met, there was no way she would've let him this close and definitely wouldn't have trusted him enough to relax in his arms. He enjoyed the pleasure of knowing he'd earned her confidence.

"Okay. Here are a few simple steps. Follow my lead."

Her eyes fluttered open and then focused on his sneakers and her fancy sandals standing toe to toe. He eased his leg out, and she followed. One by one, he moved them through the motions, working their way up to the speed of the song. And he couldn't help but admire her gracefulness even as she learned. He also couldn't help but enjoy the way she fit in his arms, as if made for this.

The music ended, but he didn't want to stop. "Should we try another? Just to get your self-confidence built up."

"I don't know, Ty." Lennox stepped back, breaking their tenuous connection. "Maybe I should just plan to sit out on the dancing. After all, my part will really be over by then. No one will care if I participate in the rest or not."

"I'll care."

She turned her back to him, crossing her arms over her middle. "Why?"

"You know why. I told you months ago." He eased up behind her, took one of her hands and tugged her into a spin and then back into his arms. With a quick tap, another song played, this one a bit faster.

"Please tell me you're not still thinking about love." She rolled her eyes before he lifted her arm and spun her a couple more times.

"I haven't mentioned it since that day in the chapel. But I fully admit I was wrong then."

She shot him an expression he hoped was disappointment, although it could also be skepticism or even anger. "Really?"

"Yes. I only thought I was coming to love you then." He wrapped her up and swayed, their noses only inches apart. "Now, I know better. Because my feelings back then are nothing compared to how I feel for you now."

Her breath caught, and he played with the idea of giving her a real kiss once more. But he held back. She still wasn't ready.

Honestly, she probably wouldn't have even let him in tonight if he hadn't needed to pick up his tuxedo. While she'd tolerated him in her kickboxing class the last few weeks, she'd also slipped out before he could catch her to talk afterward. And the disdain used when she uttered the word *love* proved she wasn't quite ready for it yet.

"But don't worry. I'm just reminding you." He spun her out

again and then leaned her into a dip as the song finished. "What you end up doing with it in the long run is up to you."

She smoothed down her tunic as he released her. He tucked his phone in his pocket. The coolness was welcome as he removed the jacket and eased it back onto its hanger. Just a few more weeks until he'd wear it again. And hopefully, once more get to hold the beautiful woman across the room in his arms.

With a few cookies in his hand, he bowed to her. "My lady, I thank you for the dances. And the lovely company over our ... dinner."

The corner of her lip twitched.

"Maybe your day ended a bit better than it started?" He cocked an eyebrow, not quite ready to remove himself from her presence, although he shouldn't push his advantage.

"You just can't help yourself, can you?" She leaned down and slid off a sandal. "You have to fish for compliments."

"Only when I deserve them." He caught her elbow as she stumbled, trying to remove the second shoe. "But seriously, Lennox, if you need anything. I'm here. Cookies, dance lessons, a listening ear ..."

She shook her head. "I think you've already done enough, but thank you."

His heart skipped a beat. Had she found out, then? Or was she simply saying that in a general way?

A wrinkle marred her smooth forehead. "What was that look about?"

"Hmm?" He raised his brows. "What look?"

"I said you'd already done enough, and you looked ... well, sort of guilty."

"Guilty?" He scoffed. "What would I have to be guilty about?"

Her eyes narrowed. "Ty Dunne, is something wrong with the chapel? Did the window not get fixed?"

"No. No. The window was re-installed weeks ago. I even

made sure all my ancestor's watches and jewelry were back in place." He snatched up the garment bag. "The chapel is fine."

She stepped between him and the door before he could make his escape. "There's something, though. Because normally you're appallingly cocky. And right now, you're looking sheepish. If it's not the chapel, what is it?"

"Lennox, seriously. What could I have done? You haven't even spoken to me in almost a month. Not since I showed up at Faye's house the night your dad was there."

She stiffened.

"I really do need to get home tonight. A few more things to do ..."

"You just said the chapel was ready." She poked a finger in his chest. "Does this have something to do with my mom?"

"I haven't spoken to your mom since that night." He drew an *X* across his chest.

She started to move out of his way, but her eyes were still narrowed. "I'm still not sure I believe you're innocent. But I'm too tired to figure it out right now. Especially after meeting Dad for lunch earlier."

She'd met her dad? On her own? His chest eased up, and before he could think things through, he pressed a kiss to her forehead. "I'm so proud of you. That's exactly what I hoped would happen."

Lennox blinked. "What do you mean?"

What did he mean? What exactly had he just said? Wait.

She poked her finger into his chest again. "You had his number."

He stepped back, despite it being farther from the door ... and escape.

"You did this, didn't you? I never did figure out how Mom got Dad's number to set that dinner up. That night we were there ... when I was outside with George. You gave it to her."

He stood silent. It's not like he could deny any of it.

"You're the reason Macy's gone."

"Macy?"

"My sister hasn't been heard from since that night. Mom's about to go crazy. It's one of the reasons I agreed to meet Dad. We're all trying to figure out what to do."

Her sister was missing. The pride that had swelled up in his chest at her admission of moving forward with forgiveness now threatened to choke him. "I didn't know, Len."

"Of course you didn't. Because you don't think things through before you do them. You get an idea and just charge ahead full-speed. Why should you worry about repercussions? Your life is perfect." She rubbed her hands over her face.

"That's not it at all."

She moved away from the door. "Get out."

"Len—"

"Get out. *Now.*"

Now what? He clumped down the stairs and got in his car, slamming his hands against the steering wheel. Not the ending he'd hoped for tonight.

He'd rather hoped to move her a little closer to being willing to spend time with him even after the wedding in a few weeks. Time was running out. And he had no idea how to fix this.

Chapter Twenty-Seven

The banging on Lennox's front door pulled her from her relaxed yoga pose. She huffed in frustration. Why couldn't he just leave her alone for a few more days? Then, the wedding would be over, and there wouldn't be any more need for him to spend time with her.

Lennox whipped the front door open as the knocking started again. "Ty, seriously—"

Sara Beth stood there, eyes puffy and red, tears dripping down her cheeks. "Sorry, Len. I didn't know … who else to talk to."

"Come in here." Lennox tugged her friend to the sofa and handed her a box of tissues. "What on earth is going on?"

Sara Beth sniffled and buried her nose in a tissue. "I don't think Brian and I are getting married."

"What?" Lennox's heart stopped for a second. Even though she'd doubted the relationship would last long, she'd at least expected it to make it all the way to the wedding. And lately, she'd even expected it to be one of the ones that hit fifty and more years. If these two couldn't make it work, where did that leave someone like her?

"Gran Nancy doesn't think I'm good enough for him." Sara Beth sobbed.

"That can't be true. You're one of the best people in the whole world." Lennox patted her friend awkwardly on the shoulder.

Inside, a little voice said, *If Sara Beth isn't good enough to marry into that family, no way would Lennox be*, but she pushed it aside as quickly as it popped up. She didn't want to get married anyway, she reminded her heart and head. Especially not to a meddling, conniving jerk. Besides, she needed to focus on Sara Beth's problems right now. Not her stupid betraying supposed friend.

Lennox unfolded herself from the couch. "Let me put the kettle on, and we'll figure this out."

"I don't suppose you have anything that's not green tea?" Sara Beth wrinkled her nose even while mopping at her eyes.

"My green tea was good enough for Ty the other night." Lennox muttered under her breath.

Evidently, not quietly enough, though, because Sara Beth narrowed her eyes. "That's the second time you've mentioned him. Did you have plans?"

"No. He came over the other day to pick up his tux, remember?" Lennox didn't mention the way he ran out for the best cookies she'd ever had and then held her in his arms while twirling her around the tiny living room. Or that he'd basically stabbed her in the heart before she kicked him out. No need to complicate things any more than they already were. She wouldn't let Sara Beth distract her from the original problem.

"I forgot I asked you to pick that up." Sara Beth sniffled again. "I guess now we'll have to see if we can get our money back on some of it. I can't imagine the boys wanting to wear such a getup without a wedding."

"There *will* be a wedding." Lennox handed her a cup of hot chocolate. "Now, tell me why you think Gran Nancy doesn't like you."

"So, it's not really so much that she doesn't like me ..." Sara Beth's voice wavered. "I don't know where to start with all this."

"Start wherever it began. Because I can't imagine Brian letting you believe his grandmother doesn't like you." Lennox leaned back into the cushions, preparing for one of Sara Beth's long stories.

It took her a minute and a few sips of cocoa before she started. "Remember when we were shopping for flowers, and I had to leave to go meet with Brian and Gran?"

Lennox nodded. How could she forget that night? She spent it with Ty. When he helped her with her mom ... and made sure she was okay after. And this wasn't helping her focus at all.

"Well, that talk turned out to be about the family house. Evidently, there's some house that has been in their family forever, and it's supposed to go to the oldest grandchild. Except Gran said she'd rather give it to the one who got married first, which is Brian. Problem is, she'd already let Ty move in. And Brian doesn't want to kick Ty out."

"Okay. I still don't really see the problem." Lennox's mind flashed to the beautifully decorated house that had lured her in during her short visit. Would anyone love it as much as Ty Dunne? Didn't matter. *Focus.* Where was the connection between the house and Sara Beth being unliked by the family?

"Here's where it gets weird. Or, weirder. I supported Brian. I don't want to come between him and his cousin. But I guess Gran Nancy had already talked about this to several others. And she's convinced the family that Ty isn't living up to his potential. It has everyone up in arms. Then, Brian gets tired of everyone harping at him and talking bad about Ty, who's been wonderful. He's restored the family chapel all summer. And now Brian sort of lets them all have it and says we don't want the stupid house. So there."

Sara Beth set her empty mug aside and then ruffled her blonde hair as if trying to decide whether to pull it out or not. "That didn't go over very well, as you can imagine. And I don't think Ty even knows any of this, because he's been so busy, he hasn't made it to many of the family gatherings. And when he did, he was rather distracted." Sara Beth shot a teasing glance Lennox's way.

"Just finish your story." Lennox nudged her with a toe.

"Brian is super stressed about all this because his family is pretty tight. I noticed, so I suggested maybe he should agree to work something out about the house after all. It's not that I want to kick Ty out, but I can't stand that Brian's so upset. My suggestion only made him madder. And we've been having little arguments. Every time we get together for the last few weeks, we've fought." Sara Beth studied the ring on her finger for a moment before continuing.

"Earlier this evening, we were at his family dinner, and Gran caught us in a disagreement. She mentioned we were off to a bad start, and maybe I wasn't worthy of wearing her ring after all. And Brian didn't disagree." Tears streaked silently down Sara Beth's cheeks. "I guess I'll give it back tomorrow."

"But the wedding is this weekend, Sara Beth." Lennox reached forward and grabbed her friend's hands. "This really sounds like you're arguing because you agree. I don't understand why you're letting his family dictate your relationship."

Sara Beth shook her head. "I really thought you were starting to understand."

"Understand what?" Lennox pulled back and fisted her hands. "What are you talking about?"

"Love." Sara Beth jumped up and started to pace. "With your dad and mom and Ty and everything that's happened in the last few months, I thought you were starting to believe in it."

"*Love?*" Lennox pounded a pillow. "Fighting with the man you want to marry because you support him in his decision— that's love? Having a grandmother threaten to take away the home of her grandson simply because he hasn't settled down yet —that's love? No, Sara Beth. I can't understand that."

"I'm not explaining this well, I guess." Sara Beth kicked at the exercise ball Lennox had used earlier. "Brian and I aren't fighting because we love each other. We're fighting because of a misunderstanding."

"A misunderstanding is enough to drive you away from the man you say you love? I thought you wanted to spend the rest of your life with Brian, but you haven't even made it to the altar yet. So, forgive me if I don't believe in love and marriage. I thought I was beginning to believe it, but ... last week ... and now ... If this is love, I don't want anything to do with it."

"What happened last week?"

"Never mind. That's my problem. Right now, we're working on yours." Lennox waved her hand in a circle. "You're trying to convince me that love means arguing over something that could be solved by a logical conversation."

"No!" Sara Beth pressed her fingers to her eyes. "This is all wrong."

Sara Beth slumped to the floor, and they both sat in silence for several long minutes. Lennox's mind spun in crazy circles, trying to work through everything. She wanted to help her friend, but she also didn't know how. She went back in her mind through the whole summer, and every conversation she'd had with George ... and Ty ... about love.

Lennox broke the silence. "Love is supposed to be a choice, right?"

Sara Beth lifted her gaze, a question in her eyes. "Yes."

"I can't remember when, but I think ..." *Was it Ty?* She couldn't let him in her head right now. "... George told me that. It's not just an emotion. It's not just a feeling. It's an action. Something you choose to do every day."

"Yes."

Deep down inside, Lennox had to admit, Ty lived out that definition. He didn't have to help her pick up her drunk mother or meet with her father again or even deal with her insecurities about participating in this wedding. And yet, he had. He'd gone out of his way to be there for her through everything. And he kept coming back, even after seeing the grittier side of her family and knowing how broken she was because of it.

If only he hadn't done some of it behind her back! Or been so cocky and self-assured. As if he knew better what she needed than she did.

Lennox forced her mind another direction. *George.* George was a great example of love. He not only assisted her mom, but he'd also been a huge help in searching for Macy. And he'd taken time out to answer any and all questions Lennox had shot his way over the last two months. Even when it seemed like his answers only spurred on more questions.

Her mind jumped back to Ty and his patient answers too. Ugh. Why did all this talk of love keep bringing Ty to mind? She couldn't deal with the tangle of emotions knotting up her insides right now. She needed to stay reasonable and help Sara Beth. The Ty mess would have to wait for another time.

"You're in love with Ty, aren't you?" Sara Beth's question was barely more than a whisper, but it was like an arrow shot straight through Lennox's heart.

"I can't be." Lennox choked out the words, refusing to meet her best friend's gaze. Sara Beth would see right through her. See things Lennox couldn't even admit to herself. Couldn't let herself feel.

"Why not?"

"Honey, if you're not good enough to marry into that family, then I sure ain't." Lennox pushed from the couch and paced. "And you're more than good enough. You and Brian just had a misunderstanding."

"Misunderstanding? He didn't disagree when Gran said I might not be worthy of her ring." Sara Beth waved her fingers in the air, but then stopped and shook her head. "No. You're right. Brian and I haven't actually talked all this through. We've been avoiding it, as if it will just go away. Instead, we're fighting about stupid things like the cake flavor and the color sheets we registered for and whether or not we should get a puppy after the honeymoon."

"Talk to him." Lennox picked up the discarded mug and walked it to the kitchen. "That's the only way you'll work this out. And I don't mean about the puppy. I mean about how his family is treating him and you. Remind him you support him no matter what."

"We won't kick Ty out of his house." Sara Beth came up and gave Lennox a side hug.

"I have no say in it."

"But you don't want him hurt any more than we do."

Maybe not completely true. Having Ty get a little comeuppance for his meddlesome ways could be very satisfying. But, Lennox agreed he shouldn't lose the house because of a lack of wife. Or for any other reason.

Scriptures George had quoted when she'd seen him over the last few months filtered back. Verses about forgiving others as God forgave you. And that God wanted His people to love everyone, even their enemies—she'd have to figure how Ty fit in that verse later. Because God was supposed to *be* love. And Christians were supposed to be like God. Now here was her best friend, a Christian, and Lennox wondered ...

"Sara Beth, why didn't you ever try to talk to me about God?" Lennox leaned against the sink, staring down into the few dishes she had yet to wash.

"What?" Sara Beth cocked her head to the side.

"You're a Christian, right?" Lennox finally glanced up.

"Yes."

"But you've never really mentioned any of that to me like George ... and Ty ... constantly do." Lennox frowned. "I was just curious why."

"You weren't ready to accept it. I believed it would drive a wedge between us, and I would much rather have your friendship where maybe you could see Christ through my life and my actions and my words than to have you not be my friend." Sara Beth squeezed her arm. "I guess that's the way I chose to love you. Maybe it wasn't the best, but I was so afraid of scaring you off."

Lennox shook her head. "Little bitty you, scare me off? I'm not so weak as that, am I?"

"No. But you definitely had your defenses built high back in ninth grade."

"I think you saved me in the long run. Without you, I don't know if I would have made it through high school or even considered going on to college."

Sara Beth was quiet for a moment. "So, are you glad I never said anything, or do you wish I had?"

"I don't know. Maybe you're right, and I wouldn't have accepted it before now. George scared me a bit at first. But then I witnessed the peace my mom has now. Something I don't know I've ever seen in her life. And a lot of the stuff George said makes sense." Lennox twisted the dishcloth in her hands.

"So, you're starting to believe?"

"I want to." Lennox lashed her hands out, soap bubbles splattering over the counter, frustrated at how hard it was to express herself. "I *want* to believe, but I don't know if I can."

Sara Beth gave a tentative smile. "There's actually a verse in the Bible where a man has come to Jesus to ask him to remove a demon from his son. Jesus says He can do it if the man will believe. And the man says, *I believe. Lord, help my unbelief.* Maybe that's the prayer you should be praying. And I'll keep praying. More than I already was."

Lennox smiled. "Join the crowd. I think even my mom is praying for me now. And I know George is. And ... Ty."

"Good."

"But we never solved your problem with Brian, did we?" Lennox turned to her friend with a frown.

"You talked me down. Talked me out of doing something stupid that would have broken my heart forever." Sara Beth grinned. "And reminded me what love is. I'll call Brian when I get home, and we'll work it out."

"Is love really worth it?" Lennox asked the question before she could stop herself.

"It is." Sara Beth squeezed her hands again. "Even on nights like this, it is."

Would Lennox ever be able to accept that as a fact? She leaned against her door jamb as Sara Beth walked down the stairs. Sara Beth said it was worth it even after almost calling off her wedding. Those were powerful words.

Would Ty think the same way if he was aware that his whole family commiserated against him living in that house he'd made his own? Would he still love them as much? Something told her he would.

And that his slipping Dad's number to Mom was his way of trying to do the same for her. *Ugh.* Why couldn't he stay out of it? How was she supposed to accept him inserting himself into her life like that?

Admitting in love was one thing. But to let it be a part of her life? That was totally different.

She couldn't take that risk. Especially with someone who would use it to run ramrod over her life, making the decisions *he* thought were best. Not worth it.

Chapter Twenty-Eight

"I thought I'd find you here." Ty's dad walked around the corner of the chapel.

Ty glanced up from where he planted mums in the flower beds, adding a bit of fall color for the wedding in two days. "Last minute things. Did you need me?"

"I just wanted to talk a little. Have a few things on my mind." His dad leaned against a cart Ty had used to wheel the new plants around. "You've been out here a lot this summer."

Ty tried not to get his hackles up. Was Dad insinuating he was slacking off on his *real* job? "Had quite a bit to do to get this place ready for Brian's wedding."

"I know. I know." Dad held up his hands as if to placate him. "I'm here because there's been a bit of talk about not only the chapel, but the house, too, among our family."

"Oh?" Ty leaned back on his heels. He had no idea his home was being discussed. "What about?"

"For some reason, Gran was trying to convince Brian that he should be the one living in the house instead of you, being the first to marry. It caused quite a ruckus for a while, but thankfully he and Sara Beth were adamant they didn't want to kick you out."

"I owe him one." Ty dusted off his hands and stood.

Dad nodded. "Gran finally told me why she wanted to take the house away from you, and what she said surprised me."

"Oh?" Ty wiped the back of his hand across his forehead to remove some of the moisture. Here it came. The old complaint about not living up to family expectations.

"Well, the part about you not settling down didn't surprise me." His dad shook his head, buried his hands in his pockets. "But she claimed you couldn't even find a real job."

Ty frowned. "What does she call what I've been doing the last six years?"

"Apparently, by working for me, you—and I quote—*are lacking backbone, letting me dictate your life, and not living your dream.*" His dad lifted a brow. "So, I'm here to find out exactly what dream I've stolen from you, because I wasn't aware that I had."

Ty let out a long breath. Gran's conversation back at Easter filtered through his memory. "Things are falling apart." Was this part of what she meant? He'd put this conversation off, trying to find the right way to approach his father, to bring up his real aspirations. But how was he supposed to do it without hurting feelings?

"You know I majored in both business and design, right?" Ty grabbed another plant so he didn't have to meet his dad's eyes.

"Yes."

"I did that because it's what I'm interested in. The design part, that is. The business part was for you." Ty stepped down on the shovel harder than he needed to. "I love seeing all the elements come together into one cohesive room or area. I love finding that perfect piece or color or pattern that speaks to the client and makes their project something that says *them* instead of *just another place.* I thought it might be neat to be one of the people you contracted out to—to work with you in that way."

Dad's hand landed on his shoulder and stilled his movements. "That explains a lot."

Ty turned to face his father. "What?"

"Remember the Joneses earlier this summer? Kitchen remodel?"

"Yeah."

"I take it you helped them pick out some things?"

Ty rubbed a hand over the back of his neck, feeling slightly sheepish. "Yeah."

"Well, they loved it so much, they've referred you to at least three of their friends."

Ty's eyes widened. "What?"

"You've got appointments all morning on Monday, so don't party too hard with all this wedding stuff this weekend." Dad's lips twitched in a smile. "But I'll still need a little help in the office until I can find your replacement, okay?"

"You've got it." Ty held out his hand and clasped Dad's.

"One question—why didn't you say something?" Dad didn't let go right away. "Why didn't you talk to me about branching out?"

Ty let out a deep breath. "I ... well, I never found the right time for one thing. And for another, I already felt I was letting you and the whole family down more often than not. I didn't want to make things worse. You'd always acted like it was only natural I step into the office and work beside you when I graduated, so I did."

"I'm sorry." Dad shook his head. "I wish you'd talked to me. I never meant to make you unhappy."

"I wasn't unhappy." A look from Dad had him amending his statement. "Not completely. But I am glad for this opportunity. And while we're shaking things up, I want to run something else by you."

"O-kaay." Dad's eyebrow lifted, and he folded his arms over his chest.

"This chapel isn't getting nearly as much use as it should. Ever since the community decided it made more sense to meet in a building closer to town, this chapel has seen neglect. I want to bring some life back to it. More than I already have. Can we start advertising it as a place to get married—a wedding venue?"

"I like that idea." Dad leaned his head back, looking up at the window. "Show me around? I haven't seen it since you got the roof fixed."

"You haven't seen a lot, then." Ty brushed his hands off once more. "Come on."

The approval on Dad's face as they walked through the chapel was almost worth more than hearing him say he accepted Ty's new role in the family business. *Almost.* Although the one person Ty most wanted to win approval from probably wouldn't be there until the rehearsal tomorrow evening.

"The window looks good." Dad stood and admired it. "I know that took a good chunk of our family chapel budget, but it was worth it."

"Did you know Gramps and Gran had hidden a watch and bracelet under the sill?" Ty motioned toward the wall where the pieces now resided once more.

"What?"

"And Great-great-grandpa Brendan and Great-great-grandma Evangeline left a watch and locket."

"Did you add to it? Sounds like it's skipping every other generation."

"*Nah.* They were all trying to move away from a past that had been rough on them. And starting a life together. I'm not in the same place they were." Ty tapped his chin. "Although, I do have a question."

"Shoot."

"Back at Easter, Gran called me Mikey."

Dad chuckled. "We do have similar hair, though yours is a bit lighter. And the same chin. Guess your Gran must've been living in the past that day."

"Sure, but she said something about you being hers before you were hers. What does that mean? I know Gran gets mixed up a lot now, but that's stranger than normal."

Dad slid onto the front pew and patted the seat beside him. "I guess I never told you that story, did I?"

Ty raised a brow.

"Gramps ..." Dad sighed. "Our family history has some blips in it. More than you know. Let's just say you're not the most disappointing person in the Dunne family history. Far from it."

Ty blinked. "Worse than the mobsters?"

"*Ha!* Different, anyway. Gramps had a relationship before Gran. A woman named Rebecca. It was a college thing, and they never actually married, but they were engaged before Gramps headed to Vietnam. Thing was, when he left, Rebecca was pregnant. With me."

That was a twist Ty hadn't expected.

"When Gramps and Gran started dating and getting serious, he received a letter explaining everything. Because my mom and her husband had both passed away. I was around three when I came to live with my dad and Gran. And she took me in as if I were hers. And from then on, I was."

"That explains it, then."

"Maybe that's why in her brain, she wants to make sure you're doing what's right. She knows what a mess can be made with relationships and families. And she knows you have a lot of potential you can live up to." Dad squeezed Ty's shoulder. "Just like I do. And I'd say you're starting to live up to it, no matter what anyone else says."

Ty walked Dad out, and a boulder-sized weight lifted from his shoulders as Dad's truck drove away. If only he could get rid of the other worry weighing on him. He'd see Lennox tomorrow, and still had no way to fix the mess he'd created.

This afternoon was booked. Ty wanted to get the rest of the flower beds completed, including adding the mulch he'd brought. Then, he would grab a quick shower before heading out for a haircut—mostly to appease his mom. Who was he kidding? He was doing that for someone else.

The evening was an early bachelor night for Brian. One of the other groomsmen couldn't do anything after rehearsal, so they bumped up their guys' night by a day. No big deal. But he hoped he could catch Brian for a one-on-one conversation before it was all over. Because, evidently, he owed his cousin a huge thanks for something he didn't even know had been an issue.

Between all the hours at the chapel and all the evenings he'd inserted himself into Lennox's life, he hadn't made it to a family dinner in months. He'd have to find more time for that in the future so he could defend himself. Although it sounded like his cousin and dad had defended him better than he could have.

Ty worked quickly and finished up his tasks, eager to celebrate with Brian. He arrived a full five minutes early at the restaurant, brushing at a few hairs that remained on his neck from the cut earlier. Brian waved him over into the corner booth, and Ty was glad to see no one else had arrived yet.

"Hey, man. Rumor has it I owe you a big thanks." Ty grabbed his cousin in a man hug and slapped him on the back.

"What for?" Confusion marred Brian's face. "Not that I'm against you thanking me."

"I heard you were offered my home." Ty raised a brow.

"Oh." Brian *pshawed*. "I would never have let Gran do that to you. That's no big deal."

"Sounded like it was more of a deal than you're letting on." Ty slid in and grabbed a menu from beside the saltshaker. "Sounded like it sort of set the whole family against you for a while."

"Well, the family is allowed to be wrong once in a while." Brian ducked his head. "Honestly, the worst part was almost losing Sara Beth over it."

"What?" Ty dropped his menu.

"We're good now. Thankfully Lennox talked her out of calling it all off yesterday."

Ty winced. Lennox was not the best option for getting advice on whether or not to call off a wedding. As far as he knew, she still didn't believe in marriage or love or any of that. Not that he was giving up. He simply wasn't sure how much progress he'd made. Especially after she found out about his part in contacting her dad.

"Evidently, Lennox reminded Sara Beth that she did love me. And that we needed to talk through the real issue and not just let it simmer." Brian shook his head. "Needless to say, no matter what you think about Lennox, I'm going to be forever grateful to her, because she kept me from losing the most wonderful thing to ever happen in my life."

Lennox had done that? She'd convinced Sara Beth that she loved Brian? There was only one way she could have done that. She'd have to believe in love—at least a little. Because Lennox wouldn't lie to her friend. Hope glimmered in his belly. He just had to gain her forgiveness so he could convince her love could be good for her too.

"You okay, man?" Brian asked. "You have this big goofy grin taking up half your face."

"I'm great." Ty was glad when the rest of Brian's friends arrived over the next few minutes. It meant he didn't have to explain why he was so thrilled. He didn't have to worry about Brian finding out he'd fanned a fire of hope that wouldn't be extinguished anytime soon. And it was a distraction from the fact that he still had almost twenty-four hours before he could see Lennox again.

"Can I take y'all's order?"

Ty glanced up into a familiar face, though it took him a second to place it. Macy. Unfortunately, she recognized him at about the same time. "Excuse me a moment."

He rushed after and caught her arm before she could duck into the kitchen. "Macy?"

She set her jaw and spun on him. "Did Lennox send you?"

"No." He'd have to tread carefully on this one. "Last time I saw Lennox, she didn't even know where you were."

Her eyes flashed with emotion, but he couldn't tell if it was pain or anger or maybe a mixture of both.

"Your family is worried about you."

"Yeah, right." She jerked free of his grip and crossed her arms.

"Seriously." Ty dashed a hand through his hair. "From what I understand, your mom is worried sick."

"If my mom cared about me, she wouldn't have been so quick to bring that traitor back into our lives. All men do is mess things up."

Ty huffed. "I'm the first to admit I mess things up. But I'm also the first to try and ask for forgiveness when I do. And your sister won't let me forget it."

Macy smirked before she could stop herself. "Sounds like her. But I still don't want to go home right now."

"I get it. Trust me. We have our own family craziness, and while it might not be like yours, it's rough at times." He gently squeezed her shoulder. "But could you at least call your mom and let her know you're okay?"

Macy glanced toward the kitchen door and chewed on her bottom lip for a moment. "I'll think about it."

"That's all I ask. Because they really are worried."

"Don't push it. I said I'd think about it."

He held his hands up in acquiescence. "Understood. I've said my piece."

And he'd learned his lesson. No more meddling. Not more than he already had, anyway. But maybe if Macy called home, Lennox would be quicker to soften toward him?

"Earth to Ty." Brian waved his hand in front of Ty's face later at the bowling alley. "Something tells me your head is somewhere else entirely."

Ty gave himself a little shake. "Sorry, man. Lots of thoughts running through my mind."

"Let me guess. Something to do with a redhead? About so tall? Blue eyes?" Brian smirked. "The one you're not interested in?"

"Yeah, yeah." Ty gave him a shove. "Before you go any further with that, just don't. It's complicated, and if you want me to be able to do all the best man stuff this weekend, I need to focus on you and not her."

"One problem with that." Brian moved to take his turn. "She'll be doing wedding stuff this weekend too."

Ty didn't need to be reminded. He was well aware that Lennox would be there, only two people away from him on the stage. That she'd be in a gorgeous dress and surrounded by flowers and candlelight. Would she let him steal a dance with her afterward?

His body basically ticked off the minutes until he could see her again. Then, he'd just to have to keep from tackling her and getting her to admit she was beginning to believe. And hope she'd forgive him. That wouldn't be hard at all, right?

Chapter Twenty-Nine

Lennox stared at the chapel from the safety of her car. It was time for Sara Beth's wedding rehearsal. Lennox was almost late, actually, but she'd crammed an extra class in this afternoon to make up for missing the next day. And then it took every ounce of self-control to force herself out of the hot shower that worked to relax her sore muscles.

Her phone pinged.

> Macy called.

Just two words, but Lennox could hear the joy in her mother's text. An answer to prayers. Lennox blinked. *Did she believe that?*

Her heart didn't rebel. All those talks with George had changed not only her mom, but herself as well.

> George, I've been thinking about everything you've said. I think I'm ready to believe.

Lennox typed the message quickly on her phone as she walked through the parking lot to the chapel.

I'm busy with Sara Beth's wedding from now until tomorrow night late. But could we talk then?

She dashed through the door and stopped, her breath catching in her throat.

The last time she'd been here, a tarp had covered the gaping hole in the front of the building and made everything seem dark and dismal. Now, the sunlight sparkled through the window, sending shimmers and rainbows all over the room, as if God Himself were blessing this marriage. And the repairs were done so well, she couldn't even tell where the glass had been broken.

Part of her missed the tarp. Much easier to deal with the dark and gloomy space than all the other memories this sparkling glass brought to mind. Particularly since they revolved around someone she dreaded facing tonight.

"Good girl, bringing your shoes to wear tonight." And there he was. Why did Ty's voice sound so ... normal? As if he hadn't stuck his nose where it didn't belong and been a general nuisance most of the year.

She refused to look his way, though he stood right beside her.

"Don't tell me this is the first time you're wearing those since—"

"Don't you think you've meddled enough? I'm a big girl. I'll be fine." She sat down on a pew and slipped off her flats, replacing them with the shiny heels.

"What do you think of my window?" His question came right next to her ear, tickling the side of her cheek and doing funny things to her tummy.

"You know, there is such a thing as personal space." She firmed her voice as she scooted farther down the bench.

Was that hurt that ran across his face? Surely not. He had to know she still wasn't happy with him. He opened his mouth to say something, but a shrill whistle at the front of the building caught their attention.

"Hey, guys. Let's go ahead and get started." Bridget Malone, Sara Beth's cousin, stood at the front, a hand on her very round abdomen. She'd agree to help Sara Beth make sure her ceremony ran smoothly, despite being seven months pregnant.

Ty offered a hand up, but Lennox ignored it. Unfortunately, these stilts Sara Beth insisted on threw her balance off. Ty caught her elbow before she could fall, a warmth spreading out through her arm and into her chest. She jerked away and found her balance on the uncomfortable shoes. Why did Sara Beth want her to wear footwear that made her taller than the bride? Ty walked beside her down the aisle, but she couldn't protest. They were headed to the same place.

"We're already practicing. Do we get brownie points?" Ty's grin came easy enough, but his usual lighthearted voice didn't come off quite as carefree.

"The only brownies people are getting tonight are at the rehearsal dinner, and we can't get to that until we're finished with the run-through here." Bridget pointed to him. "Okay, since it's bad luck for the bride and groom to play their own parts at the rehearsal, we're going to have the best man and maid of honor stand in. Up for it?"

"Sure. Anything to keep from bringing bad luck on Brian." Ty chuckled.

"Wait. What?" Lennox looked between Sara Beth and Bridget. "That doesn't even make sense. How is Sara Beth supposed to know what to do if I'm doing it for her?" She turned to Ty. "You didn't plan this, did you?"

He held his hands up. "Not I."

"It's a tradition." Sara Beth tugged at the cap sleeve of Lennox's simple blue floral sundress. "If you really don't want to do it, it's not a big deal."

"I mean, if you really want me to pretend to be you, I guess it's my job. I just don't understand it."

"It's tradition." An older woman sat on the front row and

pointed her cane at them. "The bride can't stand in that position until the actual wedding tomorrow."

"Gran," Ty whispered.

"Tell me what to do." Lennox squared her shoulders and faced Bridget as if she were a firing squad. "I guess I start in the back?"

"Let's go ahead and get all the bridesmaids and bride back there so we can do a run-through of how to space them tomorrow. Lyle, you got the music ready to go?" Bridget waved to a guy in the back. With his thumbs up, she turned and arranged the groom and groomsmen and preacher.

Sara Beth linked arms with Lennox as they walked back toward the door. "I know it's silly, but it's only pretend. Just practicing so we can make sure it's perfect tomorrow."

"I'll be fine." Lennox swallowed hard. "So long as it's *you* tomorrow when it's real."

"Oh, it will be." Sara Beth got a gleam in her eye that said she and Brian had completely made up, and she was more than ready to be his wife.

Would Lennox ever find someone who made her act the same? Her eyes lifted and met the gaze of Ty at the front, standing where Brian would be tomorrow. A war raged within her breastbone as she clung to her anger and hurt.

Bridget bustled back as quickly as her large body allowed. "Okay, let's get in order here. And then I'll show you about where in the song to start walking. We don't need to go too slowly, but we don't need to run, either. Let's do this a couple of times to get the pacing right. Sara Beth, you walk in Lennox's place so you can get an idea of how it will feel."

Before Lennox could wrap her brain around any of this, the other girls were step-pause-step-pausing down the aisle to the romantic song. Sara Beth shot her a wink before starting her own trek. Then, the flower girl was ushered toward the front, being shown how to sprinkle the artificial leaves all the way to the stage. Sara Beth's dad took Lennox's hand and gave it a squeeze.

"How's my other daughter doing tonight?" His voice was husky, as if already thinking about giving away Sara Beth tomorrow.

"We'll get through this together, huh, Mr. Miller?" Lennox squeezed his arm and took a deep breath as Bridget motioned for them to start walking.

At first, Lennox focused on making sure her steps were at the speed Bridget wanted them to be. It was awkward, and yet not. The tempo of the song lent itself to the rhythm. Halfway down, Lennox's gaze drifted up to the stage and caught Ty watching her. And the look in those brown depths nearly tripped her up. A quick glance over at Brian showed something similar in the way his gaze locked on Sara Beth. *Whoa.*

Ty's expression was mixed—hope, pain? Awe? A bit different than the bride and groom's, after all. Was it because of this farce they were forced into? It couldn't be anything else. It couldn't.

"Who gives this woman?" The minister asked.

"Her mother and I." Mr. Miller placed her hand in Ty's and then stepped back.

"Okay, then, Ty, you help her up the stairs. Brian, you watching? This is your job tomorrow." Bridget snapped her fingers. "Lennox, tomorrow you make sure Sara Beth's dress looks okay once she gets up there. I know she doesn't have a train, but it's a long skirt and might need to be straightened out some."

From there, Bridget and the minister ran quickly through how the ceremony would go. But Lennox couldn't focus on all they were saying. Ty's hair that had curled over his ears and draped over his collars all summer was now shorn closely around the bottom, but long enough on top to allow a few waves in the neat do. It distracted her, but not as much as his gaze that never wavered from her. A slight smile graced his lips, although not the normal teasing one. What went on behind those brown eyes?

"Okay, Ty and Lennox, here's something we need you to pay attention to." Bridget stepped between them, breaking the hold Ty had on her fingers as well as the intense ... whatever ... was happening between them. "Sara Beth and Brian found this old handfasting tradition they used to do in Irish weddings, and they thought it would be something fun to incorporate in theirs. They want you two to say the words and wrap their hands, so I printed it out for you and highlighted the parts you each have."

Lennox scanned the paper thrust into her hands. The words were highlighted in pink and blue. She assumed she was the former. Bridget held up a cord woven in the colors of the wedding and showed them how to drape it over the hands of the bride and groom the next day as they said the ceremonial words.

"Okay, why don't we have you practice this several times now so we can make sure you know how to drape the rope in the right way?" Bridget had Brian step over next to Sara Beth and clasp hands. From the front row, Ty's grandmother sniffed, obviously not impressed with any of this, despite it being something meant to honor their family heritage.

Ty's voice rumbled his words before he draped the cord. Their fingers brushed as she moved to do her part next, and the rope slipped to the floor. She moved to retrieve it, and Ty's hand covered hers. It took an effort to control a tremble. What was wrong with her today?

After another half an hour of going through little things, Lennox was glad to be able to sit down and slip out of the sandals. She rubbed at a spot next to her big toe that had started to get sore. Then, she made a mental note to pack a few bandages in her purse the next day. A glance at her phone showed a response from George.

> No matter how late or early, you tell me when
> and I'll meet you there.

"What are you smiling at?" Ty interrupted her, and she quickly slipped her cell back in her bag. Even though he'd had a hand in helping her reach her decision, she didn't want him to take credit for it.

"Nothing you need to know about right now." She slid her flats back on and wiggled her toes in happiness at the comfort.

"Lining up a hot date?" He wasn't discouraged easily.

"*Hot date!* As if I have time this weekend to do anything besides wedding stuff." She shook her head.

"So, you need a wedding date?"

Grabbing her purse, she left the chapel and walked toward her car. "Nope. I'll be fine on my own, just like always."

He dogged her steps, as if he still thought everything was good between them.

"Did you need something?" She unlocked her door.

"I'd offer to drive you to dinner, but since you're headed off to a girls' night afterward, I guess it doesn't make sense this time." He whispered the words directly in her ear before stepping back and holding her door open.

Her heart rate didn't slow down the whole way back to town and into the restaurant. What was wrong with her tonight? She was still mad at Ty, right? Didn't want to spend time with him or have him near her. It must be the wedding atmosphere, seeing Sara Beth so happy again, or something like that. Because she couldn't accept the alternative.

Her brain warred with itself as she discovered herself seated between Sara Beth and Ty's grandmother, of all people. The older woman lifted a knife and studied it as if looking for a spot or imperfection. Having found none, she set it back down and then surveyed the table as if she were a queen, and these were her subjects.

"Do you have a dog?" Gran Nancy nibbled a bite of potato salad.

Lennox startled from where she'd been watching Ty tell a story down the table. "What? No. My apartment doesn't allow animals."

"A shame. MC and I had several dogs through the years. I think a good pet is an asset to a relationship. Sara Beth and Brian are talking about getting a puppy later on. I promised to help them pick a good one." After all the talk about how harsh Ty's grandmother had been that summer, this was nothing like Lennox had imagined their conversation would go.

"I used to be a veterinarian, you know." Gran nodded. "Almost ruined my chances with my husband. His stubborn Irish pride didn't like that a lady doctor had moved into his promised position while he was off to Vietnam."

"I'm so glad you worked it out." Sara Beth leaned around Lennox to join the conversation. "Your family is full of so many fun stories like that."

"True. It's hard to have a boring story when you have Irish mobsters in the family." Gran smirked.

Even if Lennox were attracted to Ty and could allow herself to consider something like marriage, she wouldn't fit. Her story wasn't boring, necessarily, but it wasn't happy, either. Ty caught her attention from his seat down the table and sent her a wink. Gran sniffed again, and Lennox ducked her head, trying to hide the heat creeping up her cheeks.

Over an hour later, after several awkward conversations, listening through a few family toasts, and a huge meal of barbeque and all the fixings, the party began to break up. Sara Beth and Brian accepted several teases and taunts as people filed out, including an offer from her dad to let them elope that evening and just be done with it. Of course, they refused—too close to the actual date to renege now.

"You okay?" Sara Beth linked arms with Lennox as they walked out to her car a few minutes later.

"Fine. Why?" Lennox still hadn't disclosed everything that had happened in her family to Sara Beth. Hadn't wanted to be a downer during Sara Beth's happiest time.

"You seem distracted tonight for some reason." A gleam in Sara Beth's eyes told Lennox exactly what her friend insinuated, although Lennox wasn't about to admit anything. How could she? She wasn't even fully convinced of it herself.

Ty and Brian intercepted them as they reached Lennox's sedan.

"Don't I get one more kiss before you go?" Brian tugged Sara Beth a few steps away.

"You'll get plenty of kisses for the rest of your life." She pretended to shove him away, but then allowed him to press his lips to hers anyway.

"That looks like fun." Ty wiggled his eyebrows.

"Not sure Brian wants you to kiss him like that." Lennox shoved Ty away before he could get close enough to do anything unwanted.

Ty caught her before she could slide in the car and pressed his cheek to hers so he could murmur directly into her ear. "I'm sorry I hurt you. Sorry I pushed things and upset you. I thought I was helping. Wanted to help."

"Sometimes your idea of help causes more problems." She cringed as her voice broke. And it wasn't completely fair. Macy had called Mom, after all.

"I know. And I'm sorry about that." Ty leaned back just far enough to look in her eyes. "Will you do me a favor? At least consider forgiving me?"

Lennox blinked a few times, wishing away the moisture gathering in her eyes.

"It would make tomorrow easier, if nothing else." Ty squeezed her hand and then stepped back. "But I won't push it. You know how I feel. It's up to you now."

Lennox quickly got into her car before he could twist her heart anymore. It was too much tonight.

"The water's fine." Sara Beth giggled as she slid into the passenger seat. "Maybe you should jump in."

"Let's just focus on getting you married tomorrow, eh?" Lennox revved the engine a little more than it needed. "But first … ice cream?"

"Yes!"

Lennox drove to where they were meeting several other

friends for ice cream and chick flicks and girl time the rest of the night. Her last night to have a girls' night with her best friend. She wouldn't think about that either. Plenty of time to face those troubles another day ... along with the one with chocolate brown eyes and a heart-skipping smile, and a new haircut that only did amazing things to accentuate his jawline. The cut even revealed a scar she hadn't noticed before at the very top of his forehead.

Another day, Lennox Paige. Not today. Get him out of your head and focus, girl. Get a grip!

As if it were that easy after pretending to be the bride to his groom tonight. Not easy at all. Might not ever be easy again.

Chapter Thirty

There she was. Ty reminded himself to breathe as Lennox stepped into the doorway at the back of the chapel. The candlelight in the room made her hair look like a copper penny, the perfect complement to her sunset dress. She held her small bouquet of sunflowers and fall leaves in front of her and focused her eyes directly before her, as if afraid to look to either side.

Had she considered what he'd requested of her the night before? Was this the last day he'd ever really get to spend time with her?

"Come on." He silently willed her eyes to meet his. "Come on."

"She's going to stand directly across from you in a moment." Brian's muttered comment reminded Ty that there were others around and that maybe talking to himself wasn't such a great idea.

"You're just impatient to see your own girl." Ty teased back.

"More than anything," Brian agreed.

Lennox carefully lifted her hem and stepped up the few steps to her spot on the stage, just behind where Sara Beth would stand, and straight across from him. But she still kept her gaze from meeting his. Instead, she focused on the back of the chapel where the music had changed, and the flower girl meticulously made her way down the aisle, dropping one leaf at a time.

At this rate, they'd be here all night, and he wanted nothing more than to get to the part where he could pull Lennox to his side and maybe make her talk to him for a few minutes. It wasn't that he wasn't thrilled for Brian. He was just more ready than ever to start his own journey to happily ever after. And he couldn't imagine that with anyone other than Lennox now.

But had he ruined any slim chance of that forever?

Brian stood up a bit straighter next to him, and Ty forced his attention to the actual bride. Just like that day in the dress shop, she looked beautiful. Her hair was drawn back with little curls and wisps framing her face. The lace in her bouquet went perfectly with the lace covering her dress. And the smile on her face was one that almost outshone the sun.

Ty thought again about what Brian had told him the other night, about Lennox talking Sara Beth into giving this marriage a second chance. This wedding almost didn't happen over a family disagreement, but they were all here this afternoon. And Lennox being behind that meant more to him than just about anything else had that summer. Even more than his dream job becoming a reality.

Sara Beth took her place beside Brian, who wiped moisture from his eyes. *Yeah.* Ty could understand. He grew misty-eyed when he gazed at the maid of honor.

"Marriage is a covenant not to be entered into lightly." The minister began the ceremony, and Ty finally caught blue eyes looking his way. "It is a blessed relationship given to us by God. A partnership where you are to not only love and cherish each other, but also help each other through the struggles this life might give.

"Brian and Sara Beth know this and are sure they want to spend the rest of their lives with each other."

Lennox blinked and swallowed, but didn't look away. Had she found it in her heart to forgive him? Was she remembering the night before, when it had been them standing front and center, pretending to be bride and groom? Was she listening to the words and starting to believe their truth, that marriage really could last for a lifetime? Ty sent up a quick prayer that God would soften her heart in all those ways.

The preacher continued while Ty faced his inner struggles. Now, Lennox held Sara Beth's bouquet along with her own so the bride could clasp both hands to Brian's. The minister led them through their vows, to love and cherish each other in sickness and health, in good times and bad. Their voices were certain and sure as they repeated the words. Lennox blinked a few times as if moisture filled her eyes as well.

"And now the rings."

Brian nudged Ty's arm and held out his hand. *Oh, yeah.* Ty dug in his pocket and fished out Sara Beth's ring, passing it to his cousin. Lennox had Brian's ring on her finger, and it caught his eye as she removed it to hand to Sara Beth. A ring looked good on her. What kind of ring would she want?

After the rings, they were supposed to do the handfasting. How was the cord supposed to go again? Why did the Irish have such convoluted traditions anyway?

"Sara Beth and Brian have decided to add a little of Ireland into their ceremony today." The minister smiled and pulled out the cord. "In old Ireland, this was more of a pagan ritual, but they loved the words so much, they decided to bring it into today's ceremony. They've asked their maid of honor and best man to lead them in the promises to each other and bind their hands fast with this cord to show that their marriage will stay strong and last, no matter what."

Ty stepped forward as Lennox passed both bouquets back to the next bridesmaid. Her hand shook a bit as she took the paper from the minister. He gave her an encouraging smile and then leaned close to read the first line.

"Brian and Sara Beth, I bid you look into each other's eyes. Will you honor and respect one another, and seek to never break that honor?"

"We will." Sara Beth and Brian smiled as they answered.

Lennox reached out to help drape the cord over their hands for the first loop. Then, she read the next line. "And so, the first binding is made. Will you share each other's pain and seek to ease it?" Her voice cracked at the end, but she made it through. Was she thinking about her parents' failed marriage and all that came from it?

"We will."

Ty helped Lennox pull one of the cords through the original loop. "And so the binding is made. Will you share the burdens of each so that your spirits may grow in this union?" The words were growing on him. He liked how such a pagan ritual had a lot of Christian themes running through it.

"We will."

Lennox tugged the other cord through. "And so, the binding is made. Will you share each other's laughter, and look for the brightness in life and the positive in each other?"

"We will."

Ty and Lennox finished draping the cord, then Ty finished the words of the ceremony. "And so, the binding is made." He tugged the knot into place. "Brian and Sara Beth, as your hands are bound together now, so your lives and spirits are joined in a union of love and trust. Above you are the stars, and below you is the earth. Like the stars, your love should be a constant source of light, and like the earth, a firm foundation from which to grow."

Ty reached over and squeezed Lennox's hand before letting her go so they could each move back to their own places. Might as well take advantage of every chance he had to touch her before this day ended.

"Beautiful sentiments and promises have been made today." The minister beamed at the couple. "I know Sara Beth and Brian will keep them all. So, by the power vested in me by God and the state of Tennessee, I now pronounce you man and wife. Brian, kiss your bride."

Cheers erupted through the small chapel as Brian laid a kiss on Sara Beth that almost embarrassed Ty. He clapped his cousin on the back as they awkwardly turned to face the audience to be presented as "Mr. and Mrs. Dunne." Lennox kept Sara Beth's bouquet for now since her hands were rather occupied. Once the bride and groom were halfway down the aisle, Ty offered Lennox his arm. After only a moment, she placed her hand in the crook of his elbow and followed his lead down the stairs and toward the doorway.

"You're beautiful." He couldn't resist any longer. He had to whisper the words to her before they even made it out of the auditorium.

Her eyes cut over to him, but then darted right back to her friend.

Sara Beth laughed as she tugged at the cord. "I don't think we thought this all the way through. Can you help?"

"Considering you added that to our tasks right at the last minute? I don't know." Ty poked his cousin. "Maybe we should punish you by making you leave your hands tied together until after dinner."

"People will be coming out any minute, man. Give a guy a hand." Brian offered up his arms, and the gold of his wedding band flashed in the light.

Ty fought back a niggle of jealousy and worked to undo the knot. Who knew he'd have to reverse a knot tied this evening? Lennox reached in to tug on the other end, and as the cord came loose, their fingers collided. Her eyes met his once more.

"Oh, Sara Beth. You're just lovely, darling." An older woman Ty assumed was Sara Beth's grandmother came through the door.

Ty moved to his place in the receiving line, although most of these people wouldn't care to talk to him as much as the ones they came to see married.

As Gran exited, she greeted the couple cordially and then moved on. Lennox was next and she gave a brief nod. The glare she fixed on Ty almost cowed him.

"Don't think I can't see what's going on." She shook her

finger under his nose. "This girl here seems to have a lot of your attention. If you want to keep that house you're in, you better make sure you know what you're doing."

"I'm very sure I know what I'm doing, Gran. Thanks for the advice, though." He gave her a hug despite wanting to bat her scolding fingers instead.

She wasn't allowed to linger. The crowd behind her pushed her on, and he sighed in relief.

"Did she just warn you to stay away from me?" Lennox glanced over at him between handshakes and fake smiles.

"I wasn't really sure. But I'm not worried."

"But she threatened to take away your house." Lennox frowned. "Isn't that important?"

"One, it's not as important as you are." He met her gaze square on so she'd know he spoke only truth. "And two, my dad and uncle already started the paperwork to have the house transferred to my name instead of hers. She can't really threaten that anymore."

Her lips formed a perfect *O* drawing his attention for much longer than they should have. A cleared throat brought him back to the awareness that this was a very public event, and lots of people were around. Finally, the end of the line approached.

"Picture time." Bridget waved the bridal party and family back into the auditorium. "Come on, guys. Let's get this done quickly so we can go party."

Ty had no idea there were so many different configurations of groups and poses required for wedding photos. But he submitted to standing where told and smiling as the lights flashed in his eyes again and again. The flower girl threw a fit and finally laid on her back in the floor and screamed. The photographer shrugged, snapped a photo of the girl's tantrum, and then took a picture of the rest of them without her. Might as well capture the reality as well as the dream.

"Okay, family is done. Just a few more of the main couple."

The photographer waved his hand to release them all from confinement.

Lennox stopped at the doorway, watching Sara Beth and Brian stare lovingly into each other's eyes while the camera captured it.

"Penny for your thoughts," Ty whispered, standing beside her.

"Sorry. Mine are worth at least two cents." She drew her eyes away and walked out into the evening air. White lights strung between the tree branches gave the area a fairyland atmosphere. She paused and smelled the roses beside the front door.

"I'm so glad you picked those out." He held his breath as she straightened.

"They're beautiful."

"I'm glad you're pleased with them."

"I am." She glanced over toward the buffet tables.

"Hungry?"

"I could eat a bit."

He wasn't really interested in the food so much as just being with her. Unfortunately, she claimed a seat between two other bridesmaids with no way for him to squeeze in.

He somehow made it through nibbling a few bites of the dinner options, cheering the bride and groom as they toasted and cut the cake. But as soon as she finished her piece of cake, he couldn't take it anymore. He needed to talk, and there was only one way he could think of to get her to himself where she wouldn't easily get away.

As Sara Beth and Brian started the first dance, he grabbed the trash from her hand to throw away, and then tugged her toward the action.

Chapter Thirty-One

"What are you doing?" She hissed, wishing her heels had something to dig into on this floor.

"Dragging you out here where I know you won't make a scene and ruin your best friend's wedding." He twined his fingers with hers and splayed his other hand against her spine.

"To what end?"

"I need to talk to you."

"I've never been able to stop you from talking before." She swallowed and refused to meet his eyes.

"How are things at home?"

"*That's* what you want to talk about?" She finally let her gaze lock with his.

"I just want to make sure I didn't mess things up permanently. Did Macy ever call?"

Lennox frowned. "She did. But how did you know?"

He glanced away, spun her in a circle before moving back into a gentle sway.

"Ty?"

"I ran into her the other day. Told her your family missed her. That's all, I swear."

He had? Her belly tightened, and she warred with whether to be angry again or thrilled at his help. "There you go meddling again." Her voice stayed more friendly than scolding.

"I just can't seem to help myself when it comes to you. I want the best for you."

She couldn't answer. Didn't know what to say. What to think. What her emotions were doing.

"You're very quiet." The warmth of Ty's hand against Lennox's back sent sparks through her middle, though she tried to quench them. Couldn't let him woo her back into a sense of ease around him. Not yet.

"Lucky for me, Sara Beth decided to forgo the awful tradition of speeches." Lennox risked a smile and was met with a grin of his own.

"Too bad." He shook his head. "Although maybe not because who could've given a better speech than the best man?"

"*Ha*. Yeah, right." She started to pull away, but he held her tight.

"Not so fast. I have more things to discuss with you." Holding her fingers tight, he spun her out and then back in, making her breath catch.

"And if I'm tired of having a discussion?" She pushed the words through her lips, although she had a hunch she wouldn't be given an option.

"You're not scared of me, are you?" He gave her that smirk that tipped only half of his lips up.

"You wish." She scoffed.

"Good. Because I hope to get much closer to you."

She glanced down at the mere inches between them. "I think if we get much closer, people will talk."

"Not what I meant." He pressed his slightly scruffy cheek against hers. "Although I wouldn't complain. I don't mind people talking."

She pushed him back again. "Well, I do."

"Noted." He used their twined hands to give her a mock salute. "Now, tell me. When did you start believing in love?"

"Ty …"

"Uh-uh." His voice dropped to a more serious tone. "Brian told me what you told Sara Beth. And I know you don't lie. So, somewhere deep inside, something has changed. You're finally thinking that maybe, just maybe, love is real and is worth it."

Lennox let out a deep breath. "Ty, please don't. Even if I finally admit that, in some cases, love is real, you don't want to go there with me. I come from a messed-up family. My mom and dad fought for years before he finally walked out. Then, I watched Mom nearly kill herself trying to find someone or something to take the pain away. Macy is following that pattern. And my dad … well, you know as much as I do. Maybe more, considering how much you meddled in getting Dad back into my life."

"I apologized for that."

She shook her head. "Needless to say, I'm broken."

"You know what happens when a bone breaks?"

Not the response she had expected. "You have to wear a cast?"

"The rumor is that the bone grows back stronger as it heals. That's what I think of when I see you." He trailed his pointer finger along her jawline. "You might have *been* broken. But you *are* healing. And you're getting stronger than ever. Trust me, you're one of the strongest women I know."

She ducked her head.

"I mean it. Who else could come from a background like yours and turn out so well? You've earned a degree, started a business, made something of yourself. You obviously care enough about your mom to take care of her to the point you've been ridiculed. You've bent over backward for the last six months trying to make sure this day was perfect for your best friend, despite your uncertainty about the choice she was making. And you're obviously strong enough to control your temper, because I'm still alive, aren't I?"

She laughed and blinked a few times.

"Oh, come on. You know I'm right." He lowered his voice to a whisper. "I also think you'd believe in love even more if you'd accept the truths George and I have been sharing with you about God."

"Good thing I did, then, huh?" The words escaped before she could stop them. She met his gaze, and her breath caught. The pure joy shining through those brown eyes was almost more than she could take. Did he truly care about her that much?

"You did?" His voice came out higher than usual, obviously full of emotion.

She nodded, pressed her lips together. "George is meeting me later this evening to help me become a Christian."

Before she could react, Ty wrapped her in a bear hug and spun her around in dizzying circles, her feet flying out behind her. She held on for dear life, her face buried in his shoulder. When he finally stopped and put her down, he didn't go back to the small distance they'd had before.

"I am so proud of you." He pressed his forehead against hers.

"People are giving us funny looks."

"I don't care. If I didn't think you'd kill me, I would've let out a whoop when I did that." He squeezed her shoulders. "Can I come with you?"

She opened her mouth to object, but instead said, "Okay."

"I hate to break this up, but Brian and I are about to make our escape." Sara Beth stood right next to Lennox, a splendor in her ivory gown.

"Of course." Lennox pulled from Ty's arms, half-relieved, yet half-sorry. "I'll come help you change into your other dress."

"Thanks."

Lennox glanced around and noticed a lot of the other guests seemed ready to go too. How long had they been dancing? It hadn't felt like long, but the sunset of earlier had given way to a star-filled sky. She picked her way through the crowd toward the chapel, where Sara Beth's going-away outfit hung in one of the tiny classrooms.

She reached the chapel doors and turned back only to discover that the bride hadn't followed her. There. Across the yard, Sara Beth was still with Ty. He caught Lennox's gaze and then straightened from where he'd been talking in Sara Beth's ear. And there went that half-grin of his, sending a shiver through her belly even from this distance.

Why, oh why, had she agreed to let him come with her to the church building in town to meet George? More time with Ty, when she was already so discombobulated, was the last thing she needed. She bit back her frustration as her friend approached.

"This day has been perfect, Lennox. Thanks so much for being my maid of honor." Sara Beth wrapped her arm around Lennox's waist as they walked down the small hallway.

"I'm happy for you." Lennox helped lift the lacy gown over Sara Beth's head, then zipped up the pretty floral sundress she would leave in. A week and a half on a tropical cruise sounded lovely. A week and a half to escape to anywhere that wasn't here, honestly. A place to get away from distractions and temptations and maybe get her head on straight again.

"So, you and Ty made up, huh?" Sara Beth winked as she slipped on her flats.

"Don't even start." Lennox held up a finger.

"I know, I know. Just because you believe love really does exist now doesn't mean you're ready to accept that you're worthy of it." Sara Beth caught her finger and gave her hand a squeeze. "But you are."

Lennox swallowed a lump in her throat, her desire for Sara Beth's words to be true warring with her lifetime of experiences.

"I mean it, Len. Ty told me what you're doing tonight. I'm so happy for you. I wish our plane didn't leave so soon so we could join you. But I want you to remember something." Sara Beth put her hands on Lennox's cheeks. "You're giving your life to God even though you're not worthy of His love, either. That's the secret. None of us are worthy of God. That's why it's such a gift that He wants a relationship with us. And when we step into that relationship, *that's* what makes us worthy. When you step into a relationship with a man, it's not the same, but similar. The relationship makes you better if it's right and good. And you and Ty make each other better."

Lennox pressed her lips together, fighting back tears and hope. "Let's get you back with your groom."

They met Brian in the hallway, and Lennox went out the door first to join the rest of the group of well-wishers. Ty pressed a handful of colorful leaves into her hand, as if he'd been waiting for her to get there. And he probably had.

Brian and Sara Beth stood for a second in the doorway of the chapel, their faces beaming, hands clasped together. Then, they ran down the narrow path left by their friends and family as everyone tossed the fall flora into the air to rain down on the couple. Brian had to work a couple extra minutes before they could pull the car away, thanks to Ty and the other groomsmen's job of decorating. Someone had completely covered the front windshield in shaving cream.

Lennox swallowed another lump as the newlyweds drove away. Ty wrapped his arm around her and squeezed. She hesitated only a moment before leaning into the embrace. Right now, she needed care more than her normal standard of distance.

"What all do you need to do before you can leave?" Ty's question pulled her back to the chaos around them, and she straightened to stand on her own again.

"I don't think I need to do much. Sara Beth and Brian's moms are in charge, but Sara Beth also hired a clean-up crew, and it looks like they're already working." Lennox pointed to the tables strewn with food earlier that were now almost empty.

"I'm ready to get out of this tux." Ty tugged at his bowtie.

"Yeah. That's a shame." Lennox pressed a hand to her mouth, wishing the words back in, but it was too late.

"Oh?" Ty's eyebrow lifted. "You like the way I look today, huh?"

She pursed her lips a moment. "Always fishing for compliments."

She spun to put her back to him, glancing around to try and find her bouquet. His finger ran up her small slip of skin between her zipper and button before she could move away. Her breath caught as a shiver worked its way up her spine. She quickly faced him, afraid to let him have a chance of doing that again.

"You better watch it." Lennox stepped farther away.

He held his hands up as if remorseful, although a bit of glee lingered in the creases around his eyes. "I won't do it again."

She waited another moment, studying him.

"I promise." He drew an *X* on his chest with his fingers.

She gave a nod, gathered her things, and bid goodbye to the mothers, confirming they truly didn't need anything else before she left. Part of her was elated about what would happen in a short while, but the other part trembled at the immensity of the decision. George said this was the most important thing she could do, and she believed him.

Ty leaned against her car, hands in his pockets, his undone bowtie dangling loosely over his chest.

"You're not riding with me." She used her bouquet to motion him out of the way.

"I know. But I didn't want you to renege on your promise and leave without me."

"I never go back on a promise."

"I know." His words were matter-of-fact. He straightened, reached out to stroke her face, and then sauntered several feet away to where his little convertible sat. "I'll see you there."

This would be a night for the books, one way or another. Possibly even in more ways than she'd originally imagined.

Chapter Thirty-Two

Ty could see Lennox's hands shaking from three steps away. He longed to comfort her, but wasn't sure he wouldn't make things worse. So, he held the door for her and kept quiet.

George and Faye were already in the auditorium, although Lennox blinked several times when she noticed her mom there. Ty shook George's hand as he greeted them. George led them down to the front pew and motioned for them to sit.

"Lennox, you texted me and said you've started to believe what I was teaching. Is that right?" George's voice was easy, as if afraid to spook her.

She nodded, ducking her head. "It all makes more sense than anything else. And yet, it doesn't."

"What part doesn't make sense?" George's mustache twitched as he waited.

"I don't know." Lennox twisted her fingers together. "I see the peace and ... improvements in Mom's life since she started believing in God and going to church. I know how awful things were before. I want that. But I can't understand why God would offer such a gift to someone like me."

Ty sat behind her and laid a hand on her shoulder, but studied

George for any indication George wanted him to answer. For now, he'd stay quiet. Something told Ty she'd listen to George more readily than to him at this point. Maybe someday she'd trust him as much, but George had won her over this summer.

"Lennox, I've come to love you like one of my own daughters." George reached out and squeezed her fingers. "Was it hard for me?"

Lennox frowned. "I don't know."

"No." He shook his head. "It wasn't hard at all. Was it hard for me to learn to love your mom, even before she agreed to go to meetings with me and gave up alcohol?"

"It didn't appear so." Lennox's voice was quiet.

"It wasn't." George leaned forward. "Here's the deal. We all have flaws. We all have mistakes, problems, things that hold us back from being our best. But God loves us anyway. He looks past those things."

"Why?"

"Because we're made in His image." George tapped his Bible. "He made us to be like Him, and He made us with the purpose of being in a loving relationship with Him. When we aren't in that relationship, it hurts Him almost as much as it hurts us. And when you give your life to God, you won't have all those sins you think keep you from being worthy. Because God washes them all away and makes you into a new person. You'll be a blank slate, completely pure, and you can consider today day one of your life."

Lennox worried her lips together, and the longing for what George talked about palpably warred with the fear. "What if I fail?"

"What if you fail?"

Lennox jerked her head toward George. "Do you think I will?"

"No." George shook his head. "But I don't think you'll automatically do everything perfectly, either. We still live in a broken world. And you'll learn as you go. That's okay. God knows that. As long as you try to do what He wants, He forgives when you slip."

Lennox was quiet for several long minutes. "I want that. I want to know someone loves me, no matter what."

Faye muffled a sob in George's shoulder. Was she relieved or hurt by Lennox's words? After all, her own daughter basically said her mother didn't love her all the time. But George kept his focus on Lennox.

"Okay." George rubbed his hands together. "Let's get you buried."

"Buried?" Lennox paused where she had started to stand.

George pointed to the baptistry. "We're going to baptize you. That means, we're going to bury you under the water, just like we're burying your old body to bring you up a new creature in Christ. It's a symbol. It shows God you love and trust Him so much you're willing to follow His son's example of death and resurrection."

While he waited, Ty prayed for Lennox. Thanking God for allowing her to come to this point. Thanking God for allowing him to be here. Asking for the peace she longed for to settle on her immediately. Thanking God that George had become such a part of their lives. Praying for Sara Beth and Brian as they headed off to start their life together.

As soon as Lennox rose from the water, George wrapped her up in a bear hug, not caring that she was soaking wet and sloshing water over the edge of his waders. "I probably should've let your mom have the first hug, but I couldn't resist. I always love witnessing a baptism. Happy Birthday, Sister."

Lennox laughed, working her way through the now choppy water and back up to her mother. Faye didn't even bother with the towel. She wrapped her daughter up and allowed the cold water to soak into her clothes too.

Ty yearned to do the same, but he'd have to settle for when she came out. If he thought he loved her before, it was only a drop in the puddle of how he loved her now that she was his sister in

Christ. To see her journey from not believing in love or God or marriage or anything else of the sort to this—it was one of the most powerful things he'd ever witnessed.

"Does she know you love her?" George's question was quiet, and Ty glanced over to see George's focus on him as Lennox and her mother disappeared into the dressing room.

"She's been told." Ty cleared his throat. "But I don't know if she fully believes it or not."

"Keep working on her, Son. Just the fact that she let you come tonight tells me you're making progress."

"Thanks." Ty nodded but didn't say anything else.

He slid back onto the front pew and studied the stained-glass window above the baptistery here. It wasn't as pretty as the one in his chapel, in his opinion, but his family hadn't wanted them to move the original one out of the chapel and into town when the church moved into the bigger, more centrally located building back in the nineties. He was glad. He couldn't imagine it anywhere else, and he could admire it anytime he wanted.

So much had changed over the last few months. If George was right, then Ty really had made progress with Lennox. But was it enough? They wouldn't have the excuse of the wedding to see each other anymore. Sure, he could drop in for kickboxing class every week, but that wasn't enough, either. Especially if she avoided him again. He wasn't ready to lose momentum. If anything, he wanted to gain more.

George came out, flapping the bottom of his shirt. "Whoever decided wearing waders during a baptism was a good idea wasn't a hugger." He chuckled, his big grey mustache wiggling with the mirth.

As happy as Ty was, he also fought melancholy. In a few minutes, it would be over, and Lennox would go her way, and he'd go his. When would he see her again? That would drive him crazy.

Faye stepped from the room with the wet items in her arms and held the door open for Lennox to follow. Lennox smiled, but then worried her bottom lip between her teeth. She only stepped out far enough that her mom could close the door. It was as if she were unsure what the protocol was now.

Ty leaped to his feet and quickly walked to her, wrapping his arms around her chilled body. She'd exchanged her bridesmaid's dress for a T-shirt and leggings, and her hair was slightly messed from the water, but he didn't care. She was the most beautiful woman he'd ever seen.

"Here, we have the tradition of hugging new members." He gave another squeeze, then stepped back and rubbed his hands over her arms to help warm them up. "I feel a bit overdressed now."

Lennox giggled. "Sorry. I just couldn't bear to put that thing back on tonight."

"No worries. We'll just have to find another opportunity for you to wear it again."

She shook her head. "Not if I can help it."

When she glanced over his shoulder, he remembered her mom and George were still there. He swallowed a sigh and offered her his arm. Her mom wrapped her in another hug when they reached the back of the auditorium.

"I guess you're ready to lock up." Ty shook George's hand once more.

"Unless you need something else." George draped his arm over Faye's shoulder. "I thought I'd see if I could take this woman for some late-night ice cream. You're more than welcome to join us."

As much as Ty longed for an excuse to spend more time with Lennox, he could also see the fatigue setting in. "It's been a long day for us. I'll take a rain check."

Relief settled across her features as she agreed.

"Okay, then." George ushered them out to their cars. "We'll see you later."

"See you at church in the morning?" Ty leaned against the

open door of Lennox's car as she draped her dress across the back seat.

She didn't meet his eyes. "I thought I might join Mom and George."

"Thanks for letting me come tonight, Lennox." He ran a finger down the side of her face. "As well as the amazing dances earlier. And the pleasure of standing across from you during the wedding. And everything else we've done together over the past six months."

"That sounds like goodbye." Her gaze darted up to meet his finally.

"Only for tonight." He pressed a kiss to her forehead. "I just wanted to remind you how much you've come to like me." He gave a wink and then walked over to slide into his own car.

She frowned his direction before sitting in her driver's seat and heading toward her apartment. If he'd thoroughly confused her, it was no more than he'd done to himself. He longed to follow her and try to say something better. Instead, he prayed all the way home.

"God, if it's your will we be together, show me how to go about this."

Chapter Thirty-Three

Lennox sat and stared up at the stained-glass window from her perch on the stone bench a few feet away, at the edge of the old graveyard. The late September breeze ruffled her hair and promised cooler weather in the next month or so. It hadn't snowed in Tennessee as early as October in years, so they might be due.

Though the peace from two weeks before when she'd accepted Christ as her Savior was still there, her thoughts were unsettled. Ty had kept his distance since the wedding—to the point of not even attending kickboxing class the last two Saturdays. It was something she'd longed for back in March, but now it only left her confused ... and slightly sad.

She admitted it.

She missed him.

Maybe even more than that.

She let out a deep breath and willed her muscles to relax. As far as she knew, he wasn't even around right now. She'd wanted to get away on her afternoon off. As she steered her car out of town, it automatically turned this direction as if it had a mind of its own.

"I wondered if I'd find you here sooner or later."

His voice stirred up the churning in her gut even more. "How'd you know I was here?"

"Well, I live right over there and could see you through the window." He pointed back at his house on the other side of the parking lot. "So, you know, nothing fancy like a magic mirror or anything."

She wrinkled her nose and scooted over to make room for him. "I thought you'd be at work."

"No appointments this afternoon, so I came home to work on something else." He lowered himself to the bench, and she realized the seat wasn't quite as large as she first assumed. His leg brushed against hers, and his hand pressed her fingers where they overlapped.

"Appointments?"

Ty snapped his fingers. "Oh, I didn't get a chance to tell you."

"Tell me what?"

"I'm now a consultant for my dad's company instead of the office manager. A new employee started this week, so I'm free of all office duty except when Henry needs a sick day." He grinned. "I get to help people decide on colors and faucets and flooring and lighting and things now instead. I've already had four clients."

"Wow, Ty. That's amazing. I know it's what you really wanted." She shook her head. "But I thought you hadn't told your dad?"

"Evidently, in one of Gran's rants, she mentioned to my dad that I wasn't living up to the family's expectations."

Lennox opened her mouth to protest but he held up a hand.

"Then, she went on to say I couldn't even man up enough to let my dad know I wasn't happy." Ty shrugged. "So, Dad came to me, and we finally talked about it. I even told him about my plan to start using the chapel as a wedding venue. I ran an ad in last weekend's paper and have had three calls already."

"That's a lot to keep up with."

"It is." He nudged her with his shoulder. "Good thing I have this amazing friend who taught me a thing or two about staying organized."

"Me?" She pressed a hand to her heart. Was he serious?

"You." He held her gaze captive. "You're good for me, Lennox. I even bought a planner."

"A planner!" She dragged her gaze away and tried to lighten the mood. "What is the world coming to? Next thing you know, you'll be on time for everything."

"Let's not get too carried away." He chuckled. "Although, my planner isn't working out perfectly."

"Oh?"

"No." He hung his head and put on his best puppy dog face. "It hasn't got a single date in it."

She frowned. "A planner without dates is a notebook, Ty. What did you buy?"

"Not that kind of dates." Something gleamed in his eye, and he leaned closer to whisper in her ear. "The kind where I take you to dinner, or stay in to watch a movie, or for dancing lessons, or hiking in the state park down the road. It wouldn't matter, as long as it was with you. I've missed you terribly these last few weeks."

She swallowed against the emotion in her throat. "Ty."

"I'm serious, Lennox. I've been half-crazy since the wedding."

She shook her head. "How can you say that when you're the one who's stayed away?"

"So, you noticed."

"Of course, I noticed." She caught herself before she said more. She could tell by the smile forming on his lips that this was exactly what he wanted. "It wasn't nearly as annoying at kickboxing."

"Mm." He sat back again and studied her. "You're putting on an act right now. You did miss me. Just admit it."

"Ty." She dipped her head. "Don't you remember what your grandma said when she saw us together at the wedding? I'm not good enough for you."

"No." He pushed away from the bench and started pacing in

front of her. "For one thing, I don't care what Gran said. After all the hoopla she caused over Brian and Sara Beth, my uncle finally had some tests run. She's got early-onset dementia. In other words, it's not her. It's the disease messing with her brain." He drew circles to the side of his head. "We'd all been wondering for a while now, but the diagnosis confirmed it."

A flutter started in her heart. His grandmother didn't disapprove of her? Was that enough?

"Secondly," Ty ranted on, "I never again want to hear you say you're not good enough." He slashed his and through the air. "For anything. Good enough. What does that even mean?"

Lennox stood and caught his hands in hers to stop his erratic movements. "Ty, stop. Listen. I'm broken. I know you said I was like a bone and growing stronger. But that doesn't mean that I'll ever be whole again. I come from a past where I don't even know what a real relationship is supposed to look like. My parents' marriage didn't last. And mom's relationships afterward were even worse until she met George. I wouldn't even know how to go about ..." She motioned in the air, trying to find the right words. She wanted to say, "being your wife," but he really didn't need that kind of encouragement.

Ty pressed a kiss to her fingers. "Lennox Paige Malone, you are gorgeous inside and out. Do you see that window up there?"

"What?" The change of subject confused her more than the zings running from her fingers through the rest of her body at the touch of his lips.

"The stained-glass window right above us. Do you see it?"

"Of course. I helped move it several months ago, didn't I?"

"Okay, how do you think they made it?"

She tried to tug her hands free, but he held tight. "Ty, what are you talking about?"

"Just tell me how you think they made that gorgeous window."

"I don't know. They took all the pieces and glued them

together with the iron ... thingies." This conversation was the strangest she'd ever had.

"And how did they get all the pieces to put together in the first place?" He prompted.

She opened her mouth, but honestly had no idea what he wanted her to say.

"They broke the glass."

She blinked.

"Lennox, you can't make a window like that without breaking the glass first. They took big pieces of glass and broke them into the right shapes to put back together and become even better."

He moved his hands to her arms and gave them a squeeze. "You keep telling me you're broken, but to me, that just makes you more beautiful. None of us are perfect. You know I'm not. I don't always get my hair cut when I should. I don't always make it to things on time. And you know I'm more prone to act with my heart than my head. I'm not asking for perfection. I couldn't live up to it. I'm asking for someone to share my life with, to make me a better person. And you do that, Lennox. *You*."

He pressed a palm to his eyes and was quiet for several moments. She honestly didn't know what to say. His analogy was beautiful, but how could it be true?

"Your heart has been broken." Ty broke the silence. "I know that. But what if God allowed that to happen so He could put it together again in a more beautiful way? Think about it. If your dad had never left, you'd have never lived here, you'd have never met Sara Beth, never gone and become part-owner in your dream job. Your mom would never have met George. And you might never have learned about God. So, yes, there was a lot of bad that came from your dad walking out, but look at all the good."

Tears tickled as they made their way down her cheeks, clinging to her chin. She'd never thought of it that way before. But he left something very important out.

"You forgot to say I'd have never met you." She whispered the words.

Ty lowered his hand and peered into her eyes, as if afraid to believe what he heard.

"I'm no good at this, Ty, but we've got good examples to help us, right?" She pressed her lips together.

"Right." He crushed her to him, holding her so tight she almost couldn't breathe. "Right."

"I missed you too." She mumbled the words into his shoulder. "So much more than I thought I would."

He leaned back far enough to look at her again. "Oh, Lennox."

Then, as if of one accord, their lips met, tentatively at first, and then more passionately. She wrapped her arms around his back and held on while the emotional hurricane rushed through her, accelerating her heart rate, and leaving her more breathless than before.

And as he'd told her before, it didn't feel lustful. It was passionate, sure. And heady. But as he pulled back, she could honestly say she felt loved, cherished, and wanted.

"So, how about having dinner with me tonight? And every other evening we both have off?" He wrapped his arm around her shoulder and walked her toward his house. "I have a couple steaks marinating in my kitchen. If you're willing to help me make a salad, I'll share."

"Mm." She stopped right inside his front door and stared at the striped chairs again.

"What?" His gaze bounced between her and the furniture.

"It's nothing. It's silly, really."

He leaned against the doorframe and smirked. "Tell me anyway. If we're going to have a relationship, we have to talk about everything."

"The first time I was here, I noticed that the stripes in your chairs are the exact same shade of red as my sofa." The words slipped from her lips before she could stop them.

"I was going to ease into this, start with a few dates, work up to getting married, and then have you move your red couch over, but since you mentioned it ..." He chuckled as he closed the distance between them once more. "You know I'm really interested in getting that sofa here more than anything, right?"

She laughed as he pressed kisses all over her face. "Stop! You asked, and I told you. I don't deserve this onslaught."

"I'm willing to do a few remodels if it means you'll be my wife and live here with me." His voice was husky as he traced a finger down her cheek. "I really love the idea of melding our lives together into one."

"Don't rush me." She licked her lips. "I'm willing to work toward it, but we can't rush."

"I know." He tugged her hand and pulled her down the hall toward the kitchen.

"Although, that framed saying in the powder room would have to go if I were to live here." She pointed at the door as they passed it.

This time, he let out a full-on laugh. "Oh, Lennox. You're going to make life so much more fun. I'm so glad I found the window to your heart."

The End

Discussion Questions

1. Lennox has worked hard to escape the dysfunctional aspects of her family. But has she really escaped it? Or is holding onto her refusal to love keeping her locked in her past?
2. Ty's family might not have the problems Lennox's does, but it's not perfect, either. Why was it so hard for Lennox to see that his family had problems too?
3. Lennox bases her ideas of love on her parents' relationship. Why is it bad to have only one example to look to when it comes to relationships? Who else could she have observed in order to gain a better perspective?
4. Lennox's mom tried to fix her broken heart with relationships that never worked and with alcohol. Is it ever a good idea to fix pain with temporary relief? How are some other ways people attempt to fill the holes in their life with worldly Band-Aids?
5. Ty wants to break free of his dad's desk job, but also doesn't want to let the family down. In reality, his degree was exactly what he needed for both, but he couldn't figure out how to make it known. Have you

ever struggled to find a solution only to realize it was right in front of you the whole time?

6. The chapel fell into disrepair when people started worshiping closer to the center of town. What are some ways they could have been using it besides weekly worship services to keep the history alive?

7. The stained-glass window in the chapel has a long history, weaving faith and beauty together into one piece. Have you ever seen a stained-glass window that touched you in some way or told a story through the art of it?

8. The items Lennox and Ty find hidden in the window frame give them a peek into his ancestors' past. Do you have an heirloom that keeps you connected to those who came before? Why is it important to remember history?

9. George isn't what Lennox expects when she finds out her mom is dating someone new. Nor is he what she expects when she finds out he's a Christian. What do we risk when we go into a situation with prior expectations? What might we miss out on?

10. When Lennox's dad comes back, asking for forgiveness, her sister is unwilling to even consider it. What does Lennox discover when she starts working toward forgiving him? Why is such a weight lifted when she does?

Amy R Anguish grew up a preacher's kid, and in spite of having lived in seven different states that are all south of the Mason-Dixon line, she is not a football fan. Currently, she resides in Tennessee with her husband, daughter, and son, and usually a bossy cat or two. Amy has an English degree from Freed-Hardeman University that she intends to use to glorify God, and she wants her stories to show that while Christians face real struggles, it can still work out for good.

Follow her at http://abitofanguish.weebly.com or http://www.facebook.com/amyanguishauthor

Or https://twitter.com/amy_r_anguish

Learn more about her books at https://www.pinterest.com/msguish/my-books/

And check out the YouTube channel she does with two other

authors, Once Upon a Page (https://www.youtube.com/@
onceuponapage3326)

Window of Opportunity by Heather Greer

The Stained-glass Legacy Series—Book One

Faith and duty drive Evangeline Moore to protect her father's pristine image as a judge in Harrisburg, Illinois. Her resolve's biggest test? Dot, her childhood friend. With Evangeline beside her, Dot's desire for the Roaring Twenties' glitz and glamor leads the pair into questionable situations.

Born into a Chicago mob family, Brendan Dunne understands duty, but faith puts him at odds with his father's demands. Even when his brother James's propensity for trouble lands them in Harrisburg, the truth is undeniable. To their father, the lines he won't cross mean Brendan will never measure up.

When circumstances push Brendan and Evangeline together, unexpected events create opportunity to break free of family expectations. Will they be brave enough to forge their own path before the window closes on their chance to change?

Get your copy here:

https://scrivenings.link/windowofopportunity

Window of Peace - By Regina Rudd Merrick

Stained-glass Legacy—Book Two

Michael Connor "MC" Dunne led charmed life. He had a plan—finish veterinary school, get married, and take over the local animal clinic. Enter the Vietnam War.

MC returns home, injured, to Park Haven, Tennessee, and soon learns there's a new vet in town, hired when the local veterinarian suffered a heart attack. So much for his plan.

Violent flashbacks and nightmares pull MC away from his faith and turn him into a hermit. His safe place is the family farm, working on the old cabin and restoring the chapel his great-uncle built in the early 1900s, with the family's heirloom stained-glass window.

Nancy Jean Baker struggles to prove herself as a competent veterinarian to the small-town skeptics of Park Haven. Fighting her own demons from a traumatic past, she's driven to succeed.

But when war veteran MC Dunne returns home, wounded and wary, Nancy discovers she's standing between him and his dream.

Can they help each other overcome their hurts and horrors? Or is their hope of happiness doomed when the past threatens to ruin their future?

Get your copy here:

https://scrivenings.link/windowofpeace

Window of Time - By Erin R. Howard

Stained-glass Legacy—Book Four

Coming in December 2023

Also by Amy R. Anguish

Destination: ~~Fun~~ Romance

Roadtrip Romance—Book One

It's not every day you bring a boyfriend back as a souvenir.

Katie Wilhite is ready to settle into her new job as a librarian now that college is through, but friends Bree and Skye want one more girls' trip, and when Bree insists this is her bachelorette fling, Katie agrees. What she didn't agree to was allowing fun and flighty Skye to dictate the itinerary or for her anxiety to kick in harder than ever ... right in front of a cute guy.

Camden Malone had no idea when he agreed to be the voice of reason on his cousin Ryan's vacation that the trip wouldn't stay in New Orleans as planned. But when Ryan plots with Skye so that the guys can tag along with the girls all week, he isn't nearly as upset as he should be. Not with Katie's fiery temper and flashing eyes intriguing him more by the minute.

Can Katie relax enough to trust Camden and a possible future, or will she continue to push him away as only a vacation fling? And can Camden move past a rocky history of his own to be able to jump into a better future? For a trip that was supposed to be all about fun, there's a lot of romance going around.

Get your copy here:

https://scrivenings.link/destinationromance

Roadtrip for ~~One~~ Two

Roadtrip Romance—Book Two

Recovering from heartbreak is hard when

the ex-fiancé tags along ...

Dallas wasn't in the plans when Bree Henley set out to use the nonrefundable honeymoon tickets from her canceled wedding. Nor was running into ex-fiancé Nathan Hart. But their mutual friends and the weather have other ideas. A hurricane cancels their cruise and Bree decides to turn the disaster into a roadtrip for one, never imagining Nathan would object.

Nathan is furious when he uncovers the plot to get him back with Bree.

But he can't just let her go roaming around the big city of Dallas alone. Though he knows calling off their wedding was the right thing to do, he still cares for Bree. And before he knows what hits him, he's volunteered to tag along. Suddenly, it's a trip for two.

Spending the week together might remind them of why they fell in love. But is it enough to overcome the obstacles standing in the way of "til death do us part"?

Get your copy here:

https://scrivenings.link/roadtripfortwo

Operation Find a ~~Job~~ Guy

Roadtrip Romance—Book Three

by Amy R. Anguish

She's set on saving her car ... and her heart.

Skye Jones has one goal for the summer—keep her father from taking away her convertible. That's the *only* reason she agrees to work at her sister's bridal shop in Boulder, Colorado, while she searches for a non-boring job. Why else would she have anything to do with weddings when she has no interest in marriage?

Benjamin Smith somehow ended up as a groomsman in two weddings over the summer, so he's spending a lot of time at Happily Ever After events. Falling for a blonde with no dreams of settling down wasn't in his five-year plan, yet the more he sees Skye, the more he wants to figure her out.

But all she sees him as is a boring attorney–her complete opposite.

Besides, romance is supposed to be for Skye's friends, not her. And she's in Colorado to get a job, not a guy. Right?

Get your copy here:

https://scrivenings.link/operationfindaguy

Love Delivered

A novella collection, including "Romance at Register Five"
by Amy R. Anguish

Mack McDonald isn't happy about the Grocerease app coming to his grocery store. But he's committed to the sixty-day trial period, and braces himself to lose money. Kaitlyn Daniels loves how the Grocerease app helps her make ends meet so she can assist her mom, the reason she moved to small Sassafras, AR. Mack and Kaitlyn struggle to overcome differing opinions on the perks of the app. But if they don't, it could keep them from something even better.

Get your copy here:

https://scrivenings.link/lovedelivered

No Place Like Home

Can love secure Adrian's wandering heart?

Roots are overrated, at least to someone like Adrian Stewart, preacher's kid, who has never lived anywhere longer than six years. That's why her job with MidUSLogIn Inc., is so perfect for her—lots of travel, and staying nowhere long enough to have it feel like home. But when work takes her to Memphis, closer to her family for the first time in years and in the same small office as Grayson Roberts, she starts to question her job, her lack of home, and even her memories of her rocky past with the church.

Gray is intrigued by Adrian from the moment he sees her, and he's determined to get to the bottom of why this girl, who loves old movies and hums when she works, won't go to church with him. As they grow closer, he wants more too, but how can he convince her to stay in Memphis when she doesn't believe in home—or God? Can he use his own broken past to break through hers?

Get your copy here:

https://scrivenings.link/noplacelikehome

Saving Grace

Michelle Wilson's one goal in life was to become a top journalist at the local paper back in her hometown of Cedar Springs, AR. But on the way to bringing that dream to reality, a life-changing wreck interrupts Michelle's plans and adds an orphaned baby into the mix. Now, she has tough decisions ahead—did God put her in that accident to save baby Grace? And if so, why is it so hard to convince everyone else she should be the baby's new mommy?

Greg Marshall has been Michelle's best friend his whole life. He's thrilled she's moving back home, but not so sure about her sudden desire to be a single mom. His feelings for her have grown through the years, but she's never seemed to notice. Can he help Michelle with the adoption and grow their relationship at the same time?

Get your copy here:

https://scrivenings.link/savinggrace

Faith and Hope

Get your copy here:

https://scrivenings.link/faithandhope

An Unexpected Legacy

Get your copy here:

https://scrivenings.link/anunexpectedlegacy

Stay up-to-date on your favorite books and authors with our free e-newsletters.

ScriveningsPress.com